Cella

Cella

OR

THE SURVIVORS

Franz Werfel

TRANSLATED FROM THE GERMAN BY
JOACHIM NEUGROSCHEL

HENRY HOLT AND COMPANY
New York

Published by Henry Holt and Company, Inc.,
115 West 18th Street, New York, New York 10011.
Published in Canada by Fitzhenry & Whiteside Limited,
195 Allstate Parkway, Markham, Ontario L3R 4T8.

LIBRARY OF CONGRESS CATALOGING-IN-PUBLICATION DATA
Werfel, Franz, 1890–1945.
[Cella. English]
Cella, or, The survivors / Franz Werfel; translated from
the German by Joachim Neugroschel.—1st ed.
p. cm.
Translation of: Cella.
ISBN 0-8050-0907-8
I. Title.
PT2647.E77C413   1989
833′.912—dc19   89-2040
                                                        CIP

Henry Holt books are available at special discounts for
bulk purchases for sales promotions, premiums, fund-
raising, or educational use. Special editions or book
excerpts can also be created to specification.

For details contact:
Special Sales Director
Henry Holt and Company, Inc.
115 West 18th Street
New York, New York 10011

First American Edition

Designed by Kathryn Parise
Printed in the United States of America
1   3   5   7   9   10   8   6   4   2

Foreword

BY OTTO FRIEDRICH

Though Franz Werfel is not very widely read today, he once was one of the most celebrated writers in the world. Born in 1890 into that oddly claustrophobic world of the German Jews of Prague, that world of *The Castle* (by his slightly older friend Franz Kafka), Werfel was almost exactly the opposite of Kafka—outgoing, fecund, sentimental, worldly. His first success came as a lyric poet. His early works, *Der Weltfreund* (1912), *Wir Sind* (1913), and *Einander* (1915), won high praise from the most distinguished of Prague poets, Rainer Maria Rilke. But Werfel had many interests. He was teaching philosophy at the University of Leipzig when the outbreak of World War I swept him off to the Russian front, and he returned to Vienna as an ardent believer in revolution and the brotherhood of man. Turning to the stage, he wrote adaptations of Euripides and Verdi; his *Juarez and Maximilian* reached Broadway in 1926. He achieved international fame with his novel about the Turkish oppression of the Armenians, *The Forty Days of Musa Dagh* (1934), and then again with his paean to Catholic faith, *The Song of Bernadette* (1942).

At a point about halfway between those two commercially successful novels, Werfel worked hard on *Cella,* which he conceived as a major work, possibly a trilogy, but which he finally abandoned in April of 1939, forever unfinished. The only reason he ever offered for this abandonment was that *Cella* had been overtaken by events. It was certainly written at a time of great turmoil, both personal and political. Werfel was already an exile when he began drafting it at Sanary, in the south of France, in September of 1938, five months after Hitler's *Anschluss* had devoured Austria. Some of the later chapters bear the notation that they were written in the Paris suburb of Saint-Germain-en-Laye in the early months of 1939, just before France itself went to war (and suddenly began treating German refugees as dangerous subversives). And Werfel's health was failing. A pudgy man now nearing fifty, smoking and drinking rather heavily, he suffered a series of heart attacks. "His condition is getting worse," his wife, Alma, wrote in her diary after Werfel nearly fainted during a prolonged police interrogation. "He is completely enfeebled, senescent, in fact—and very hopeless. Exile is a terrible disease!"

Yet when works of art go unfinished, it is rarely because of physical difficulties. More often, there is something in the work itself that remains unresolved, something that the artist either has not figured out or cannot face. *Cella* is an ambitious attempt to explore two difficult themes that were extremely important to Werfel. One was his love for a daughter who was not his own child. The other was his effort to escape the fate of being a Jew.

The girl was Manon Gropius, the third and last surviving child of the celebrated *femme fatale* of that time and place, Alma Schindler Mahler Gropius Werfel, who, in between her famous husbands, conducted a tempestuous affair with Oskar Kokoschka. The man she seems to have cared about least was her second husband, Walter Gropius, the architect, and founder of the Bauhaus, but as she wrote in her memoirs, *And the Bridge Is Love,* "I had wanted to know what it means to have a child from a beautiful, beloved man. I had my wish now. My curiosity was at an end." She had married Gropius in 1915, given birth to Manon in 1916, and by 1917, she was already in love with Werfel, whom she described as "a stocky man with sensuous lips and large, beautiful blue eyes under a Goethean forehead." She saw all of her various admirers while they were on furlough from the war, but Werfel, who was twelve years her junior, soon became the only one who mattered. "My mind is full of Franz Werfel," she wrote in her diary. "The music I make with him has become the air I breathe." She became pregnant again, but the premature birth was difficult, and Werfel's only son did not live long. During her confinement, Lieutenant Gropius hovered at her bedside in the country, while Werfel remained in Vienna. "Yesterday Walter Gropius found out everything," Werfel wrote in his diary. "When Alma phoned me in the morning, he heard us calling each other by our first names. . . . Then he asked—she remained silent—and he knew."

The result of all this intrigue was that after Alma's divorce and remarriage, Manon grew up with the Werfels, and grew into a remarkable girl, always a little shy but charming and gifted and beloved by everyone who knew her. "She was the most beautiful human being in every sense," Alma wrote in her memoirs. "She combined all our good qualities. I have never known such a divine capacity for love, such creative power to express and to live it." Manon loved music, and writing, and the theater—she dreamed of becoming an actress—and she was just eighteen when she collapsed with shattering headaches that were diagnosed first as meningitis, then as polio. Her legs became paralyzed, then her whole body. The Werfels did everything they could think of to keep up her spirits. When they brought in famous theatrical people to rehearse their parts with her, Manon said, "I never knew that you were all so fond of me."

Werfel spent much of the summer of 1934 coaching Manon to play the leading role in his adaptation of Verdi's *La Forza del destino*. "She looked quite regal in black tights, doublet, and hose, and spoke from her wheelchair like a consummate actress," Alma wrote. "Werfel played opposite her, and I had to provide the music." But there was nothing anybody could do. On the day after Easter, Manon felt herself failing. "Let me die," she said to her mother. "I'll never get well; and my acting, that's just what you make up for me out of pity. . . .

You'll get over it, Mummy, as you get over everything—I mean, as everyone gets over everything." After a year of suffering, Manon Gropius passed away, and of all those who wanted to commemorate her brief passage, Alban Berg did it best when he dedicated his new violin concerto, his own last work, "to the memory of an angel."

Manon was obviously much in Werfel's mind when he began writing *Cella* three years later, when his central character, Hans Bodenheim, tried to express his rather inarticulate love for the piano prodigy who, he mistakenly thought, was his own daughter; but all these memories were engulfed by the disaster that was overtaking Austria. After about the first hundred pages of Werfel's novel, Cella virtually disappears from sight, and the only question is whether her father can get her out of Austria; and then, for many pages, the only question is whether her father can get himself out of Austria, or can save himself on any terms.

In many ways, the most interesting element in *Cella*—and what makes it so evocative of its time—is the portrait of what might be called the pre-Holocaust mentality, the mentality of the myriad German Jews who did not fully understand what it meant to be Jews. Though the German Jews had been granted their basic civil rights only a century earlier, many of them were, in Werfel's time, passionately dedicated to the idea of assimilation, to implicitly denying their own origins, or perhaps more accurately, to denying that their origins made them forever different from their neighbors. Not only did such notable figures as the Mendelssohns convert to Christianity, but an exemplar like Walther Rathenau, industrialist, diplomat, connoisseur of the arts, looked on the impoverished inhabitants of the Polish ghettos with something akin to horror. "An alien and isolated race of men," Rathenau said of them, "loud and self-conscious in their dress, hot-blooded and restless in their manner. An Asiatic horde. . . ."

Werfel, whose father was a wealthy glove manufacturer, grew up in that tradition. From his earliest student days, he pursued a dream of the brotherhood of man, which is another way of dreaming that the differences between Christians and Jews are less important than their common humanity. Werfel flirted with Christianity all his life, and, like the skeptical doctor in *The Song of Bernadette,* wanted to believe but did not believe. Questioned about the slightly saccharine pieties in that huge best-seller, Werfel finally sent to a Catholic bishop a statement that said: "I am . . . a Jew by origin and have never been baptized. On the other hand, I wish to profess here that . . . I have been decisively influenced and molded by the spiritual forces of Christianity and the Catholic Church. I see in the holy Catholic Church the purest power and emanation sent by God to this earth to fight the evils of materialism and atheism, and to bring revelation to the poor soul of mankind."

If Werfel's relationship to the Christian majority was ambiguous, he was almost equally ambiguous about the onrushing force of fascism. Cella's father, Hans Bodenheim, could certainly see that something new and terrible was happening in Vienna, a terrible process of revenge and destruction: "There were two kinds of people in the streets: a colorless mass, flowing to work, graver, more depressed, more hopeless than ever; and a number of uniformed figures weaving . . . into the crowd, apparently in order to keep an eye on the people and terrify them. . . . Modern tyranny . . . is not so much a domination of an individual, a clique, a class, as a serried despotism of opportunists culled from all ranks of society." Yet when that despotism first came to power in Germany in 1933, Werfel was one of the writers who signed a declaration of loyalty to the new regime. When he applied for membership in the Nazi–run Writers Association, he described himself as a "member of the German minority in Czechoslovakia" (one of those Sudeten Germans who were soon to be heard from so loudly). This was not at all uncommon or unusual, of course. It was an expression of that spirit of deferential acquiescence that had brought the Jews out of the ghettos and brought them to the point at which Sigmund Freud's father could calmly report that when a Gentile knocked off his new hat and ordered him to get off the pavement, "I stepped into the gutter and picked up my cap." Yet when the Nazis staged their mass burning of books in the early days of 1933, they burned Werfel's books along with all the rest.

Werfel seems to have thought—it is not certain, because he never publicly said so—that *The Forty Days of Musa Dagh* was an artfully disguised sermon on the need to resist oppression, but the Nazis probably saw no such message when they banned the book; they banned it simply because its author was a Jew. Yet even in 1938, when Werfel began writing *Cella,* he felt compelled to rely on euphemisms. "Avoid the word 'Jew' if possible," he wrote in one of his first notes on the novel. His narrator, Bodenheim, refers only to "our people," or even "one of us, the accursed." And Bodenheim's Gentile wife ("I am married to an anti-Semite," Werfel once said of the Wagnerian Alma) speaks of "your people." Bodenheim is similarly unable to identify the oppressor as Adolf Hitler, only as "the archenemy" or "the dragon." The Nazis are "the race protectors" or simply "them."

This unwillingness to name the forces of evil reflects an unwillingness to confront them. The wealthy Jews in *Cella* keep protesting that their arrest must be some mistake, a violation of the law. They keep demanding to see some supervisor who will fix things, give them back their top hats and their privileges. Like Werfel himself, Bodenheim is intensely proud of the war medals that he won in the Austrian army. It is a fact that a disproportionate number of Jews served in the German armies, as soon as they were allowed to do so, and that a disproportionate number of them died in combat. It is also a fact that a number of Jews carried their war medals onto the trains to the death camps and died convinced that there must be some mistake.

Werfel may possibly have foreseen the consequences of this blindness. The *Kristallnacht* pogrom in November of 1938 clearly demonstrated that his hero's discreet anxieties were becoming irrelevant. In the final pages of the unfinished manuscript of *Cella,* when a banker aboard the train to Dachau is savagely beaten for protesting that "they did not mean me," Bodenheim finally exclaims (though only to himself): "They do not mean you, Freudreich! They do not mean me. Whom do they mean? Israel is not a nation, Israel is an order of the blood, which one enters by birth, involuntarily. . . ." It is possible, in other words, that Werfel had finally realized what the Jewish destiny was to be, and that the purpose of his novel was to show Bodenheim gradually acquiring that same knowledge. Yet a few pages after his outburst at Freudreich, Bodenheim is allowed off the train, rescued by an old school friend who is now a high Nazi official. In other words, it *was* all a mistake. Things might still be fixed if one knew the right people.

The pages on Bodenheim's imprisonment after the Nazi takeover seem so grimly realistic that one assumes Werfel had experienced the *Anschluss* at first hand, had experienced the fear, the degradation, the isolation, the need for flight. It was not so. Werfel spent those frightening months in Capri, which was in fascist Italy, but which had always deferred, ever since the days of the Emperor Tiberius, to the pleasures of the rich. It was Alma who packed up and closed the house in Vienna and met Werfel in Switzerland so that they could proceed to a rather comfortable exile in the south of France. It was there that Werfel wrote *Embezzled Heaven,* another big commercial success, after deciding to abandon *Cella.*

Only when France fell, in 1940, did Werfel realize that his money might not save him. He and Alma took a taxi all the way from Marseilles to Bordeaux, where the panic-stricken government had gone in order to flee from Paris, and where they found that there were no hotel rooms at any price, and no exit permits either. Hence the retreat to Lourdes, and Werfel's desperate pledge that if he ever escaped from this town where young Bernadette Soubirous had seen her vision of the Virgin Mary, he would somehow repay her in the best currency he had.

It was primarily Werfel's own celebrity that saved him, however, that and the heroism of a young American Quaker named

Varian Fry, who had made it his mission to rescue intellectuals from the wreckage of France. One little band that he led out over a wooded pass in the Pyrenees included the ailing Werfel and Alma—he carrying the manuscript of *Cella* and she the score of Bruckner's third symphony—and also the 69-year-old Heinrich Mann, his alcoholic wife, Nelly, Thomas Mann's son Golo, and the novelist Lion Feuchtwanger and his wife, Marta, who had both been virtually kidnapped from a French internment camp. "It was sheer slippery terrain that we crawled up, bounded by precipices," Alma recalled. "Mountain goats could hardly have kept their footing on the glassy, shimmering slate. If you skidded, there was nothing but thistles to hang onto."

Safe in neutral Spain, the Werfels could pay their way to America, where *Embezzled Heaven* was flourishing on the bestseller lists, and Werfel could buy a handsome house in Hollywood, and Alma could entertain "local" musicians such as Schoenberg, Stravinsky, Bruno Walter, and Otto von Klemperer. And while the song of Bernadette called out from the miraculous grotto in Lourdes, the song of Cella seemed increasingly faint, fading in the distance. That was probably what Werfel meant when he said that his novel about the anxieties of self-definition and flight had been overtaken by events. Yet that judgment was more true than Werfel realized. Not until three months after the Werfels reached America in October of 1940 did the Nazis' secret Wannsee Conference outline the plan that became known as the Final Solution. Not until the following year was the first trainload of Jews taken to be gassed in Auschwitz, whose commandant, Rudolf Hess, had once made a pilgrimage to Lourdes. It was with the coming of all these complexities, the news of which hardly reached Franz Werfel or anyone else in Hollywood, that *Cella* was finally and forever overtaken by events.

Chapter 1

Prelude and Fugue
Number 12

Cella is seated at the piano. Her real name is Cecily. But we call her Cella, a name that suits the child nicely. "We" are Gretl and I. Gretl is hunched over some needlework. She can never keep her hands idle when she listens to Cella playing, which always irritates me. Gretl is wearing her strong glasses with their bulging lenses. Her eyes, alas, have not improved during our sixteen years of marriage. Without her glasses, Gretl is still a beautiful woman; her slender body has not changed. She is slightly taller than I. Of course, her blond hair has recently lost much of its former glow, and it looks dull now. I often wish that Gretl would spend more money on remaining beautiful. She could do so, even though our circumstances are rather modest. But her austerity seems motivated by a severe principle, something I do not understand about my wife. Perhaps she does not care to be attractive. Perhaps it is just her nature and nothing more. How odd that there are undiscovered facets in a person even after one has lived with her for such a long time. Perhaps our small town is the reason. Although we are barely an hour from Vienna, Eisenstadt is still an obscure nest.

Cella spends two days a week in Vienna. For a year now, she has been studying with Scherber, a world-famous teacher. Professor Scherber is considered the top man in his field. Supposedly, he is only a mediocre pianist, but as a teacher he has beaten out the competition everywhere. He is very expensive, for his prices are determined by his American students. If Cella were to attend the National Academy of Music, her training would require a far smaller sacrifice. Not only does Scherber demand very high fees, but his teaching method involves expensive paraphernalia, including scores, books, concerts, opera tickets, and above all, the social activities. Scherber himself is at the hub of this socializing, which he considers indispensable for the artistic progress of his pupils. How I thank Heaven that I can make this sacrifice for my only child.

I recall the words that Scherber growled at Cella's audition after she played a Chopin étude and Liszt's Second Rhapsody: "The girl is not ungifted, but she's dreadfully sloppy." Connoisseurs told me that this praise meant more than if a normal musician were to cry out: "The girl's a genius!" Scherber is a tiny, hydrocephalic manikin. Everything about him seems dingy gray: the unkempt hair, the droopy suit, the worn-out boots. Only his face is brownish-red, and his eyes virtually shriek with life. One can see instantly that he is special, a unique man, for whom music holds no secrets. His pupils swear by him. So do I. Ever since he took Cella into his private circle, he has proved correct about her a hundred times. Generally, he sends home ninety-nine percent of the applicants. And the girl was barely past fourteen. Yes indeed, I agree with that international expert: Cella is a major talent. I won't say that other word, if only to avoid challenging fate.

Cella's hands, heavy with restraint, are still in her lap as if unable to decide on taking up the weight of the music. These are no longer the child's sweet hands that snuggled so warm, so trusting, in my hand just a year ago. The highly gifted child who, just lately, seemed to belong to me as a branch belongs to a tree, has become a person in her own right—why, in a certain sense a stranger. But such is the fate of all parents, and there is no use belaboring it.

Cella has announced in a soft voice: "Prelude and Fugue Number Twelve from *The Well-Tempered Clavier.*" Her body pulls itself together, as if jolted by a very grave decision. She raises her hands, hesitates for an instant, then drops them on the keyboard, as if throwing them both away, as if letting them take their own, independent route, completely detached from her. Next, Cella closes her eyes, bowing her head slightly. She frowns as if focusing her thoughts; her face grows older and older under the invisible rays of the approaching music, which seems to descend upon her lowered head from all sides of the room. I can feel the brief pause precisely, that moment of filled emptiness when the Bach piece begins without yet sounding, the way an oar slices the air before the other oar actually smacks into the water. Then comes the second turn, mournful and decisive.

It is always the same. Whenever Cella starts playing, a curious thrill shoots through my nerves. I do not believe I am blinded by paternal love. Besides, I am unmusical, though not completely unmusical, for I have always been delighted by music. There is something peculiar in Cella's touch, in her tone, addressing me beyond the sound of the music, as when someone is called in the soughing of the wind. Unfortunately, I cannot put my finger on it. It must be something peculiar, for only I, her father, can hear it. Even her mother seems untouched by it, for she does not look up from her sewing.

My nerves shuddered the very first time Cella, an eleven-year-old, gloomily knitting her brow as she does today, played Schubert's well-known Impromptu. My inexplicable bewilderment is a blend of terror and amazement. How astonishing that God granted us a child like Cella. I am an utterly ordinary, insignificant person, and Gretl, who may be a beautiful woman, has no other exceptional talent. In addition, I am terrified of the danger inherent in an excessive favor of destiny. The union of two ordinary people has produced Cella, that creature over there, whose fingers draw knowledge from the white and black keys, draw experiences far beyond a child's ken. Granted, I might find a bit of myself in Cella. There is a certain tenacity that has allowed me, without much ado, to keep my small family afloat, even in very difficult times. There is a certain reserve, which has caused me so much bitterness in life, preventing me from letting others know me fully or from fully knowing others, including Gretl. And then there is my deep, burning ambition, a tormenting mania to be and to do something extraordinary. But in the course of my life, almost fifty years, I have had to bury my ambition quite early. A lawyer can amass neither honors nor riches, and certainly not here, in this provincial nest, where I was born, and where I have been kept by my sedentary nature. But the ambition buried within me only *seems* dead. It bores and gnaws and thinks and takes care of Cella. She is to achieve what I have never even dared to dream. The world will lie at her feet.

The huge throng of wishes that I nurture for my child often causes me sharp sorrow. At such times, I suspect the purity of my paternal love. Unjustly, I hope. Otherwise, why have I been so wracked by these constant anxieties about Cella ever since the day she was born? I am never fearful about myself. All kinds of medals are gathering dust in my desk: the Great Silver Cross, the Gold Medal of Courage, the Signum Laudis; and I was recommended for the Order of Leopold with the swords—a rare exception for a reserve lieutenant, as anyone will agree.

But in regard to Cella, I am a miserable coward. When the child takes the bus to visit Scherber in Vienna, I suddenly picture a collision and I hear a scream. If she is ever late, I nervously pace up and down like a prisoner. If she has an autumn cold, and her fever does not go down within three days, I send for a well-known Viennese physician, despite my strict budget. Our local doctor is not good enough for me. A small town distrusts itself. "You're overreacting again," Gretl then says, almost glaring at me. Words like *scarlet fever, measles, diphtheria* are a constant nightmare for me, not to mention *polio.* That is why I am glad that Cella is no longer attending school this year.

Aren't these worries and deep anxieties easy to explain? Do I not bear a grave responsibility? I, a nobody, have been gifted with Cella. We know how destiny loves taking back such an undeserved present at the very first opportunity. As a practical man, I have learned that in life, property is always lost, but debts are never canceled. The injustices we endure are legion. Does any injustice ever work out in our favor and not turn against us? I can scarcely believe it.

Cella's face is immobile. She has closed not only her eyes, but all the shutters of her being. The music arising from under her hands, which have become independent, makes her narrow body tremble. It trembles like a ship when the engines are throbbing far below. The prelude charges ahead; Cella charges ahead. Scherber has performed a miracle. And it took him only a year to unearth the spirit of music from the child. A force seems to live in this spirit, defying any age. The spirit does not care whether one of its chosen few is twelve years old, fifteen, or eighty. Cella shows only one childlike trait while playing: at times, her pointed red tongue unwittingly emerges between her teeth. Scherber simply has to be made aware of that. I had best write him a tactful letter. It will not do for a great artist to cling to childish peccadilloes. The international public is cruel, and even while showering its minions with applause, it maliciously keeps a sharp lookout for their foibles and vulnerabilities. Any success in life, commercial and probably also artistic, usually faces the threat of revenge from those people who all too easily feel hoodwinked. Granted, I cannot speak from personal experience, but I am warned by my gift of observation.

The prelude is in full swing. With Bach, one never knows whether he means to be cheerful or desperately sad. Only the chord that always concludes his pieces is usually as positive as a sunrise. One would like to have more of that final chord. To be perfectly honest, Bach is too lofty for me. His music is like a blind giant with a gnarled stick, walking heedlessly through a crowd, sometimes fast, sometimes slow. Anyone who does not make way is shoved aside without even realizing it. The blind giant has a grand goal: that final chord, which is a sunrise. But the teeming crowd, which does not consider itself blind, has no goal. I myself am part of that teeming crowd. Perhaps that is why my favorite composer is Puccini. I feel truly moved when I listen to him. His melodies affect the very core of my breathing. In general, operatic music is my cup of tea. (Of course, ever since Cella began studying with Scherber, I have had to cut out opera and theater for Gretl and myself.) I like some things by Wagner. But he drags on too long. Frankly, all music drags on too long for me. It tires me quickly, especially when I resolve to focus hard. After the first twenty measures I feel sleepy, as if I were being forced to listen to an extremely lively conversation in an utterly foreign language. My own thoughts and fancies grow impatient, they start tugging at the reins of my concentration. This is happening now, when my beloved only child wants to show me what she has learned recently from Scherber.

I light a cigarette. My eyes, needing some diversion, follow the smoke as it drifts toward the window, floating past Gretl, who is busy with her sewing. November is here already. It is past four o'clock, and twilight is thickening. The windows of our four-room apartment face the main square of the town. The houses here are ancient, with courtyards, nooks and crannies, winding stairs, and thick walls. This is the best section of Eisenstadt. Goodness knows why I recall my parents' home now of all times. I grew up in a house that was torn down long ago. It faced the so-called Haydn Church. A beautiful view for a rather thoughtful child: that pilgrimage church with its many domes, humps, and conchlike protuberances. There was something eerie about the church of my childhood, and yet I sincerely loved it, even though my parents had nothing to do with any church. Indeed, to put it bluntly, we were not even allowed to enter one. Burgenland, my native province, has many churches, chapels, and countless wayside shrines in front of which the pious folk cross themselves. There are also a lot of brown-skinned Gypsies in our Burgenland. They are left over from the Hungarian period. We, that is, our people, are neither brown-skinned Gypsies nor pious folk who cross themselves in front of shrines and churches. Yet we have lived here as long as the others, if not longer, for we were already here when the Turks were ruling and the predatory Cumans invaded the land. At least, that is what the history books tell us.

In the past, no one ever dreamt of making such a great fuss about belonging to the native soil. But now things are completely different. Because of these disastrous years in Germany, dim questions, dim anxieties nestle in all minds. Even in me, although I have moved far away from my origins; if only through my marriage with Gretl. . . . As far back as anyone can remember, our people have been granted our own street in Eisenstadt. This street consists mainly of small, lovely, cultivated baroque houses. At either end, one can still see the heavy cast-iron chains that closed off the roadway during the Sabbath. My father left that street at a very early age. He was a freethinker, a very upright freethinker. He always preached that there are no distinctions between human beings, that all such differences are merely the backward remnant of medieval ignorance. I tried hard to live by his words. And yet, in my heart of hearts, I could not help noticing a certain difference between our people and the others, even though no one at home told me who was this and who was that. The farmers, market vendors, cattle dealers, wine salesmen, artisans, innkeepers, indeed, the province officials always greet our people with a respectful flourish of their hats. Even Prince Esterhazy, who resides at the Eisenstadt Citadel, as well as his entire household still wave to our people, condescendingly familiar, as if in complicity.

But why do I now recall a completely insignificant episode from my school days? One Sunday, when Father and I were strolling through the Castle Park, we ran into a high official. (He was, by the way, related to Gretl.) He and Father got into a conversation. I can still remember the slight malaise I felt throughout their indifferent exchange. I sensed that my father, whom I honored, that model of male pride, was being inauthentic in a very convoluted way. He had lost his composure and was acting both arrogant and toadyish at once. He was sort of clapping the man on his back while anxiously fawning on him, assuring him of his good will. And yet, goodness knows, my father could never have been accused of even a touch of that undignified bustling that is said to be characteristic of our unpleasant mentality. I must confess that as Bach's prelude races toward its final chord, nothing worthier has occurred to me than that very trivial incident, which has still not lost its embarrassing aftertaste, even decades later! The bizarre effects of music on an unmusical man!

Gretl has leaned back, taking off her glasses. She looks tired, under stress. I keep begging her not to sew in twilight. No use. I am moved by a tender feeling for Gretl now, almost a quiet sense of guilt. I am familiar with this emotion, but it usually comes over me only when we are separated. After all, we have a good marriage. But lately, there have been more and more tiny misunderstandings. They are only differences of opinion about trivial things, barely worth mentioning. But they conceal an irritability that I cannot quite explain. At such times, I become vicious and torture her.

Gretl now seems not untouched by the same tender feeling that flows through me. She smiles and blinks at me, saying, "Cella has made a lot of progress since the summer. Don't you agree?"

Cella appears not to have heard her mother's praise. The

short breather she inserted following the prelude is over. Her hands plunge into the fugue; Bach, the blind giant, charges off. He dashes up hill and down dale, toward his ineluctable goal. While I may not know very much about music, I am beginning to have an inkling of what such a fugue is all about. It is a fabulous game of tag—escaping over and over again, getting caught over and over again, utmost confusion amid utmost order, something cosmic and strategic at once. For a time, I listen spellbound. But then my mind is swept off again by the powerful rhythm. My child's great artistry—her progress is truly astounding—suddenly takes me back, for no visible reason, to the happiest time of my life: the war.

Yes, that terrible war was a wonderful time for our people, despite everything. We lived more lightly than ever. During the war years, the specific weight of our people decreased. I picture a large, deep mountain lake, where you swim far, far out. The powerful water carries your body, which no longer weighs itself down. The lake is dangerous, but magnificent. And the war was like that lake. One might almost speak of a social displacement of water. This was, of course, completely different for a highly decorated first lieutenant than for a modest lawyer. No one, not even Gretl, knows how much I suffered in my youth for being a hopelessly average person, who could not even write poems and emulate the teachers. How often did I dream of finally arousing the admiration of my friends and schoolmates, of being marveled at by Myslivec and Pramer. And especially Zsoltan Nagy.

Regarding the latter, my dream came true in the war—to a certain degree. Nagy began a military career after graduating from Gymnasium, and, as a dragoon captain (I do not know what his duty was), he was in the young Kaiser's suite when the Supreme Commander honored my company by addressing us near the front. This took place behind the lines, near Tolmein, in a small village that had been battered by gunfire. We had been stationed there after several months of extreme exertion and the most dreadful casualties, and now we were waiting to regroup. I can see the Kaiser's clear, blond face. It seemed to be suntanned by sheer good faith. But, in that great moment of my life, I probably could not have seen his face; I was too excited. After my breathless report, the Kaiser held out his hand, squeezed mine, and clutched it for a long time, as if to thank me rapturously for a very personal achievement. With truly imperial generosity, the Supreme Commander-in-Chief transcended military ritual. "Herr Lieutenant," he said, "I thank you for your courageous action against the enemy. I shall never forget you. I can be proud of such men. You are one of the bravest company officers in this sector." And then once again: "I thank you, Herr Lieutenant Bodenheim!" His majesty's entire retinue smiled and they all shook my hand: the corps commander, the division commander, the brigadier, the staff officers, the adjutants. It was a tremendous sunrise of goodwill; it almost scorched me. But men need goodwill. It is the nourishment of our poor souls. Without it, one all too easily becomes a nightshade plant, as many of our people are.

Eventually, Zsoltan Nagy came and hugged me. "Bodenheim, you goddamn bastard," he laughed, "just look at you— to think that you've become the biggest hero of us all, and you're in the military roll of honor! Congratulations, old boy, but don't be a fool, put in for a furlough and try to get a better position."

I admit that despite his irony, the word "hero" made me happy. My ardent boyhood wishes had come true; I was admired by my friends. However, I did not deceive myself for an instant. I was no hero by any stretch of the imagination. I had acted no differently than a calm and collected, or rather a not very temperamental, spectator during a panic in a theater. I had remained in my place, thereby preventing worse things from happening. Of course, I was the responsible man in the position, for my superiors had been killed in the very first minute, and, within half an hour, I was the only officer left far and wide. My sole thought was: No one must retreat, otherwise we are doomed. And I planted myself at the entrance to our communication trench. If anyone was a hero, it was the corporal with the second machine gun, a stupid, repulsive fellow who, out of sheer obstinacy, kept firing into the Alps as if we were having an artillery drill. But I did not realize I was suddenly in command of a tactically crucial point—all communication lines had been destroyed. And so I, First Lieutenant Bodenheim from Eisenstadt, wiped out the broad Italian operation, and I was a hero; my name was listed in the military roll of honor, and I was decorated in front of thousands of other men. Perhaps that is the gist of all so-called "great deeds": their successful aftermath makes them great. I do not know. In any case, the reality of the whole war was not deeds, but thirst, hunger, filth, lice, lack of sleep, lack of cigarettes, lack of mail. What a pleasant feeling even after twenty years: I proved myself.

I stretch out in this awareness. Something in my life had universal value and was publicly recognized. Only something? Is not Cella my child? Her name, my name will some day be listed in an army roll of honor that will not fade as soon or be forgotten as quickly as the poor Kaiser's praises. Cella is graced; I will not say it aloud, but I truly believe it. She will shine before the entire world. If only fate has nothing bad in store for us! If only no illness gets in the way! Cella is pale, under stress, she practices too much, eats too little! It is torture watching her eat. I will live and work for Cella. My life is not futile. How violently Bach shakes the girl! The way a god shakes his prophetess. The trance of music yanks her to and fro. A strand of hair dangles on her forehead, her chin and cheeks are trembling. Once again, the fugue rises ominously. A mountain of clouds blocking the sun. It breaks through. A winter sun. This time, it is not a chord, but a single empty note, a goal different from normal.

Cella listens to its vibrations. She has slumped slightly, narrow-chested, her fingers still on the keyboard. The room is almost completely dark. Standing up, I go over to the piano.

"Bravo, Cella," I say, "that was really very good. You've

matured tremendously. . . . What does Professor Scherber tell
you?"

I then think to myself that a true father should not jeopardize
a beloved child with total recognition, so I add:

"Incidentally, I think you ought to watch your posture a
little. It's not perfect yet."

Only now do Cella's hands loosen themselves from the keys.
She looks at me, thoughtful and dissatisfied.

"Was it really all right, Bulbul?" she asks.

"I was impressed," I hear my measured answer. She smiles
slyly.

"But I totally messed up three times, I just plunked down.
Didn't you notice, Bulbul?"

"I kind of thought so," I state dishonestly and vaguely,
squinting at Gretl, whose shape almost dissolves in the deep
twilight.

But Cella suddenly leaps up and tempestuously throws her
arms around me. She is getting taller than I, I think, an indescribable delight in my heart. Then I feel her familiar girlish
lips on mine. But for the first time in her life, they are a woman's lips. This moves me profoundly. Like a fulfillment and
like a departure.

Chapter 2

A Dear Visitor

And now, all at once, Zsoltan Nagy is standing in our living room. The man I happened to think about just half an hour earlier. He disappeared at least five years ago. We are all glad to see him. Cella has not forgotten him despite his long absence. She is not the least bit bashful, she is jubilant. To her, Uncle Zsoltan has always been the epitome of all festiveness. And indeed, he has brought her a gift, generous as he is. Some kind of Asiatic bauble, jade, depicting a god with many arms. Cella instantly puts the necklace on, saying it will always be her amulet, warding off all evil. Gretl is handed a huge bouquet of long-stemmed roses, blood-red and yellow. They must be awfully expensive, now in November. A frivolous spirit—that Nagy!

I too am delighted by his visit. It now seems to me that he was my only friend among all my schoolmates. That is to say, I have always had a special affection for Zsoltan, almost unconditional warmth, which prompted me to court his friendship, even though I could never take him quite seriously. After all, our personalities were too different. Gretl seems least delighted by Zsoltan. I know my wife well, especially when something arouses her opposition or troubles her. She does not

show it. She shows nothing at all. But at such times, she becomes restless, bustling. And that is how she is acting now. As
soon as our first hellos have been exchanged and Nagy is
seated, Gretl leaves, to return with a pitcher. Pouring water
into two vases, she divides the roses between them, intent and
assiduous. This activity takes an amazingly long time. Yet it
was Nagy who introduced me to Gretl and actually brought
about our marriage. My goodness, that was in 1922. Naturally, I know everything even though we have never spoken
about it—I mean, Gretl and I. She must have been in love with
Nagy once. What young girl, what woman has not been in
love with Nagy? Yet there is no man of whom one should be
less jealous. Nagy spells no real danger for a woman precisely
because he is so handsome, so dazzling, so successful, probably
even today. I am somewhat touched to notice that Gretl put
on some lipstick while she was out, something she does not
exactly do every minute.

The old boy is incredibly well-preserved. He does not look a
day over thirty-five. People tell me I have not aged either. I
steal a glance in our Venetian mirror. The comparison is in
Nagy's favor, a hundred to one. I am not bald, but Zsoltan's
narrow cavalier's head has kept all its beautiful hair, the thick,
silky chestnut hair he had at school. His teeth glitter roguishly.
Even the creases at his lips and eyes look like an adornment
of boyish merriment. Yet Nagy must have gone through worse
times than I. Just imagine: an active officer, a good-for-nothing
ex-cavalryman after the collapse of the Empire. And next fall,
this indestructible Apollo will be fifty years old. He has had a
somewhat checkered career between thirty and fifty. His life
cannot have been easy; it is even admirable, measured by a
country law office. I admire Zsoltan, just as I admired him at
school and then always anew.

Nagy's fresh eyes wander through our living room, smiling.
"Well," he says, "so the Bodenheims still haven't been hit by

the crisis. You're blossoming and thriving, an immortal hero, like . . ."

I do not find his tone, the old tone between us, altogether pleasant. We have not seen each other for too long a time. But, needless to say, I go along with his banter.

"And you, you old con man, you've managed to escape and come home safe and sound?"

"In triumph! The prince has invited me to hunt a few stags." This sounds a bit disparaging. "I may stay a few weeks or even longer."

We are alone. Gretl is in the kitchen, preparing a somewhat more festive tea. She has sent Cella over to the pastry shop. To my surprise, I realize that I no longer feel so comfortable when I am alone with Zsoltan Nagy. At the same time, I know it has never been otherwise, despite my sincere affection for him. The Nagy of my memory and imagination has always been different from the real one. Every time I see him again, our meeting arouses certain anxieties in me and tires me out. Our personalities are all too different.

I get him to tell me about himself. That is the best approach. With a conceited gesture, Zsoltan places the long, brown fingers of one hand on those of the other. His attractive eyes gaze past me indifferently. I am offended (an old boyhood malaise), sensing that I barely exist for him. He tells me about his travels during the past five years. He has seen a great deal of the world, nimbly and, no doubt, rather victoriously. A boastful string of cities penetrates into my strangely inattentive ear: London, Paris, New York, Los Angeles, Shanghai. It is only the name "Berlin" that dispels my slightly painful absentmindedness.

"You were in Germany?" I ask, and perhaps my question unwittingly contains a lurking emphasis, for he hesitates a single instant, gaping at me in surprise before answering, "Yes, I was in Germany last summer. You see, there are more hard-of-hearing people there than anywhere else in the world. And I was a sales representative for a hearing-aid company." Then he obligingly adds, clearly to please me: "Awful conditions in Germany."

"We've experienced a few things in Austria too," I remark vaguely.

"I can imagine. I've thought about you people often."

Nagy says this with sympathetic indifference. Then I see golden sparks in his eyes, but the sparks instantly vanish.

"Listen, Bodenheim," he inquires, "you're a big man in the local Iron Soldiers Ring, aren't you?"

I resolutely reject the role of "big man." Granted, at the last general meeting of this legion of Dual Monarchy veterans, I was elected secretary of the provincial section. But this so-called honorary title is more of a burden than an honor. I can afford only one assistant, and my office is overwhelmed with the agendas of the Ring. I do not know why Zsoltan's question makes me a bit uneasy. I toss it back at him:

"What about you, Nagy, don't you belong to the Ring, being a veteran and all?"

Nagy's laughter is as appealing as everything else about him.

"You know me, old boy. I'm a Hapsburg to the core! True unto Death! But when it comes to clubs, thanks but no thanks. First of all, because of the dues. Secondly, I'm a vagabond. And thirdly, my needs are met by my membership in the London Pacemaker Club."

And he scrutinizes me to see whether this name elicits my due respect.

The tea cart is rolled in. Gretl, hospitable as she is, has not forgotten that Nagy is a passionate coffee drinker. She has brewed him a very powerful coffee. Cella sits right next to him. Her hand enthusiastically clutches the jade god.

"You don't even really know me yet, Uncle Zsoltan," she says, "and you've brought me such a beautiful gift?!"

He stares at her in surprise.

"What do you mean, Cella, I've known you since your birth."

"Oh, well. . . ." She pouts disdainfully. "You knew me when I was little. But now I'm an adult."

"You really are, Cecily," he solemnly says, putting his arm around her shoulder. For an instant, Nagy's head nestles against my child's head. I squint at the two of them through half-closed eyes. My girl's brown hair flows into the brown hair of this prince charming. Behind them, I see a golden background blazing up. A thought fragment flashes through my mind—no, an emotion that I cannot untangle, and that fortunately vanishes right away, although leaving behind an astonished pain for two minutes. The last time Cella saw Nagy, she was ten or eleven. Cella is truly a big girl already, and I am troubled by their present intimacy, which has no solid basis. Ignoring my resolve, I begin to talk about her great gift, about Scherber, about my hopes for her, and I tell her to show Uncle Zsoltan how much progress she has made in music.

Cella does not act coy. She hurries to the piano and opens it resolutely. That is one of the great differences between my daughter and myself. She has not, thank goodness, inherited the melancholy and timidity that weigh me down. If ever I am forced to speak unprepared on any occasion, I have to muster all my strength to overcome the paralyzing anguish that almost robs me of my voice and makes me sweat profusely. Cella does not know the meaning of the words "stage fright." Music is the element in which she truly feels secure, even dominant. If I did not keep protesting vigorously, she would spend the whole day at the piano. Should I not recognize this naive devotion— which is never inhibited by any false timidity—as the happy sign of her authentic gift, as the harbinger of the future champion? Only a person without joyous confidence in his power and destiny will simper, make excuses, have qualms. But not Cella! Her greedy fingers are already sniffing at the keys, and the unchildish furrow of contemplation and willpower is already forming between her pure eyebrows.

To forestall her decisions, I firmly admonish, "But please, no Bach."

Looking at us, she laughs.

"Bulbul" (one of the nicknames she has devised for me), "Bulbul is afraid of Bach. What about you, Uncle Zsoltan?"

Gretl steps in. She judges Nagy correctly.

"Something brilliant, Cella," she says. And Cella plays two pieces by Liszt with a truly amazing fluency and almost virile force—I must admit that in all objectivity. Her final selection is a waltz by Johann Strauss. But such light music, I feel, is beyond Cella's ability. For a performer, this waltz probably requires more life experience than classical music does. Cella's hands hammer the waltz beat all too regularly, all too precisely.

But Nagy is truly carried away. He is so enraptured that I have to banish Cella from the room, sending her on some trivial errand. For a fifteen-year-old mind, rhapsodic praise from this sophisticated uncle is unconditionally dangerous, as anyone will agree. I do not want the corrupting arrogance of expertise to strike roots in Cella too early. Sometimes I fear that she, in strong contrast to myself, already tends to overestimate her role. Nagy strides up and down with long paces. His still youthful face beams with astonished approval. All in all, my friend Zsoltan is really a very dear man.

"What a splendid job you've done with the girl!" he cries. "She'll run rings around us all, she'll have fame and fortune, you'll see, fortune."

I put my finger to my lips, for I do not want Nagy to tempt the gods, and I am also bothered by his exultant "fortune," which ardently leaps from his heart. But he pays me no mind; he clutches Gretl's hands.

"My God, you've done a marvelous job. Congratulations!"

Nagy's mind was always teeming with ideas, even in his boyhood. Now that we are gathered around the tea cart again, he expounds on the idea that struck him during the Strauss waltz. Despite my initial resistance, Zsoltan's idea begins to make sense to me.

Everyone knows that cultivating music is part of the illustrious tradition of the princely House of Esterhazy. One need only recall Joseph Haydn, who spent years as a conductor and protégé in the service of this family of magnates, which has salvaged its sovereign power by maintaining it in the field of art. Today, the younger son of the current Esterhazy, a title devolving by primogeniture, embodies that old tradition. Prince Ernst is not only a music lover, but also a performer and composer. Now and then, one can find his name in newspaper reviews of concerts. Recently, Nagy tells us, Prince Ernst announced his plan to sponsor a musical academy in the magnificent hall of the Residence. It is scheduled to begin during the coming Mardi Gras, in late February or early March. A renowned quartet has offered to premiere its latest chamber music creation for this event, and the participation of two opera stars is as good as assured. Furthermore, says Nagy, and this is especially important, there is no celebrity in Vienna's music world, no famous conductor or influential critic, who will not feel flattered by an invitation to this academy. Such an event, in part artistic and in part dazzlingly social, will, in Nagy's opinion, form the most felicitous background for the debut of a young pianist, who is almost a *wunderkind*. She will never, he says, have a more tasteful or more effective chance to perform in public. He will take care of speaking to the prince about Cella and getting everything afloat.

Although, as I can remember, Nagy has always been a born arranger and *maître de plaisir,* I would never have expected this unselfish warmth for someone else's child.

Has Cella's personality, Cella's talent, inspired the restless bachelor with a tender need to help her, to promote her career?

I am surprised at Gretl. She seems to have given up her strange resistance to Zsoltan, and she now gazes at him through her thick spectacles, attentive and grateful.

"It would be very nice of you to do that, Nagy," she murmurs, suddenly blushing for no reason. Like most women, Gretl has the weakness of admiring everything that is higher socially, and here this weakness blends with her wishes for our child's success. Occasionally I can sense such feelings in her, even though we lead a very withdrawn life, seeing few other people. Our isolation and exclusivity, which constitute my vital element, have often caused her suffering, as she admits to herself. Her willing gratitude in accepting Nagy's offer forces me to show some restraint. It does not sound like such a bad idea, I say. Above all, I greet the possibility of a debut that will take place not in an ordinary concert hall, but in front of a parterre of connoisseurs. I tell Nagy to do some cautious probing, but not try to overcome any possible resistance. Cella is the one who behaves most correctly when we call her in and Nagy tells her about his plan. Once again, her conduct strikingly justifies my faith in her. She is neither very excited, enthusiastic, hungry for fame, nor anxious or cowardly. She faces the academy, calm and collected, whether or not it may come true. What a feeling of strength in the girl, who does not doubt her own direction, and yet what a childlike nature that is not confused by beguiling prospects!

"It's not up to any of you or me, it's up to Professor Scherber. Recently, he allowed a pupil to play somewhere, but he wouldn't allow another one. He's very particular about that. But if Bulbul speaks to him, maybe . . ."

I will speak to Scherber.

We ask Zsoltan to stay for dinner. But he has other plans, an important appointment in Vienna. When he leaves, as self-satisfied as Father Christmas after distributing presents, Cella accompanies him to the front door, laughing and chattering. We stay up late, Gretl and I. The table is cleared. A few files lie before me; I wanted to go through them, but I have not opened them. Gretl has likewise pushed her sewing basket far away. A touch of stress in her face shows me that her eyes must be aching again. The door to the next room, where Cella is asleep, is open. It is always like that. Cella claims she can fall asleep only when she hears us talking. And indeed, we *have* been talking, mainly about Nagy, over and over—his adventurous life, his unclear circumstances, his eternal youth, his high connections, his generosity. We are haunted by Nagy all evening. He is hard to read. Should one believe his stories?

What does he live on? Is he a parasite or does he simply know how to make the best of everything?

One cannot, as I remind Gretl, deny that there is a touch of flimflam in Nagy's background. His father, a tall, extremely elegant man, whom I still remember very clearly, also had a rather obscure profession. The small, philistine town viewed him with both awe and scorn; people saw him as a dangerous, debt-ridden gambler living in constant bankruptcy. Yet old Nagy had five children to feed—no minor task even for the most tenacious cardplayer. This large family lived in a rather small home which, during my boyhood, struck me as the epitome of aristocratic taste. Their home was filled with strange, scalloped antique furniture, of which no one understood the purpose. The walls were crowded with innumerable small paintings in huge gold frames. Every single picture was dark, almost black, and no image was recognizable. The place looked as if it had been won by its tenants in a bizarre lottery. The craziest knickknacks could be found everywhere, but no bedsteads. It remained an enigma where the Nagys laid their weary heads at night. And yet Zsoltan's home made a powerful impact on me when I compared it with my parents' sober, practical, and old-fashioned home.

Whenever I visited Nagy during our school days, he would never forget duly to point out the various treats and treasures of his father's museum: This bronze inkwell once belonged to Metternich, that brocade foot rug used to warm the lap of old Cardinal Richelieu, and so on, all of which I believed with respectful faith. He also kept explaining to me that the "Y" at the end of his name was the sign of an aristocratic background in Hungarian. Nor had I any reason to doubt him, for of all my schoolmates only Nagy had those brilliant traits that one ascribes to the frivolous and daring blood of horsemen. When we graduated from the Gymnasium, I myself urged him to exploit his many connections and take up active service in a cavalry regiment, which he then did, although his funds were more than limited. I keep recalling things from our adolescence, for whenever Zsoltan is absent, my feelings of friendship for him increase. Gretl probably knows all these stories ad nauseam. She sits there, silent and absentminded, as if making an enormous effort to listen to me. And then something surprising occurs.

"Bodenheim," she says (in earnest moments she does not call me by my first name, Hans), "don't you think we ought to move away from here?"

"To Vienna?" I ask, dumbfounded. "You of all people? When I suggested that a couple of years ago, you didn't want to leave Eisenstadt. You said you wouldn't feel at home anywhere else. And at that time, we had a marvelous opportunity—"

Gretl breaks in.

"No! I don't mean Vienna at all. I mean: move away entirely. . . . Somewhere else. . . . Abroad."

I am stunned. Gretl, such a homebody, so afraid of traveling, Gretl, who can barely be talked into going on a small summer trip—*she* wants to put an end to what we have here, *she* wants to leave Austria, *she* longs to live abroad? I am so perplexed by her desire that I cannot speak. She stares at me with huge eyes that glow brighter than usual.

"How can such an intelligent and educated man like you be so blindly trusting, *so* blindly trusting. . . ."

"Darling, you're speaking in riddles."

"Don't you sense what I sense, Hans? This sick atmosphere . . . You, I mean you people, should have more instinct for danger than we. And yet you're all so devoid of instinct."

Now I understand her. She is talking about the future of our fatherland. This is the first time that I have heard her speak such words of desperate anxiety. Is she upset by Zsoltan's visit? In our little town, one can encounter this political despair now and then. But such talk always angers me. Ever since German despotism passed those cruel laws, I have become more of an Austrian patriot than ever. I went to war for a great Empire, of which only the core has survived, and it is no claptrap to say that I shed my blood, for I was seriously wounded twice.

The ruler of our great Empire decorated me in front of many others, not only with several medals but with his personal words and goodwill. Is it conceivable, is it humanly possible that any power in the world could challenge my right to live in Austria and force me to consider the precaution of fleeing? I jump up and, with a pounding heart, I dash around our table, where Gretl is sitting motionless. At the same time, I know— and it infuriates me—that, in my agitation, my arguments are not quite logical. The real issue is not my own rights, but the eruption or absence of an elemental event. Neglectful of Cella, who is asleep, I shout, "No one has the right to speak like that, Gretl. We have to have faith, faith. The slightest lack of faith weakens our position. I admit the government has made one mistake after another. But the workers won't desert. Austria will live forever, I'm sure of it. The Austrians aren't obsessed barbarians, they're good people. Prussia is on the move, of course. And yet despite their big mouths, the enemies of our state are only a tiny minority—a very tiny one if it could be counted. We mustn't let ourselves get confused. That would be the worst misfortune."

Gretl heaves a conciliatory sigh, but she is not fully convinced. "I hope you're right. . . . But I'm better than you at telling when people are lying. . . . And very many people are lying."

Cella's voice comes from the next room: "Bulbul, what's wrong?"

I hold my tongue. I am sorry that my loud words have awakened her. Slowly I tiptoe into her room and over to her bed, which shows the rectangle of light from the parlor. But Cella does not notice me; she has instantly drifted off again. Oh, how tempestuously she still sleeps the sleep of childhood. Her hair hangs into her passionately reddened face. Her hands, chosen hands of art, are clenched in a little girl's fists. In her impetuous slumber, the blanket has slid from her feet. Covering her gingerly, I feel with strange devotion that I am her father.

Chapter 3

Castle Park, Reed Lake, and Gypsies

According to the calendar, we should have had frost and snow by now. But at the start of the new year, the fateful year, our Burgenland was quite warm. A resigned drought lay on the cracked stubble fields and highways all around. Every morning and evening, a brown fog rolled in from the direction of Hungary: eastern fog, *puszta* fog, filling the streets of our little town. "A sick atmosphere," Gretl had said, and I was forced to agree. It was like the cosmic accompaniment to some still unknown event. When these fogs came, it was difficult to breathe.

We had not heard from Zsoltan Nagy since his visit. I must confess that I was deeply upset by his unreliability, his infidelity, and not only because of Cella's debut. Popping up, vanishing, always unexpectedly, reeling off lavish promises, then forgetting them by the time he reached the threshold—such has always been his way. This—how shall I put it?—this iridescent morality may be very effective for driving women crazy. But among men, it constitutes a despicable hindrance. It is all profoundly related to the deceptive small black painting in the ostentatious gold frame, to Metternich's rusty inkwell, Richelieu's cheap foot rug, and Voltaire's shoe buckle (my father worshiped Voltaire), for which I, a dreamy-eyed fourteen-year-old, once swapped my rather large stamp collection. I hoped that this time Nagy would stay away forever. I was fed up with him.

I was sorry that the business of the academy in the House of Esterhazy was nothing but empty braggadocio. It would have been an excellent framework for introducing my Cella to the influential circles and leading musicians. Although she was not yet sixteen, a sense of disquiet within me said that I should miss no opportunity to launch such a talent. After all, the times were very bad. The prospects for a young artist could worsen crucially overnight. Anything that could be won today might be lost irrevocably tomorrow. Such thoughts blatantly revealed that my wife's pessimism, which had erupted so surprisingly after Nagy's departure, had already infected me against my will. No! Naturally, I did not admit these feelings, even to myself. In my own eyes, I remained the old upright, sanguine believer, the superior optimist, although a bit too emphatic. After all, as far as the eye could see, there was no adequate reason to take a gloomy view. Nevertheless, general anxieties now mixed into my usual worries about Cella.

On the afternoon of the second Sunday in December, a disquietingly warm sun was shining. Contrary to my normal habit of spending my free day at home, I went out right after lunch. It was two P.M. Following a long hiatus, I again felt a need to stroll alone in the Castle Park. The previous night, I had had very vivid dreams about the park. Slightly overgrown in my dream, it had appeared like a warning, a reproach, a rebuke, as if I had neglected it in some way. Naturally, I mean the Castle Park that rolls down the mountain like a dense green firebrand behind the princely Residence. Now, in winter, all that was left of the firebrand were the thick, trembling fumes of the branches. In my childhood, the park had not been open to the public. But since my father, an accountant and estate administrator, was deeply involved with the princely house, he was granted the privilege of taking his family strolling along the paths of the huge grounds on Sundays and holidays. We had to share this honor with several other residents of Eisenstadt. But still, when I was a boy in the Castle Park, I delighted in being slightly above the great mass of the local population and my schoolmates. Nagy, for instance, or Myslivec or Pramer, could not enjoy such a distinction.

In my dream, I saw the trees in the Castle Park again after a long absence: the century-old planes, elms, oaks, and lindens. They seemed to have grown to a supernatural width and height. Their crowns articulated spaces as solemn as cathedrals. In moss leggings up to their knees, in colorful autumn coats and robes, they stood as rigid as mighty Cossacks awaiting important visitors. Normally, the city dweller does not notice the trees that grow along the roads. But I felt as if I recognized each and every one of them, and they recognized me. My feet passed over a rolling terrain, softer than any other in the world. It was a voluptuously springy soil, a dry, fragrant swamp; for the fallen leaves remain on the ground here, forming yearly strata over the more remote paths and labyrinths of the park. Everywhere, cracks, adits, corridors opened up, blasted into the malachite mine. Sometimes it was like a long, narrow bazaar of silence, with the motionless branches stretching out their hands and peddling diverse and particolored brands of stillness. I kept coming back to the two pools, these stagnant waters of my drowned childhood, with their venomous films of coppery verdigris. Sudden holes gaped in these films, full of black, gurgling water, in which large tadpoles and tiny fish frolicked wildly.

And all at once, from the depths of one of these ponds, I was struck by Cella's voice. It sounded muffled, as if coming from a well-insulated adjacent room, and rather than calling for help, it politely announced, "Prelude and Fugue from *The Well-Tempered Clavier.*" And the same words over and over again. But I ran to the rotten boat that was moored there, in order to row across the dense water and reach my Cella's voice. "Bulbul, Bulbul," it gurgled, rising like bubbles around me. I could not tell whether Cella was still alive or had long since died of one of those feared childhood diseases. Yet oddly enough, the pain of knowing she was no longer on earth was not as dreadful as I had imagined.

That is only a minor feature of my dream, a detail I have salvaged in waking, for it was an unbelievably complicated dream, although the setting of the Castle Park did not change. Indeed, the main subject, the protagonist, was not Cella, but the park itself, its warning, its reproach, its rebuke. I had an embarrassed sense of guilt, like a man who suddenly remembers that his old parents still reside in the same city, and he has not visited them for years. This absurd sense of having neglected a filial duty reverberated deep into my Sunday, impelling me to leave my home at around two P.M., even though Gretl and also Cella made awful faces, for I was abandoning them to the hopeless boredom of the day of rest in a small town.

I found the Castle Park far more sober and normal than it had appeared in the lush autumn of my dream. December had defoliated it, unmasked it, the way reason exposes a poem. It is stupid that a man of almost fifty is still susceptible and measures ordinary trees in a dream with the wondering eyes of a child. Not even my near and dear, Gretl and Cella, knew that I had run out on them today because of a silly dream. One cannot say such things aloud. I am a thoroughly practical man, I have trained myself in precise planning, punctuality, schedules, consistency. The budding energy that prematurely faded in me has been inherited by Cella in the form of her musical gifts. And yet, were I to reveal only one one-hundredth of what goes on in me, I would be a universal laughingstock, and professionally I would be even worse off than I am now. The same must be true of other people, for goodness knows I am no exception. One's mind, one's good conduct, one's conventions seem to be merely the scab that has formed over a burning wound.

The anachronistic sun of that December day had lured many people into the Castle Park, mostly elderly gentlemen and a few noisy petty-bourgeois families. On one of the side paths, I ran into Jacques Weil. His name was actually Jacques Emanuel, Lord von Weil. The Weils played more or less the same part in our town as the magnate family of the Esterhazys played in the province. The Weils had been granted their nobility way back during the eighteen sixties in gratitude for the vast sums that they had contributed to the building of the Austro-Hungarian railroad network. Their home on the specific street, a delightful baroque mansion, was a designated landmark. Jacques' art collection and his grand library were even listed in the Baedeker. Weil was only three years my senior. But because he had been in a much higher year during our school days, I was in the habit of viewing him as far more mature than myself. He was very tall, very fat, bald, clean-shaven, wore large horn-rimmed glasses, limped slightly on his right leg, and therefore always walked with a black cane. His suit and fur coat sat stiff and creaseless on his body, as if someone had decked out an enormous mannequin in a store window. The old-fashioned black derby looked too small for his skull. He held his hand out to me in brown kid gloves, but then instantly pulled it back. Aha, I promptly thought, the rumor about Weil's germ phobia is true. People say he wears gloves even when he sleeps. But I find it odd that the well-known piety of his family coexists with this godless scientific fear.

I had not seen Jacques Emanuel Weil for ages. The peculiar thing about a small town is that it appears to keep us far more solitary than a big city and that people see one another far more seldom here. We reeled off our formulas in turn. What a miserable human fate it is that we always greet one another with the question a doctor asks at a sickbed: "How are you?" Both of us were so-so. One must be satisfied that things are not worse. He asked about Cella, about her progress at the piano. Is not a good memory for the traits, gifts, and cares of others a vivid proof of loving kindness? My heart warmed. I felt at peace, something I can never feel in Nagy's presence. Yet Weil's dark face remained stiff, motionless, an image of painfully self-absorbed indifference. His eyes never looked at me when he spoke to me.

We strolled on together. All the people who crossed our path saluted Weil with broad swings of their hats. It was the respectful homage one pays to legendary wealth, to a secluded and inaccessible prestige that was tongue-lashed at political gatherings, decried as alien and destructive. He was greeted even by people who were blatantly uncomfortable about acknowledging him. Jacques's space-displacing presence, his name, and the force of traditional habit compelled them to doff their hats. They had no choice, their arms twitched. Later, they could be ashamed of their weakness, which was not *yet* overcome. After a long promenade, we reached the lower pond, where my confused dream had taken place the night before. A shallow rowboat was actually rotting there in the thick soup of the swamp water. Since it was so warm, we settled on one of the benches and stared at the pool, which probably also signified something in Weil's dreams. A bunch of young boys strode past us, discussing something in their rough dialect. All at once, they fell silent. Their faces showed secretive contempt. They all wore shorts and white stockings. Everyone knew that those white stockings signified a certain political belief. When the group was gone, I turned to Weil. "What about you? What do you think of these matters?"

Smoking and ardently pensive, but without looking at me, he replied, "Can anyone still have any doubts, my dear friend?

What we see before us has nothing to do with political decisions made on the basis of any sort of interests or logic. Such motives can lead one to be a Democrat, a Republican, a Conservative, a Liberal, or even a Socialist, for all I care. But this is something biological, something physical. Don't they all look alike? These are faces off the assembly line, clichéd faces, a collective of faces that has suddenly formed without our noticing it. *One* single mother could have given birth to this entire generation—an inconceivable mother, to be sure. There is no remedy against this—above all, no intellectual remedy."

I was irked and agitated. "You must admit that this bunch does not have the slightest pretense to any sort of nationalism. Their fathers were Croats, Czechs, Hungarians, Turks, and goodness knows what else. Our population is an omnium gatherum of some fifteen races. Almost no one speaks an honest German as his mother tongue."

"Who is talking about nationalism," said Weil, unmoved and quite apathetic. "That is the most external of all signboards. Once these people have conquered the entire world, they will be more international than any Communist world revolutionary has ever dreamt. The truth lies behind the surface. In flesh and blood! Damn it all, it's true! The spirit of history always seems to prepare the physicality that it needs for its purposes."

"My dear Herr von Weil, I cannot and do not wish to think that objectively."

"Objectively or subjectively, what does it matter, who cares! All at once, they are here, the way the Huns or the Tartars were here! Except that they do not come from just one direction, they come from all directions!"

"And you consider their victory inevitable?"

"Call it a victory if you like, dear Bodenheim! It is really a remolding. Science tells us that each early period was ruled by a different animal species. The saurians, for example, and then the more advanced reptiles. Now it is the turn of the white-stocking species to conquer the earth and remold it. Just take a good look at the photographs in all illustrated newspapers, whether in America, Russia, Germany, or even Africa. Always the same type: slender, handsome, muscular, with blank eyes, a small skull, an activist chin, and glittering cinema teeth. Swimming, jumping, running, boxing, motorized from A to Z! All alike. It is easier to distinguish the faces of horses and dogs than the faces of the white-stockings. The collective drive, the hostility toward individual personality, is not the consequence of this remolding, it is the cause, just like the accompanying politics."

"But that does not explain the evil, the diabolism," I argued.

"Is it not splendid," said Weil, not moving a single muscle in his face, "is it not true bliss to be a primordial animal again, a boar, a hippopotamus, a bull, cloaked by the tattered drivel of a political ideal?! To let oneself go, to satisfy the inner criminal instinct, always in the intense feeling of one's own great worthiness and the noblest heroism?! Who is the enemy? Latin and Greek and mathematics and study and speculation and all the printed paper in the world since Gutenberg. The haughty printed paper is the archenemy, for it contains the hardest overexertion of mankind. Revolution against the mind! Mankind is going on vacation. Presumably, it needs to relax. And the white-stockings are in the lead, for they are weaklings like all rebellious truants. And then there is still one more enemy, the worst one of all: We!"

I looked at him. Did he mean us as a race? He smiled at the pond without waiting for my question.

"We are said to be hasty, but we are slow, so slow and so monotonous. The clock in our blood is very different from theirs. We are, to a certain extent, omitted from the course of history. Then too, they can remold everyone, but not us. They can kill us, drive us away, plunder us, but not make us bend, even if we help them in their efforts to do so. For we are completely immune. This immunity, willed by God, is the reason why they are so unhappily 'in hate' with us. As long as even one member of our tribe is still alive in the most remote nook of the world, the power of the white-stockings cannot be total."

I cannot say that I was satisfied by these views. Granted, Weil was a splendid man, a sage. After all, he had the leisure and wherewithal to devote his life entirely to study and contemplation, unlike myself. Even in times of crisis, a house like S. Weil & Sons, Agricultural Machines, effortlessly yields a profit from which several families can live in a princely style. A factory almost a century old, working smoothly for generations now, and never having lost its markets in Bohemia, Hungary, or the Balkans. There are brothers and cousins working there. Jacques Emanuel is troubled only with the most important decisions. Around noon, he looks in at the office, but normally he sits in his amazing library, letting nothing divert him from his thoughts, for he is unmarried. How easy it is in this way to attain scientific and scholarly omniscience as well as abstract indifference. I was also disturbed by his downright pathological cleanliness. For prior to sitting down on the bench, he spread out his large silk handkerchief.

"Dear Herr von Weil," I declared in rather ill humor, "your ideas are probably correct. But things have not yet reached that pass, thank goodness. Our Austria is still here. And she lives and wants to live and is defending herself. It is extremely dangerous to present the principle of destruction as an ineluctable fate. We cannot indulge in the luxury of viewing the devil in scientific terms. Our passivity affords the greatest opportunity to the white-stockings. Did you yourself not say that they are basically weaklings? Hence, no justice, no compromise—just bare your fists and fight, fight! I will not have anyone tell me that this is not our fatherland and that *we* cannot defend its freedom without compromising that freedom. We should therefore all think of the fight rather than a destruction which must not come."

"Fight, of course," Weil murmured absentmindedly, "by all means, but how, and with what?"

He suddenly looked pale and decrepit. His broad face slackened. He nervously squirmed about on the bench while talking toward the ground. "All at once, some people are standing in the sun and the others in the shade. For several years now, it has been growing cold for us, and the shadow keeps spreading more and more. Can one call this 'victory' and 'defeat'? Is this happening above or below? Then let us fight the position of the sun, by all means, it must be . . ."

As if at a cue, the treacherous December sun vanished behind clouds, and the air instantly turned very cool. Weil quickly stood up as if worried about his health; he pedantically folded his silk handkerchief with his stiff gloved hands, and, without glancing at me, he began to move.

"Come, Bodenheim. My car is waiting outside. Let us take a little ride in the country, to the lake, if you wish. Who knows when we shall meet again and have time. How about it?"

Weil's car, a long, heavy American limousine, was waiting across from the castle, near the low barracks. Here, until the start of our century, the Princes Esterhazy had been allowed to maintain their own bodyguards, merrily bedizened operetta soldiers with shakos, busbies, and broadswords, to the delight of all the children. A lordly chauffeur, cap in hand, opened the door of Weil's limousine and helped us in. Jacques, with his lame legs, arduously wedged himself into the car. Suddenly he looked old and unhappy. At worst, he might lose everything with his riches. I had no riches to lose and, if worst came to worst, I would still have the most important thing of all: Cella. No, better think no further along those lines.

We sat soft and deep in the seats. A passenger in such an automobile loses part of his physical weight and thereby a piece of mental gravity. Luxury is no delusion. It banishes certain anxieties and feelings of inferiority. Of course, it replaces them with other feelings, especially for a man like me. One is ashamed. I am ashamed. For we live in a wretched world.

We had already left our little town. The road wound through the sad and lovely countryside of grapes and colorfully painted wayside shrines—my homeland. Villages opened their shabby arms. Although the cold of winter had not yet broken in, the church towers stood gray and frozen stiff. Poor land! Even the naked acacias were grieving, and the village ponds were filled with hissing geese, mud, and mire. The villagers were loitering outside their shacks, lined up in a Sunday row and staring after us, hollow, curious, and reproachful. They appeared to be waiting for something that would not come, and by no means along this road. It was certainly not us they were waiting for. I knew such people from my law practice, doomed souls, hesitant, taking one step forward, one back. All too many nations had poured their beverage into this melting pot. And the East with its empty eyes peers over the horizon. But once the local wine comes into its own, these doomed souls lose all control, they grow violent, and the results are murder, mayhem, and politics. However, the populace drinks many wines that do not come from grapes.

We drove through a workers' settlement. Here too, the people stood in rows. But these were different human beings. A severe melancholy prevailed. They could not forget that they had been robbed of their strength four years ago, when the government ordered its militia to fire at them. This annihilatory work had been both absurd and inadequate, for they were still alive and still had the last word in their hearts. A miserable human condition! I let out a painful remark. Jacques Weil, the rich man, glared sick and gray, as if shouldering the blame.

The motor excitedly crooned its way up a slope. Weil told the chauffeur to halt at the top. Before our eyes, Neusiedl's lake of reeds spread out, one of the largest inland bodies of water in Central Europe. It stretched from north to south, its end invisible. Over on the Hungarian side, it melted into the shapeless gray of December. We drove slowly through the winemaking town of Rust, down to the shores of the lake; then we had to walk a great distance along a gully in order to reach

the shallow water. Were the inconceivable to happen, the re-
alization of Gretl's fear and Weil's theory, I would lose the
oldest part of my homeland with this lake, for a thousand
experiences, memories, impressions of my childhood play on
its banks, even more than in the Castle Park. It was here that
I first encountered nature. Now the head-high reeds, circling
the lake for miles around from spring to fall, had been har-
vested. Instead of the mysterious forests, an exposed marsh-
land stretched everywhere. But if I shut my eyes, everything
was as in May and June, when a dense, muggy, tropical heat
fills this virtually Asiatic basin. Purple herons and silver herons
and spoonbills fluttered from the gigantic masses of reeds and
flocks of them soared across the sky. In venomous green holes
in the reeds, I saw the Egyptian ibis standing on one leg, for
it nests only on the Nile and here. When I was a child, how
proud I was of my homeland, proud that the Egyptian ibis,
this cousin of the exotic flamingo, nests in my area and nowhere else. I could hear the croaks and cries of the bitterns
and the large aquatic birds, which lived in the deepest, most
internal sanctum of the reeds, tolling incomprehensible ave
bells. How deeply I wished that it were June. And that all the
memories gathering in Weil's soul and mine were a summer
reality. But instead, that strange brown fog suddenly rose and
encompassed us. Nevertheless, we stood there hushed, unable
to leave.

Then all at once, on the edge of the brown fog, a shallow
rowboat landed, gliding out unnoticed from behind one of the
reed islands. An old peasant couple, dressed in black, got out
and began trudging into the mist. They were followed by a
young woman, coarse, strong, and very tall. She was carrying
a child's coffin in both arms, the tiniest coffin I had ever seen.
Sometimes, the old peasant turned around and signaled his
desire to help. The young woman did not seem to notice; she
kept taking long strides with her solid feet, her eyes staring
blankly ahead. A symbol! Jacques Weil must have felt it too.
But what was the symbolism of the tiny coffin that the young

mother was carrying in her own arms from one of the deserted hamlets to our shore? I am not a sentimental man. But I am always horrified by the sorrow and death of a small child, perhaps because I am reminded of Cella and all the dangers that she has escaped so far. I suggested to Weil that we go home.

Upon leaving the tiny village of Sankt Margarethen, Weil told the chauffeur to stop again. For centuries, a small settlement of Gypsies had survived there, on a small hill above a pond. Usually, three wretched, roofless shells teemed with a dirty, gaudy mob, and half-naked, brown urchins pounced on every passerby with their greedy jargon, begging for "kreutzers" and stretching out their earthy claws. They still asked for kreutzers, a currency of times long past and, in the incomprehensible conservatism of all that is ancient and outcast, they seemed not to realize that the kreutzer had been replaced by the heller and the heller by the groschen. But today no beggar boy was to be seen. No suspicious smoke curled up from the ruinous chimneys, and no ragged laundry flapped in the wind. We drew nearer. The ruins were stiff, lifeless, and empty. Only a few rusty, battered pots were lying in the mangy winter grass, pots that had been too useless for even the Gypsies to take along. With a despairing expression, Weil wiped off his shoes before reentering the car.

"They are gone," he said. "They have the instinct of rats."

And I had to think of the way Gretl reproached me and our people for not having that instinct.

When I returned home, a surprise awaited me. I had feared being greeted by reproachful faces. But I was welcomed at our very door by loud voices and laughter. When they heard the grating of my key, Cella came dashing toward me. "Bulbul," she cried excitedly, "I had to play so many things for them: Schumann's *Carnaval* and two Chopins and Debussy's 'Reflets dans l'eau.' If Professor Scherber knew, my goodness, we haven't had anything like it." Her hot hand pulled me into the room. There, at the festive table, sat Gretl with Zsoltan Nagy and two strangers. Gretl is a slow, deliberate person, who does not have an easy time improvising. I was therefore astonished that she had managed to dig up such huge amounts of cake and candy and sandwiches on a Sunday. There were bottles of cognac, whiskey, and kirsch on the table; these beverages were a great rarity in our home since neither Gretl nor I drink such strong liquor. A glass of wine at lunch and another at dinner are enough for us. Where did those bottles come from? Had Nagy brought us more presents? The guests drank from water glasses. I was amazed that Gretl too had joined in. Her face glowed from the unaccustomed alcohol. She had put away her spectacles, although she is helpless without them, unable to see more than two feet ahead of her with her naked eyes. How pretty, how girlish she looked without the thick lenses—ten years younger and twenty years more attractive. Nagy sat right next to her and seemed to have been courting her. Goodness knows, I would have granted her a more serious admirer. I was annoyed by the words he greeted me with. Always the same stupid irony: "You have kept the supreme assembly waiting for a long time, bold war hero. . . ."

Can he not get over the fact that a nobody like me was once honored and decorated before his very eyes? Now he stood up, and so did the two other gentlemen. Both were tall; one had black hair and a small, trimmed moustache, the other blond hair and a goatee.

"My dear Styxi," Nagy said to the black-haired man, "this is *the* Bodenheim, the *pater familias*. . . ."

Then he introduced them to me. "Prince Ernst Esterhazy, whom you know of, and this is Professor Lateiner, editor of *Die Abendzeit*—who does not know him? I have brought all this glory into your humble abode."

We shook hands.

Despite his overlifesize and well-padded heaviness, Prince Ernst (Nagy familiarly used his aristocratic nickname, Styxi) was a man with delicate bones. One could tell by his wrists. His feminine joints could barely carry the mass of this body, and he tended to look for support, something for his weight to lean on or slump against. The head with the thick, black, parted hair was extraordinarily tiny, and it swayed to and fro on its long stalk. The broad mouth under the small moustache had bulging and astonishingly naked lips. The prince's shiny eyes were rigidly fixed on me. Effusively earnest, they bored into some point on the left half of my face, as if it had something stunningly important to reveal. At the same time, these mindlessly sparkling eyes showed that Esterhazy was resolutely determined to gaze at the other person to the point of exhaustion, but not listen to him. For if anyone else began speaking, the prince's eyes were instantly flooded with a wave of painful impatience.

"Extraordinary," Prince Ernst said to me, without going into Cella's performance. "Extraordinary. The other participants are all prepared. It will be a marvelous academy." He counted on his fingers. "The quartet . . . the two singers . . . Lateiner was good enough to speak to Suchoda. . . . Suchoda agreed to play. . . . I daresay I regard Suchoda as the premier violinist in the world. And then the surprise . . . The little girl . . ."

"Suchoda, oh well, Suchoda," said Lateiner with a weary gesture, and one could not tell whether he was being derogatory or merely absentminded. If the young prince had conspicuously frail wrists and joints, then the critic looked utterly boneless. He twisted to and fro in a bizarre way, obligated to perform such serpentine movements by a distinct malaise with the world and with himself. He kept chewing his lower lip incessantly, peering as if, at times, he were deeply offended, and at times, resigned to God's will. I wondered why he was disgruntled, but could find no reason. Only little by little did I realize that this offended air was Lateiner's natural expression. Everything he said appeared to be wrested from his inner annoyance, but then it was quite vague and empty, as now: "A decision must be made. . . . There are still all sorts of things

. . . Hmm . . . And the program . . . Along with your highness's works, there would also have to be a fresh touch. . . . Your humble servant, at least . . ."

The prince's burning eyes again drilled into a point on the left half of my face.

"Who is more in favor of a fresh touch than I? I have already conferred three times with the minister of education. All music has to be reformed, if you please. That is my viewpoint. You do know my paper, Professor. . . ."

"Just take it in hand, Styxi," said Nagy. His tone—I did not know why—offended me. But the prince seemed delighted at Nagy's confidence; he raised his glass and drained it. And now the three of them launched into a conversation that the three of us, Gretl, Cella, and I, could barely follow because of the names and events in high politics and art, to which modest people like us had no personal access.

I observed Cella. Her earnest and attentive eyes were gazing at the mouths of the speakers. With all her strength, the child realized what these moments could signify for her future. I will not conceal that I too was on tenterhooks. After all, we know from various life stories that the fate of a talent often depends on sheer chance. In peaceful times, one can calmly wait for a fluke. But today, when the future lives of all children appear more somber, more frustrated, more hopeless than ever before, one has to seize any opportunity. Not to mention the life of one of *our* children! Cella looked more like her mother than me. Everyone said so. And yet, what if the inconceivable were to come about, the things that aroused Gretl's innermost fears, and that an intelligent man like Jacques Weil awaited as a natural catastrophe—what then, yes, what then? But if by then Cella had crossed the first threshold of success, if she had already evoked the public astonishment that I felt certain was bound to come, then she could not be so easily deprived of her ascent and give way to mediocrity. In any case, there would be a contest between the unthinkable (in which, despite everything, I still did not believe) and Cella's debut. The conversation of the experts drifted farther and farther afield. The prince decreed with rigid, sparkling eyes that did not pay attention. Lateiner twisted like a snake, producing nothing substantial whenever he spoke. Zsoltan Nagy seemed to be poking fun at both of them. There was nothing serious, no conviction in any of the three. I interrupted their conversation.

"What date have the gentlemen set?"

I was irked by my choice of words, the legal terminology that had slipped out of me. Prince Ernst added some cognac to the whiskey in his glass. It must have tasted awful. His reply was imprecise. "The last week in February, I think."

"Should it not be earlier?" The words escaped me, to my own amazement.

Gretl eyed me strangely. "My, you're impatient!"

"He's right," laughed Nagy, "the child has to be launched early."

A dreadful locution! No one spoke like that in our area. It did not fit Zsoltan, who normally cultivated an aristocratic accent with a slight Hungarian tinge. Lateiner, pulling a diary from his pocket, read out all the important dates of the great concerts, opera premieres, and festivals in Vienna, which would prevent him and all other celebrities from accepting the invitation to Eisenstadt. Since, contrary to his nature, he had drunk a lot of whiskey, but only in order to keep up with the prince and Nagy, his response became longwinded and chaotic. It took me quite a while to get them to choose and fix the nineteenth of February for the academy.

Nagy had lapsed into silence and seemed not to be listening. All at once, he turned to Gretl. His lips twitched, and his eyes sparkled incomprehensibly. "Now I've made up for it, haven't I? You must have been very angry that you didn't hear from me for three weeks."

Although he had not addressed me, I replied, "To be frank, Nagy, we *were*. You did not behave at all nicely. We were at a loss to understand. Is that not so, Cella, you were very disappointed with Uncle Zsoltan."

"But now he *is* here," said Cella, grabbing Nagy's hand and smiling at the guests. Zsoltan sighed.

"Cella is the only one who has a little faith in me. I just got back three days ago. Styxi can confirm it. I was called away right after visiting you, I had to go out of town."

"And where, if I may ask?" I inquired, sounding like an investigator, against my will.

"Actually, no one may ask," Nagy jeered, "when someone travels to Geneva. People usually go there on confidential missions. Unfortunately, I am not one of those decent souls, so you may be as indiscreet as you like."

To my astonishment, I saw that Gretl had poured herself some more kirsch. Her cheeks were burning. She repeated "confidential mission," running her tongue over these words as if they were a taste sample that she had to savor thoroughly. However, she appeared to find the taste extremely comical, for she suddenly leaned back and burst out laughing, a long, alien laughter that was not like her.

Chapter 4

Many War Veterans

After a long debate on all the pros and cons, the musical academy at the House of Esterhazy was scheduled for the twenty-first of February. On the whole, Zsoltan Nagy had proved himself after all, and I felt I had judged him too harshly. One cannot expect a darling of the gods to show the stolid consistency of a government official. He now visited us frequently, even on weekdays, when I was not at home. Cella and Gretl conferred with him about all the problems having to do with the recital. Cella even maintained that he was not at all superficial, and that he had a very fine musical sense, despite his lack of knowledge.

Meanwhile, the prince's office had sent out brochures and invitations far in advance, so that the guests, who were overwhelmed with obligations, could fit all the events into their schedules.

Several days later, Nagy reported that not a single one of the musical celebrities had begged off, and that Cella would catch all birds with one stone—an opportunity that seldom knocks for a beginner. We were also invited to the castle twice: once for tea, and once even for dinner. Cella had to play. She was not intimidated by the dazzling circle. On the contrary, it intensified her energy, just as I had expected it would. Never had her touch been more powerful, her absorption in the music more profound, her indifference to all externals greater than at this moment. My faith in her inherent strength was solidified beyond all measure. I had difficulty concealing the moist happiness in my eyes. Cella did not court cheap applause: despite our agreement, she had selected chiefly rigorous pieces. Lots of Bach. Her performance elicited more than loud admiration. I could almost use the word "bewilderment" for the mood that took hold of this unfeeling and superficial company after the final chord. Prince Ernst, slumping frequently, walked from one guest to another, playing the discoverer and accepting congratulations. Cella was showered with expressions of goodwill and assurances of a wonderful future. It was the first time that I saw the child's brown hair surrounded by the warm, trembling air of triumph.

Gretl too was simply overwhelmed with love, especially by the ladies of the house. They did not act aloof, they displayed not a smidgen of the distrust that one usually shows toward the stage mother of a child prodigy. Indeed, Gretl seemed to evoke something like an emphatic warmth. It apparently did her a world of good. She blossomed. The excitement reverberated in her for days on end. To my surprise, she looked like someone to whom amends have suddenly been made for an old injustice. This gave me food for thought. Despite our domestic peace, our marriage was apparently not as simple as I often assumed.

I was the only one who did not feel all that comfortable in the overpowering rooms of the Residence. Although I was treated with the greatest kindness, I could not free myself for even one instant from the hateful awareness that I did not belong here: My father was an employee of the prince's. I am a small lawyer. Outside my sphere, I feel oppressed. Perhaps this is just an awful arrogance on my part. But for Cella, for the omnipotence of art, all doors fly open, all distinctions are an-

nulled, and there is no such thing as high and low, rich and
poor.

Needless to say, I had written a letter to Scherber about all
this, making Cella's participation in the private concert dependent on his permission. The child herself had delivered my
letter to the professor. He had barked something about "eating
fire prematurely" but raised no other objection. After her lesson, he had casually indicated that he was expecting a visit
from me very soon. However, Christmas passed, and then the
first week of the new year, before I managed to call on him.
The reason for my delay was a welcome development in my
career.

One day, Jacques Emanuel Weil had turned up in my office:
large, gray, creaseless, and stiffly gloved. Suspiciously testing
the chair on which he settled and gazing numbly past my face,
he asked me to process a drawn-out transaction for the firm of
S. Weil & Sons.

It was a major deal, involving a very considerable fee for the
negotiating attorney. This single case not only altered my eco-
nomic condition thoroughly, it enhanced the prestige of my
small law office. It certainly meant something that this important matter had been entrusted not to the major attorneys of
the capital, who were normally hired by the house of Weil, but
to me, a modest provincial lawyer. I did not know how I had
earned such honors. Had our meeting at the Castle Park that
Sunday and our brief drive to the lake of reeds aroused Weil's
active liking for me and given him something to think about?
After all, we were as good as neighbors. No matter! As he sat
next to me, heavy and dismal, I could not stifle my joy at this
success or maintain the professionally indifferent face of the
legal advisor. How happy I was for the sake of Cella and Gretl.
This was only a start. And the connection to one of our largest
industries would make me a rich and influential man. New,
shimmering possibilities of life floated past my inner eye, as I
casually leafed through the papers that Weil had handed me.
At last, all our limitations and straitened circumstances would

be overcome! A larger home! A first-class grand piano for Cella, a Bösendorfer, a Steinway, or even a songlike Blüthner. For Gretl, a fur coat; she needed one badly—if not mink, then perhaps Persian lamb. Curly black goes wonderfully with soft blond hair. But most important of all: Cella's musical training would no longer be a sacrifice weighing down our budget. My hands would be free to do a lot more for the child than previously; I would be able to calculate and prepare her road to victory more clearly. Rosy dreams of the future smiled at us. The anxieties of the past few weeks took a backseat.

I plunged into my work eagerly and ardently. I had to take three trips: one to Prague, another to Belgrade, and the last to Bucharest. I traveled third-class and always at night, in order to keep my expenses as low as possible. A joyous obsession forced me to pinch every penny, so that I would net a large profit, which would finally—and belatedly enough!—establish our prosperity. I intended once and for all to end our old life, that small-town rut. The newspapers wrote about various measures taken by our government to fiercely protect our independence against any high treason. Optimist that I am, I breathed sighs of relief. I blessed all the anxieties that had prompted me to sturdily take my fate in hand. (Naturally, if one thinks about it, Weil was responsible for this revival of my energy.) But seldom had I experienced more cheerful times than on the hard wooden seats of the sooty night trains, which ground to a screechy halt every ten minutes. The gods were favorable to me. My negotiations were successful. The adversary's lawyers proved amazingly easy to negotiate with. My ambition made a powerful impact. Everything went like clockwork. I attained much more for the firm than Weil had expected. I came back from Bucharest with the exhilarating certainty that I had brilliantly demonstrated my abilities and shown that as the attorney of a renowned industrial firm I was second to none of my colleagues.

The day of my return—it was the eighth of January—I found a letter from the Iron Ring on my desk. This letter was the

reason why I instantly made an appointment with Myslivec,
Johannes Myslivec.

$\mathcal{I}$f I am not mistaken, I have already mentioned Myslivec
once or twice as the name of one of my school friends. We
shared a desk for eight years, he as an excellent student, I as
a mediocre one. I can easily evoke Myslivec's earlier image: a
fat boy with the thick, pink hair of an albino, swollen eyes,
very pale eyebrows and lashes. His heavy, large-pored face had
begun forming jowls at an early age. Myslivec knew everything
without acting like a grind. Whenever he was tested, he would
dauntlessly translate his knowledge into strange, fluent, unc-
tuous words. In those days, he impressed me as an unattainable star; after all, he was the only talented student in our class
and, aside from Zsoltan Nagy, the only unusual one. We saw
him as a future judge, for his compositions radiated "style,"
and the teachers always read them aloud as unsurpassable
models. Above all, Myslivec was a master of quotations. His
essays always teemed with the most sublime and most powerful names in world literature, and the glory of these involun-
tary collaborators elevated his style to heights that were
inaccessible to the rest of us, who were just average students.
This occasionally annoyed some of the others. However, since
Myslivec was never arrogant, but always cultivated a formal,
gingerly courtesy toward everyone else, he almost never got
into a fight. As the son of a small elementary-school principal,
he was—how shall I put it; "thrifty" is not the right word, nor
is "precise"—the epitome of caution. His textbooks, borrowed
from the school supply room, were covered with blue glossy
paper and sported calligraphic labels. In the highest grades of
the Gymnasium, when other students proudly began flaunting
stiff collars and striped cuffs, he always wore yellowish cellu-
loid protectors on his collars and cuffs. Never have I met anyone in whom everything was as thoroughly "in order" as it was
in Myslivec's life. While the rest of us forgot something almost

daily, he always had everything with him. Nothing about the wordsmith Myslivec was unintentional or uncalculated. His class schedule was a miracle to behold. He always had time for anything and everything, although he omitted none of the elective subjects, including singing and drawing, which the other students avoided. Yet he sang like a drill press and handed in drawings—vases and plaster heads—whose lack of talent was hard to surpass. Although we sat side by side, he, who knew everything, never lent me a hand in my most helpless moments. Likewise, during tests, his arm shielded his notebook in such a way that I could not steal even the tiniest word or number from his masterwork. However, his avarice was not malevolent; it derived from an invincible sense of personal property and an eternal anxiety about his own success in life. Nevertheless, we were good neighbors for eight years. I know the weakness of my self-confidence accurately; it all too easily makes me admire the abilities of other people and deadens my critical faculties. However, Myslivec seemed to like me in return. He visited me at home every Sunday, while I entered his home only once. In those days, a "liberal" era, our people were not publicly acknowledged to be different. Nor did Myslivec and I ever allude to such things. Except that once—we were fifteen years old—he asked me the following question in his hard, solemn Slavic accent: "Is what my mother says true? Are there still real magicians with real books of magic among your people?" I, the son of a freethinker, was so outraged by this stupid question that I have not forgotten it, even today.

That was Myslivec the student. Myslivec the man—Government Councilor Dr. Johannes Myslivec, chairman of the Burgenland Office of Landmark Protection, editor-in-chief of *The Eisenstadt Herald,* head librarian of the province, founder of the Association of Local Costumes and Customs, director of the Catholic Amateur Theater, and so on—Myslivec the man had evolved physically and mentally from the albino-colored boy. His face seemed unchanged, only the fat jowls had grown. Although both of us lived in the same small town, our paths seldom crossed. It was only when Myslivec was elected vice president of the Iron Ring—in addition to all his other titles—that we occasionally got together. I simply cannot fathom how he ever achieved that honorary office in the veterans' association, since he allegedly spent the entire war in the press barracks. Oh well, it was none of my business. I do not poke into other people's affairs. Nagy hated Myslivec; he called him a goldbrick and a busybody. That could be, but I still envied my former schoolmate's work energy and his ability to set up schedules.

I had offered to meet Myslivec at the White Rose. He rejected this idea with the most modest courtesy and instantly came over to my office from the provincial government building, where he had his office. He shook my hand emotionally and protractedly, as if expressing his condolences for a mysterious cause of grief. He wore a brown, sacklike smock with a leather patch on his right sleeve. His buttonhole sported the red-white-and-red sign of Austrian patriots and government supporters—an emblem popularly known as the "worm of conscience." All of us wore it; many of us only pro forma, alas. However, I was unnerved by Myslivec's tie, which boasted the same colors, until I persuaded myself that this was only a silly coincidence.

I handed the vice president of our provincial section of the Iron Ring the letter from the central committee, asking us to dispatch a delegation consisting of two members to the important conference of all nine provincial sections that was to take place in Vienna on the tenth of this month at the conference hall of the Österreichischer Hof hotel. Myslivec read the letter in his usual precise and solemn manner, folded it neatly, and raised his priestly baritone to a lengthy and elevated speech.

"Honored friend, allow me to make the following suggestions. Sergeant Jupenigg—our honorary president—is a venerable old man of the staff, who should not be exposed to any inconveniences. Lieutenant Schuster—our president—has been ailing for a long time now and generally does not care to desert his sickbed. What then is left to do, given the relative lack of time? *Quidquid agis, prudenter agas et respice finem.* We shall have an ad hoc election, *sponte nostra,* and choose a duumvirate that we shall represent at the plenary session, you, my honored colleague, and my own humble self. . . . If you agree, and if you, as a veteran, are filled with true virile courage, then entrust yourself to me and my senile vehicle, which I shall drive to our capital the morning of the day after tomorrow. *Urbem petimus. . . ."*

His speech by no means sounded ironical or comical. Myslivec listened to his own series of words earnestly and attentively. I accepted his invitation. Since the conference was slated for three in the afternoon, it gave me a convenient possibility of calling on Scherber, as he wished me to do.

I sat. Scherber, on the other hand, moved restlessly about the room, so that I, being seated, had to keep turning my head to follow him. The winter sun fingered its way through the room, making the thick dust glow on all objects. His place lacked a woman's touch. Scherber's unkempt gray hair blazed red whenever he crossed the rays of the sun. The gold pince-nez danced on his nose. The wan lips under his moustache showed saliva bubbles. He wore a velvet housecoat, greasy and spotted. His left shoulder was higher than his right. His footsteps smacked sloppily in worn-out slippers. This was Scherber, the most important piano teacher in decades, one of the three surviving disciples of Franz Liszt, highly esteemed by the Master and constantly recommended in his letters. Several years ago, Scherber had left Berlin for obvious reasons and been forced to return home to Vienna. He was always excited, but today far beyond the usual measure. I had probably not chosen a favorable time for my visit. "Herr Doctor Bodenherz," he snapped at me (how embarrassing to hear one's own name altered), "Herr Doctor Bodenherz, I have to talk to you about the girl. Do you know what is going on with that girl?"

"I do believe I know, Herr Professor." I smiled, with mild assurance in my heart. "I see my daughter every morning when she gets up, every evening when she goes to bed, and in between, at every meal, except on the days when she has lessons."

"Lunch and supper, so you know something about the girl's appetite. But otherwise . . ."

I was a bit terrified.

"Do you have something unpleasant to tell me about Cella, Herr Professor?"

Scherber interrupted his stormy movements and guffawed.

"Not at all. I am utterly uninterested in private lives. Cella is an innocuous child, an adolescent with no special features, quite in keeping with her age. But that is just it. I must say that her conception far surpasses her age."

My chest swelled. I claimed—no doubt a bit too arrogantly—that the professor was telling me nothing new and that I was profoundly amazed, over and over again, by her abilities at the piano. My words aroused Scherber's anger. His pince-nez danced and flashed.

"What do you mean, Herr . . . ? How long did you have to study in order to obtain your doctorate? A physician, right? Oh, an attorney! So four or five years at the university, then a year as a legal assistant, right? Do you believe that music is attained any more cheaply? It is more expensive, Herr Doctor Bodenhaus, music is a great deal more expensive. Music is a sacred order with the strictest labor vow. A musician goes to sleep at night, believing he has everything in his fingers, and when he wakes up early in the morning, his fingers are empty, stiff, stupid, mindless. . . . Talent? Just one precondition among many, that is all! . . . Incidentally, there must have been some musical raw material in your family or your wife's?"

Not that I knew of. I have never heard of even the slightest musical gift among Gretl's people or mine.

"Is that necessary?" I asked, astonished, "To explain a phenomenon like Cella?"

"As a rule," Scherber growled vaguely, and all at once he looked tired and absentminded. He pushed a chair next to mine and sat down, groaning, a very old man.

"How do you like living in this country, Herr Doctor?" he asked in a solemn, hollow voice, and without waiting for my opinion, he answered conspiratorially, "I find it filthy. Filth everywhere, character filth, opinion filth. Wherever you step, it is soft and mushy. I know whom I am dealing with, good Lord. 'Kiss your hand' and 'The pleasure is all mine' and 'My compliments' and 'I am honored' and 'A thousand thanks.' They have no honor, believe me. In public, they bow and scrape to the cross, but in private they have prepared their crooked cross, their swastika, just in case. . . .''

He waved me off as if unwilling to hear any reply, then moved closer, touching my knees.

"No prospects, Herr Doctor, no prospects for your girl. Or do you believe that I am dependent on this filthy country? Scherber is part of an undesirable past here, although I bring foreign money into their country and they have lured me here with a hundred promises. But across the ocean, among the Indians, Scherber is someone, you probably know that too. Music, sir, left our country long ago, acquiring the immigration papers of a new homeland. . . . My motto is: Better one year too early than one day too late. In short, do you wish me to take Cella along when things reach that pass?"

I was dumbstruck. Another man without faith, without hope, more desperate than Jacques Weil. Only gradually did I comprehend the honor that this great teacher was paying Cella by asking if he could take her along to America. He was placing her above all his other students. Understandably, I was made slightly dizzy by this turn of events. Thoughts of salvation, anxieties of separation assailed me chaotically. Scherber did not wish any immediate decision from me. He said that everything was still up in the air and he hoped there was still time.

"Think it over at leisure, Herr Bodenherz, for a few

weeks. . . . Come back at the end of March. I shall then give you more detailed information. . . . For the time being, not a word to the girl, needless to say."

He was interrupted by a knock. Lateiner, the critic of *Die Abendzeit,* twisted in through the door, filled with his humility and malaise. A lurking tension appeared in Scherber's face.

"What's new, Lateiner?"

The critic's blond moustache quivered. His long, boneless figure sank into an armchair without his shaking our hands.

"The All-Christian government . . ." the journalist bleated, ". . . Kupka has gotten the master class. . . . Kupka, the Teutonic believer in Wotan, a notorious traitor, a piano sergeant of agility and rapidity . . . Gentlemen . . ."

Scherber suddenly faded into utter indifference. "Did you expect anything else, Lateiner? Could you possibly have thought that they would ask *me?*"

Lateiner pointed an exceedingly long forefinger at Scherber. "A directive has been issued concerning you. We have to write that you are an international celebrity, but that you can no longer be considered because of your advanced age. You will be awarded a medal the first chance they get. It all means: Knocking the wind out of the enemy's sails."

Scherber seemed highly amused; he laughed. "Murder with mitigating circumstances for the victim—that has always been an Austrian specialty."

But Lateiner leaped up, stretching his arms to the ceiling and shaking his fists. Given his swaying figure, I would never have imagined him capable of this gesture of tense resolution.

"Gentlemen," he cried, "if we could only charge ahead once more, as in the past."

This unleashed my temper, too. "Believe me, we *shall* charge ahead. I am hopeful and confident—"

A jeering growl from Scherber's lips: "We *shall* charge ahead, gentlemen, but in a different way, a very different way."

In his flapping slippers, he dashed over to the window, rattled it open, stuck his head out, and inhaled deep gulps of the winter air, which, rust-colored and full of the cold smell of burning, filled Mondscheingasse, the street on which he lived.

I walked through the streets of Vienna. I had a lot of time. Until three P.M. I was not plagued by hunger. My head was in a vise. I made a useless effort to focus on the most crucial thing: Scherber's plan to whisk Cella off to America. How could I think! My mind was a tense, crouching animal that sniffed danger. Images, lights, shadows, emotions passed through the animal, never quite cohering. Flags hung from all buildings, red-white-and-red flags: people were celebrating a patriotic holiday. The afternoon traffic moved leisurely. It was quite early. But the sun inundated the tremendous main thoroughfare, and the people enjoyed it. These people hurried or strolled, crowded onto the trolleys, thronged the rich shop windows, the wealth of goods delighting their hearts; the people chatted, laughed, read the afternoon gazettes while walking, and together formed the "public," the spitting image of the public in any other metropolis in the world. These people were no less dissatisfied with the prevailing government than people anywhere else. They did not yearn to lose their independence and freedom. And yet! If only I had been able to penetrate their innermost hearts in order to find the truth. But did their hearts know this truth? They all seemed unspeakably indifferent. Their eyes, sweeping ahead, were filled with passivity, everyday cares, everyday playfulness. Were their old imperial city, their old Austria not worth clenching a fist for? Not even in their pockets?

Oh, I knew the language of indifference precisely. One could hear it everywhere. Even Gretl brought it home after visiting her family. *That* country has a population of seventy million, and we have only six. Such were their words. And also: Our hydrocephalic country is not capable of surviving. The peace treaties are to blame for everything. A mutilated Austria has no choice. People argued, cited the best reasons, the most cogent evidence. But the arguments of indifference could not be dislodged from their ruts. The line between letting things happen and wishing for them is extremely hazy. Perhaps Weil was right, and only our people were completely immune. And even I, just a few weeks ago, had belonged to the passive ones, if not to the indifferent. I suffered, I suffered, as I strolled through the beautiful city of Vienna. It was still *my* city. Since my childhood, I had been intimate with every mansion, every gap between buildings, every tiny side street. I greeted the museum domes, which melted into the grayish-blue sky. You still belong to me, I still belong to you. The enemy was not to be seen far and wide. The white-stockings did not dare to penetrate the depths of Vienna. Cowards that they were, only tiny groups of them marched through the small towns and suburbs on Sundays. They were a minority, a weak minority, no doubt. But is not history always decided by minorities? The great masses have nothing but their tremendous gravity. They lend it to him who develops the most tenacious determination.

Here, on this famous corner, they are constructing a scaffolding. One ought to stand there and stop the torrent of indifference, transfix it with a thunderous voice, appeal to it. Danger is brewing. Do not surrender! Protect the work of centuries! Defend yourselves!

But who shall appeal? I? I, a little lawyer from Eisenstadt. Even if I were a great orator, the voice of paralyzing tact would be bound to whisper to me: Not you! Certainly not *you!*

It was an impulse as strong as it was alien to my nature. I tore myself out of it. Several people were in the German Travel Bureau on Kärtnerstrasse. Three or four very patient women stared with hungry eyes through the window, into the room, where the flower-lined, lifesize portrait of the dictator hung on the wall. I shall never pronounce his name as long as I live. That is a small revenge that I owe to my human dignity. I too halted and stared into the plate glass, yet perceived nothing but my own transparent and alien face. Then, a silvery voice chimed near me, "C'mon, handsome, how about it? Wanna have a good time with Mary?"

Embarrassed, I looked at the young, slender streetwalker, who, though all decked out, appeared to be freezing miserably under her short fur jacket. My astonished gaze was misunderstood as a punitive response to the untimely moment of her approach. Her voice chirped softly, "Yes, Mary is a daybird."

And the daybird, a skinny water wagtail, flounced off, pushing through the male portion of the torrent of people. However, this minor incident had sliced through my thoughts, which were absorbed in fantasies of oratorical effectiveness. Can this be, I wondered; can some innocently born mortal be deprived of the fundamentals of life by some dark power, to-day, in the year of our Lord 1938? No, it cannot be! We are here to live—and the right to live must be guaranteed. The homeland in which I first saw the light of day is an inalienable part of this right to live. More than a right! It is a part of my nature. Like breathing! How many times does a human being draw his breath? Several million! It is mine, mine, such as nothing else is mine. I breathe for Cella. And for Gretl, too. Nothing else really concerns me, for I am merely an average person, and I have nothing to do with the cares and perils of the state, thank goodness. Jacques Weil sent me the twenty-five thousand right away. Now I can get going. Be happy, be happy! I have a new lease on life. Gretl is modest and thrifty, that I have to admit. She has never complained and never longed for wealth.

But when I showed her the check, which was only a beginning, how she lit up!

My goodness, here I am in front of Hoffmann, the world-famous leathergoods store. Nagy, you're not the only one who can give presents. Inside myself, I feel a wave of happiness that wants to make others happy. Goodness knows why my recent moods have changed so maddeningly fast. I'll buy Gretl a handbag, black patent leather, and Cella a new briefcase for her scores. The gift for her mother has to be more expensive, that's only proper. Gretl is considering a fur coat. She is so decent that she does not want to spend too much. And what about the piano for Cella? I will purchase it despite Scherber and America. I am banking on Austria. Just look at the people inside Hoffmann's. Patrons and salesclerks. How rapturously they listen to the man on the radio: "Austria is an eternal value. Austria cannot be lost. Austria is Mozart's voice in the concert of nations."

Johannes Myslivec was already standing on the corner of Rosenturmstrasse and Fleischmarkt at the entrance to the Österreichischer Hof. With his tremendous skull and his straddle-legged mass, the government councilor for costumes, customs, and landmarks himself resembled a monument. With a grandiose swing, he doffed his inexplicably Alpine hat, which, for the sake of cultivating costumes and customs, was adorned with artificial edelweiss even in the middle of the metropolis. Myslivec greeted me with a soft baritone, a hard German, and exquisite verbal artistry. What an enormous effort it must have cost this uncommon brain to deck out even the simplest words with curlicues. (Did he employ his sonorous calligraphy in order to gain time, conceal his own intentions, and fathom the other person's?) "I have been awaiting you, domine, quite stationary, in front of this portal. Let us, as delegates of the Burgenland, the most recent state in Austria, enter the Capitol. I propose the following: It will be wise to lend our ears to the bold speeches of the heroes. . . . I would find it unwise to confuse and prolong the struggle of the experts with our own advice. . . . I, as an official of the government, am bound by strict oaths of allegiance, and, consistent with my nature as an observer, ill-disposed toward Catilinian orations . . . *Sapienti sat* . . . I am counting on you. . . ."

The meeting place of our Iron Ring was of medium size and amazingly shabby. The sordid penumbra of the advancing winter hours was frostily darkened rather than illuminated by a few bare, ill-humored bulbs. A large horseshoe-shaped table covered with green, ink-splotched cloth monopolized all the free space. By now, twenty gentlemen had arrived, forming groups within the horseshoe. The cigarette smoke was already thickening into cloudbanks. Waiters brought in black coffee. With unmannerly haste, they rattlingly set the cups on the table and demanded payment on the spot. These waiters did not seem imbued with great awe of the many war veterans gathering here. At first, I remained at the door, while Myslivec instantly joined the groups, loudly raising his voice and his style everywhere. Timidity when entering a social function is one of those serious character defects that I have not yet learned to overcome, even at a more sedate age. I knew one or two of the gentlemen from earlier conferences and saluted them with a bow. But most of the faces were unfamiliar. Among these veterans, a martial figure was a rare exception. All around me, I saw care-ridden heads of families, mostly in the prime of life. Some were already white-haired, wrinkled, worn, shabbily dressed, and tired. Others were well-groomed, setting store by chic elegance and emphatic youthfulness. But for everyone, the war or even a long-thwarted military career was now an ancient fairy tale, gone with the glorious army of the Kaiser, a dream that one evoked on holidays in order to confront an incredulous and ice–cold younger generation by sprucing oneself up a bit with one's own grand time—a uniform, carefully preserved in a chest, but, despite the faithful mothballs and protective covering, revealing more and more alarming wear and tear. (Last year, I myself had had a Viennese military tailor make me a new old uniform, but secretly, since I was ashamed of admitting my vanity to Gretl—and besides, it was a superfluous expense.)

I moved closer to the others, for I had recognized a local colleague with whom I had once had some business dealings. We were exchanging the usual questions and answers when a hand descended on my shoulders.

"Thank you for coming, Herr Doctor. The situation is such that we must absolutely count on every single member."

The man speaking these words to me truly cut a martial figure: tall, erect, lean, with the narrow, shrunken head of a soldier and a tremendous hooked nose protruding from its autumn-colored mummy shape. Lieutenant-Colonel Dagobert Grollmüller, Lord von Podhajce, a Maria Theresa knight, was, as universally conceded, the soul of the Iron Ring. As captain and battalion commander of the Forty-Seventh, he had won military laurels in one of the first battles on the Eastern front, and, as the youngest officer in the army, he had been awarded that highest decoration, which was established by Empress Maria Theresa for daring heroic deeds performed without or against the supreme orders of the military leaders. During the early years of the war, the glorious heroes could be counted on the fingers of one hand—the few who were granted the empress's medal after their deeds of honor had been meticulously sifted and combed. Emaciated and exhausted as he looked, our lieutenant-colonel did not show the countless humiliations he had suffered in all kinds of professions after the war, until, several years ago, he had begun playing a certain role in public life. The civilian jacket still looked short and awkward on his desiccated military frame, as if he had taken off his uniform only an hour before and not twenty years ago. Grollmüller had bold, blue eyes, whose depths sometimes revealed a peculiar, anxious kindness that we had once known among the best of our active warriors. His eyes made a profound impact on me, and I could understand why the pretender to the imperial throne had evinced his paramount confidence in this officer among all his loyal followers—a man who was neither an aristocrat nor a member of the general staff.

Meanwhile, our gathering had grown to thirty-five members. Grollmüller clapped twice.

"Gentlemen," he said, without raising his voice, and the room grew still, "gentlemen, may I ask you to be seated. There is no need to stand on ceremony."

We sat down. Naturally, the delegations from the individual provinces stayed together. As did Myslivec and I. Myslivec suddenly looked sleepy. He breathed heavily, rhythmically, as if he were bored before the meeting had even started. A lot of time was spent on the roll call. Lieutenant-Colonel Grollmüller had left the room. More than a quarter hour passed before he returned with an old man in a general's full-dress uniform. Holding the frail officer's arm, he guided him almost tenderly. The old man wore an azure tunic, red stripes on his trousers, and a green hat with feathers. We all leaped up as one man, in military fashion. A command seemed to have whipped into our bones, even though we were elderly officials, engineers, lawyers, businessmen. Nonexistent spurs jingled inaudibly. Trudging along on Grollmüller's arm, the little old man reached the table. He nodded and smiled amiably in all directions, utterly unlike a general.

"Thank you, thank you, my deepest thanks, gentlemen. Please make yourselves comfortable."

And he fell into the only armchair at the table; the seat had been raised with several cushions. The bicorne with the green feathers of a general lay before him, a garish emblem of a dead, very dead past, an emblem in which the wind of a proud history played softly. A very great name of the old army still lived in this blinking old man who sat in our midst. After an awe-filled shudder, I felt that a ghost had turned us into ghosts. Field Marshall Baron Dudenovich, army commander in the world war, the last of that glorious Croat dynasty of soldiers who, for three centuries, had fought for the Hapsburg colors on all the battlefields of Europe—now with a trembling hand, he put on spectacles in order to read a note that Grollmüller pushed over to him. Then he raised a tight little voice and opened the meeting. "Very praiseworthy that the gentlemen have heeded our call not only from here but from other places. I give the floor to Herr Lieutenant-Colonel Grollmüller. Let us listen to his report."

And, in order to obey his own request more effectively, the

old man cupped his hand around his defective ear. Grollmüller
jumped to his feet. His voice sliced through us, clear, sharp,
yet not without concealed warmth. It aroused my affection and
that pleasant confidence with which superior resoluteness always manages to imbue a weaker character. Such a voice cares
for us and takes responsibility for us, and one stretches out in
it with the certainty of not being deserted.

"The board of directors of the Iron Ring," Grollmüller began, "would naturally not have asked you to convene, if certain political developments did not seem to make it imperative
that we meet today. I know only too well that most of us war
veterans are not in the fortunate position of easily sacrific-
ing the time and money for the journey. Our alliance is poor
and cannot cover anyone's expenses; the former—imperial—
government subsidies no longer exist. You members have
demonstrated by your appearance here that you truly take our
sacred cause seriously. However, this cause is threatened more
earnestly than ever, if the clouds thickening on the horizon do
not deceive us."

He was absolutely convinced, Grollmüller went on, that this
aforementioned darkening of the horizon was not deceptive,
and his conviction, he said, was based on reliable facts. Prussia
was arming herself, in order to make up for the defeat she had
suffered and to reach out once again for world domination,
this time under better conditions. To this purpose, Austria, as
the closest European bulwark, would have to fall, that is, she
would have to lose not only her political and historical auton-
omy as an independent state, but also her human sovereignty,
down to the last vestige of the slightest memory. Anyone fear-
ing only halfhearted measures in this respect did not really
know the ruthless enemy, who was truly not enervated by
moral pangs of conscience. Anyone who indulged in the illusion of a partial fog would be an accomplice to the entire catastrophe. The enemy needed Austria not because of any bogus
ideals, but for extremely solid tactical and industrial reasons.
The new border would form an invincible base for the planned

military advance, and Austrian steel would considerably strengthen the material foundation of this venture. One did not require the gifts of a prophet to foresee a complete fusion, a complete pulping of Austria, down to the minds of the youngest schoolchildren, whereby every last soul would be absorbed by a throttling state, far worse than in present-day Germany. Such was the true development of things, as was already being announced by certain speeches and events in Berlin. What must take place, and indeed take place without further delay, since every instant was precious? He, Grollmüller, like all his comrades gathered here, stood behind the government heart and soul. Our federal chancellor, an honorable man, was doing his best, no doubt. But could he see everything, supervise everything, despite the authoritative constitution? There were forces at work, secret forces (some of the gentlemen gathered here must have had their professional experiences with them), forces that—what is the scientific term?—forces with a neutralizing effect, wiping out every good intention with less good considerations. And these forces, alas, were reaching very far up. The government had to be helped by an act of will from below, to prove unambiguously to the entire world that Austria was not just some tiny German state that could exist or vanish without a ripple, but that the Austrian people had absolutely no intention of being incinerated for all eternity.

I listened to Grollmüller's words, which lucidly, passionately, and heartwarmingly articulated the anxieties that I had been feeling for weeks, and which had been eliciting only weary, numb, desperate, or mordant responses on all sides. Here stood a true, battle-tested hero, who would not surrender, but who, clutching a flag, wanted to take up the struggle and lead us all the way. Did the others here not feel as I did? Myslivec, next to me, was still breathing in his heavy rhythm. Dudenovich, the great marshal, sat there, a dazzlingly garbed bundle of old age, his exertion making him smile. My Viennese colleague—his name was Dr. Brandeis—was gazing at the speaker with a face full of rapturous readiness. Not just his but several others' eyes hung with excited faith on Grollmüller's every word. However, while the majority of these engineers, officials, and businessmen from the mountain provinces listened closely, their features did not reveal approval. I was puzzled. Were we not all united by a single thought? Or did these men also belong among the weary and indifferent, the sight of whom had so deeply unnerved me in the streets of Vienna? Perhaps, I told myself, they feel no weaker than you, but they are semipeasants or complete peasants, and the rustic mentality prohibits any display of emotions. And one more thing. I was tormented by the fact that not a single young man was among us, although my qualms were extremely silly, for how could a young man have been a veteran of 1914?

Meanwhile, Grollmüller had forged ahead to his conclusions. The Iron Ring, he said, would now have to be truly iron, no longer a droopy veterans' club, but the invincible core of patriotic resistance to extinction. Every single member had to take undauntedly the initiative in his own group. Two goals must always be borne in mind. The first and greater one: "The young imperial gentleman in Steenokerzeel is looking at us. I can assure you all that the young gentleman is worthy of his great name and heritage. I am thoroughly convinced that some day he shall enter history as a true Hapsburg ruler. However, the government cannot summon him to Austria, this is prohibited by the situation of our foreign politics. *We* must call him, *we* must prepare the way for him when the time is ripe. And I tell you, the time *is* ripe. We are on the razor's edge between not yet and too late. If we miss the moment, our life task will be buried forever."

In all frankness, I am no blind monarchist. This form of government has its pluses and minuses like any other. I joined the Iron Ring years ago because its principles were consistent with my personal situation and my general way of thinking— if not entirely, then at least more than the principles of any other group. As young as I may have been, the old days had been my good days, my best. In that time, our people were

considered human beings and fellow Austrians, unconditionally and not just relatively. And then! Hapsburg! In his heart,
every Austrian born before 1890 retains the awesome, knight-
like picture of the aged Kaiser Franz Joseph as a loyal dream-
guardian of childhood. Did not Dudenovich, that grizzled
general, still wear the sideburns of the idol of an entire era?
However, my relationship to the Hapsburgs was even closer,
warmer, more personal. After all, the last ruler—the "dead
man of Malaga," the "martyr of Funchal," words repeatedly
used by Grollmüller—this human embodiment of goodwill,
had granted me my great moment of honor, the only one in
my entire life! My blood was surging. Whenever this happens—and, alas, it still happens all too often—I begin to see
images and feel emotions. This weakness may be suitable for
an artist, but a lawyer approaching the age of fifty ought to
have overcome it long since. Of course, without this weakness
of her father's in her blood, Cella might not be what she is.

Thus I once again saw the young ruler's face emanating
warmth, I felt my hand in his two warm hands, I felt the bliss
of the goodwill he had heaped on me, which filled the whole
world like a strange southern springtime. But these images were
disrupted by Scherber's jeering voice: "Yes, we *shall* charge
ahead, gentlemen. But in a very different way."

A large color photograph interfered. I had seen it today in
the window of a shipping line. The skyscrapers of New York,
resembling the Dolomites, dipping their heads into the rosy
clouds of dawn. And in front of them, astonishingly tiny, the
tremendous ocean liner that has whisked Cella off to America.
Is there no other solution? Cannot Cella begin her triumphant
advance here and in Europe, under my care? Styxi's academy.
If Grollmüller gets his way, if he unites all well-meaning men,
the overwhelming majority, in an oath of allegiance . . . No
doubt about it! I felt as if I had to jump up and keep shouting
just one word over and over again: "Yes, yes, yes!" However,
someone else forestalled my tempestuous desire. It was Brandeis. He kept nodding and then exclaimed several times in a

squeaky voice, "That's right!" This cry amid the overall listening and pondering struck even me, I must admit, as importu-
nate and unpleasant. A few members exchanged quick glances.
Grollmüller paused briefly. Then, hurrying to finish, he offered
a plan: a petition was to be circulated by all of us in our individual provinces and precincts. These signatures—an irre-
sistible avalanche of names—would be the concentrated voice
of the entire nation shouting for freedom, independence, and
the restoration of a sacred monarchy that had proven itself in
the course of centuries, that stood above all classes and parties,
that knew no distinction of person, that was objective in an
otherwise unattainable sense, and that could reestablish the
equality of all citizens as the sole power in this world of gross
utility and cruel tyranny.

Grollmüller had not resorted to the usual oratorical device
of concluding in an elevated tone and with grand words. Instead, he merely offered a few prudent suggestions about the
petition he was asking for. After a quick bow to the marshal,
he promptly sat down. Dudenovich made an abortive effort to
rise from his pillow. His hands, virtually welded together by a
very long life, reached toward the chairman's bell and swung
it to and fro.

"May I express my gratitude to Lieutenant-Colonel Grollmüller," he began; no one could tell whether he was smiling
out of fatigue or satisfaction. "His discourse was, if I may say
so, highly illuminating, and I would like to declare that I am
completely in agreement with him. If any of the members
would like to have the floor, please feel free."

Several of the men raised their hands like schoolboys. The
marshal gave them the floor by nodding toward one or the
other with his lowered head. The things we got to hear were
indeed anything but enlightening. No, indeed, no one opposed
Grollmüller's appeal or quibbled with its viewpoint—that
would have meant betraying the cause to which they had committed themselves by joining the Iron Ring in the first place.
On the contrary, each speaker kept reemphasizing his loyalty

and patriotism. Yet again and again, the circuitous and thread-bare rhetoric hinted at naked laziness, lethargy, pomposity, perhaps even an ambivalent fear, and also a cautious and insidious something that I did not yet understand. All these men, who were heads of families and way over fifty years old, did not want to ruin their chances in a future that might be just around the corner.

Only a good youth ruins the future, even though or precisely because it has so much future. But youth, heaven knows, was not siding with our just, but backward-looking cause, whether in small towns or in the metropolis. It was dismal, very dismal.

To my amazement, Johannes Myslivec had disrupted his sleepy, heavy breathing to wave his hand and then get to his feet. Actually, he was breaking our agreement that only one of us would speak. Resting his weight on his hands, he leaned on the table, his upper body rocking back and forth. How well I knew this gesture of the knowledgeable honor student.

"Above all," he commenced with his usual unction, "I would like to give tongue to the profound awe with which we are imbued at the sight of His Excellency, Field Marshal Duden-ovich, who has made the great sacrifice of presiding at today's assembly. There is no patriotic Austrian with any knowledge of history in whom the immortal name of Dudenovich does not evoke feelings of enthusiasm and gratitude. His Excellency will not prohibit a military nonentity like myself from responding to Lieutenant-Colonel Grollmüller, our bearer of the highly venerable Ribbon of Maria Theresa, by quoting the words of the great poet:

> *Austria is in your camp,*
> *The rest of us are nought but ruins.*

The highly respectable assembly of officers, in which we have the honor of participating, in a way resembles that well-known assembly of officers in Schiller's drama *The Piccolominis*, Act four, Scene seven, in which, as we know, the issue is likewise signatures, although there the cards are shuffled in a different manner than here. . . . I would like to ask my tried-and-true comrades a modest question: Is there such a *conjuratio,* a conspiracy, that eludes the approval and concurrence of the authoritative offices?"

Breaking off, he groped for his red-white-and-red tie (blatantly distasteful, in any case) and loosened it because of the heat. His baritone darkened painfully.

"The well-constructed ship of state is now wending its way between Scylla and Charybdis. I am one of those faith-filled persons who will not be dissuaded and who do not doubt that our frigate will escape the strait without a leak and with proud masts, and that it will soon reach the open seas. All hands aboard, I say so too. But nothing without the skipper, gentlemen, if you please, nothing without the pilot of the ship of state, the man whose expert eye sweeps ahead, that is a seaman's duty. . . . I am but a harmless dreamer, devoted to profound contemplation. Nevertheless, I must weigh the following considerations. Since, in the opinion of our venerable Lieutenant-Colonel Grollmüller, we are menaced all around by reefs and depths, should we truly, unlike Darius, also unleash a tempest of our own choosing?"

With his inexhaustible stylistic howlers, Myslivec had said nothing that sounded disloyal or contrary to Grollmüller. As a lawyer, I could even understand the qualms he voiced as a government official who felt beholden to the state. Nevertheless, I was seized with wild resentment, surprising myself; indeed, I have to admit that it was not just resentment, but genuine hatred. I despised him from the bottom of my heart— that careful, cautious, circumspect creature, that class genius, that exemplary boy, that collar-protector of life; and my hatred greeted me like an old friend. Once, I had not dared to challenge him, during eight years, for Myslivec was great and prestigious, and I, I suffer from crestfallen admiration for anyone who is greater than I and enjoys more prestige. But now! I cannot quite pinpoint how I unexpectedly managed to overcome my timidity and my sense of worthlessness. To make a long story short, I stood there, hearing myself speak; I even heard the trembling of my own voice, not without disapproval. I probably did not speak all that badly—indeed, I most likely spoke better than on other occasions. I used the expression *levée en masse,* which I had found in my newspaper that morning. Must one put up with what human beings can do to another, as if it were a flood, an earthquake? Twenty years ago, we were stationed at the front and, without batting an eyelash (an exaggeration), we shed our blood for Austria. It is inconceivably dreadful that the millions of heroic deaths should have been as senseless as a mere accident, claiming not a limited number of people, but an entire generation. My anger carried me away beyond Grollmüller's goal. No, after twenty years, after a brief inhalation of history, we should not allow those millions who died in good faith to be made ridiculous, nor should we permit the extinction of what they died for. It would be better to seize arms once more and aim them at those who attack us, no matter who they are. Not just we but tens of thousands of veterans live in this land. If His Excellency, Field Marshal Dudenovich, gives the order, then they shall all join us as one man, and the younger generation, still lingering on the sidelines, shall follow us. But an indomitable will must rise to electrify the nation!

Grollmüller had interrupted me twice with a very loud bravo. And my words seemed to have made an impact on the others, too, an impact, however, that was not quite clear to me. A few men came over and shook my hand, Brandeis in the lead, of course. Others put their heads together, launching into noisy murmurs. My head roared, and I was filled with astonished uneasiness. That was how a man must feel when he has lost his way in the mountains: the cliff above him, the abyss beneath him. In the repulsive light of the meager bulbs, I saw a new speaker at the extreme end of the horseshoe. He was a robust, highly jovial man with a light crewcut, a native of Salzburg. The murmurs died down, and we heard the following:

"It is very odd that certain men . . . please understand me . . . that, at the end of the war, when our nation was felled by treachery, certain men . . . well, certain men devotedly and patiently accepted the circumstance, they were satisfied, those men were, for, gentlemen, they were pacifists and international. . . . Now those same men are no longer pacifists, quite the opposite, those certain men are advocates of war and bloodshed, because, well, because . . . If only—"

Grollmüller jumped up. His lips disappeared. His face looked even more mummified. But his voice sounded muffled. "I would like to request once and for all that such allusions be dispensed with at our meetings. In the old army, they were entirely unknown. And we are the representatives of the old army and its traditions."

His words were followed by a more than repulsive hush. The air in this ugly hotel room was loaded with smoke, dry heat, dull confusion, and indecipherable cunning. Who would take the floor now? No one! Dudenovich, who looked as if he had been sleeping, raised his head slightly, aroused by the silence. All eyes turned to him. He wearily jingled his little bell again. But then an amazing jerk galvanized his body, he straightened up, quick and stiff, and was no longer frail, and his voice no longer came from beyond the grave. His wrinkled cheeks turned crimson, and some sort of pain flooded into his bloodshot blue eyes.

"Let me sum up, gentlemen," he said, pulling over his green general's cap. "I look back, alas, upon a very, very long road, as you gentlemen can imagine. When Bismarck began his criminal war against us in '66, I was already wearing the uniform of a second-year cadet. When Philippovich occupied Bosnia, I was a young captain in the troops, and when His Majesty entrusted me with commanding his army in the world war, I was already a rather old general. And I have then had to live twenty more years, twenty, until this day. And it has gotten worse and worse since the collapse, baser and baser, in general and personally, the human material and so on. You gentlemen must have experienced to some extent for yourselves what it means to grow very old in such times. Every single day is an achievement, a strain, an exertion, far worse than during the battles of Isonzo, and the moment comes when one has even missed the chance of putting an end to things. I simply have no idea why I am telling you gentlemen all this. And yet, I must say, at the risk of repeating myself . . ."

He paused as if he had forgotten what he was about to say. His hand went to his forehead. A deathly pallor covered his small, shriveled face.

"I would like to sum up, gentlemen. . . . Sum up . . ."

Dudenovich could not sum up as he planned. Suddenly, he reeled. His neighbors leaped to his side and held him fast. Otherwise he would have sunk to the floor. They shoved a few chairs together and bedded him on them. Was it his longed-for death that had grabbed the old man after his bizarre lament? The stunning death of this pompous ghost of the old army would not have been an unsuitable end to our meeting, and, even more, it would have been a sorrowful symbol of the confusion, the impenetrable things that were happening, indeed, congealing, in the city and the provinces. I felt ashamed and horrified. Myslivec, next to me, also looked bewildered.

"Leave him in the museum," he whispered, "do not touch him, just leave him in the museum."

But death had no intention whatsoever of carrying the marshal off from our midst. Grollmüller, kneeling at his side, had unbuttoned the general's beribboned azure tunic and his shirt. We saw an old man's tawny chest studded with tufts of white hair, calmly rising and sinking. Waiters with curious, impudent faces had burst in and were standing around. Grollmüller clutched a glass of cognac, from which he let drops ooze between the lips of the exhausted man.

A poignant sight, these two survivors of a long-beaten army, the younger man assisting the older one on the gray and indifferent battlefield of everyday life. Dudenovich looked past us all, as if we were the ocean. He tried to smile. His melting little voice indicated how embarrassed he was.

"Please excuse me, gentlemen, please . . . This is utterly embarrassing . . . Do not worry, just feeling a bit weak, that is all . . . Very mortifying, thank you, thank you, gentlemen . . . I just shouldn't . . . I simply shouldn't socialize."

The marshal recovered rather quickly. Grollmüller took him home, where the former lord over the lives and deaths of hundreds of thousand of people led a lonely, modest existence under the command of a pitiless housekeeper. The meeting disbanded. Most of the members were presumably quite happy that the dreadful incident had interfered with their reaching any clear decisions or commitments. I drove home with Myslivec through the misty winter night. While he sat at the wheel of his car (which was by no means as shabby as he always claimed), he gave free rein to his eloquence. He spoke enthusiastically about highway construction, agriculture, literature, Mardi Gras, but not about the one thing that was crucial. He did not say a word about the meeting. My attempts at bringing it up were warded off with the most courteous skill. Congratulations, I thought. Two days later, I received a certified letter from Johannes Myslivec, informing me as secretary of the Iron Ring that he was resigning from his office in the association and also terminating his membership.

Chapter 5

Will the Academy
Take Place?

Myslivec and the dismal outcome of our meeting were responsible for the agonizing fervor that robbed me of time and peace during the next few days. Myslivec must have shared my views, he could not think otherwise. And yet, he had skipped out on us, in a dreadfully craven fashion, like the obsequious official that he was. Why? Presumably, a wind was blowing "up there" that was hostile to the aspirations of the Iron Ring. How tormented we were by that upper stratum, that government in its authoritarian clouds, with its big hollow words and small hollow deeds. Every patriot became a Tantalus, and the government kept holding out to him the water of fresh opinion and clear decision—only to pull it back again from his lips. There were shamefaced bows to moderate traitors, an understanding wink at the white-stockings, a muddled parroting of the same slogans and the same thoughts—enough to drive one to despair.

Why should you care, I thought at night, controlling myself and lying silently, so as not to awaken Gretl. Is it any of your concern? My concern. The words boomed through me. It was more my concern than any other concern had ever been. And so I proceeded to carry out Grollmüller's plan. I am speaking about the petition, which was supposed to call the savior into our land. The lieutenant-colonel had handed me a tremendous number of mimeographed appeals—me and not Myslivec.

I collected 1,507 signatures. A trifling number, and one that is easily written down. But this number cost me a good portion of my nervous strength. The reader may know me a little by now. I hope that I can at least manage to depict some of my failings truthfully between the lines. One can therefore probably imagine what a difficult time I had going from door to door, even though I was working for a noble cause, making a desperate attempt to save our country. (It was already so difficult to put up with minor inconveniences, to get oneself to make such trivial efforts.) Yet I was functioning not with a lucid mind, but with a numb urge to act, a drive that both burdened and liberated me. At least something was happening, I was active, I flailed about in this slough of ambiguous paralysis and viscous stagnation.

As chance would have it, or rather the luck of the draw, my career began to flourish during those weeks. The good graces of S. Weil & Sons had blazed a trail to my door. For over twenty years, I had been scraping by with a rather modest clientele. After all, we were so close to Vienna that people preferred retaining lawyers there. But now, all at once, other prominent industrialists, for instance, Bohlmann and the United Leitha Works, were also remembering me. There was a contradiction that I could not unravel: Why was it happening, especially to one of our people at this time? While my good old desk used to remain fallow for days on end, now the dossiers piled up across it, and I never got to bed before midnight. In the daytime, including Sundays, I was always out somewhere. As secretary of our Veterans' Association, I had a huge list of names and addresses. Anywhere, even in the most out-of-the-way nests, there was always someone who might be sympathetic to our cause and willing to help us.

That was the reason I now saw my little family rarely and only briefly, for I would gulp down my meals at the office or in restaurants. Even my anxieties about Cella abated. Incidentally, I had spoken neither to her nor to Gretl about Scherber's upsetting proposal. I did not wish to make them uneasy before it was necessary. Yet nothing could have been more necessary than preparing our escape. It would still have been child's play. And had Gretl not spoken about going abroad, in a moment of premonition, before I even admitted the danger to myself? Gretl, whose background in no way helped her to sense what was brewing? However, the goal of my activism was to preserve our homeland, not tear myself away from it.

I launched my action, as was appropriate, at the prince's Residence. The old gentleman, Prince Ernst's father, one of the most brilliant courtly cavaliers of past days, did not appear at all surprised to see a little man like myself advocating a cause that was more his than mine. He found my zeal—as he put it—quite laudable, thanked me, called his household together, his children, grandchildren, guests, domestic staff, read them Grollmüller's appeal, a bit affectedly and arduously, in an old man's halting voice, and then added a little speech for good measure. (People say that the old prince, to universal dismay, did not like to neglect any opportunity to take the floor. Indeed, the first time Cella performed at the Residence, he paid her his homage in the guise of an after-dinner speech. I was deeply impressed by his free-flowing, benevolent manner.)

Thus, I obtained thirty-two signatures at one swoop. And, even more important, all the great families were instantly informed of our action—which meant something, for our Burgenland, literally the "land of castles," was named for the many castles and fortresses that adorn it. Styxi and Nagy were the last to sign, for they arrived from Vienna just as I had taken my leave.

Zsoltan hesitated, looked at me, and asked sotto voce, "And you truly believe that history can be made with signatures?"

"If nobody makes a move," I retorted, "if nothing happens, if everybody gobbles everything up, what should one do? Can you think of something better?"

"I don't know of anything better. But I know that there is only one way to make history: with fear!"

I did not quite understand. He helped me. "The fear that one arouses, my friend. Today, politics is the art of forcing every citizen into a tight squeeze between life and death."

I said nothing. I gazed at him. He looked as if he were still in his late twenties, with his thick, slightly wavy chestnut hair, narrow cheeks, curving lips, and that roguish smirk, which had gained my affection so many years ago, the morning we had first met in the classroom at the Gymnasium. (In those days, the yellow gaslight was still singing over the school desks.) That smile, pouring out of slightly swollen, half-closed eyelids, now grazed across me.

"You know, Bodenheim," he said, appending his signature in delicate penmanship, almost embroidery, "you should leave me out of this business. All I'm really interested in now is Cella's and Styxi's academy. You're certainly a marvelous father, one only has to hear what people say about you; they sing your praises, I swear. But Styxi and I have put together Cella's program—a terrific program, by the way. . . ."

No mockery, not even kind-hearted teasing, was to be gleaned from his words. Styxi focused his penetratingly empty gaze on my necktie and began to list the pieces on the program and to explain why they had been selected. I understood nothing. For an astonished pain began to spread through me, a burning, incomprehensible pain. . . .

𝒯he balls in a small town have their own peculiarity. During Mardi Gras, there were many such balls in Eisenstadt: the Garrison Ball, the Vintners' Ball, the Government Officials' Ball, and whatever the names of all those mediocre vanity fairs that took place at the two large ballrooms in town. A dense throng in stuffy air. Cheerless faces for the most part, since a provincial feels he is compromising himself by showing merriment. He needs the local wine in order to lose his everyday grouchiness, and once he has lost it, things become a lot worse. The girls and women, even the pretty ones, are awkwardly dressed. There is something wrong with nearly all of them; they are either a bit too fashionable or a bit too unfashionable. On the whole, they are ungraceful. Yet they seem to flaunt this lack of grace, as if it were the fruit of a moral conviction rather than a hard life. And then there are the merry entertainments that these philistines insert during the recesses between dances. The cross-eyed daughter of the notary public squawks out some ditties, and the accounting counselor from the tax office parodies a magician. As if we were at the other end of the globe and not just a short hour from the capital. No thank you!

I obtained my law degree in Vienna and lived there for seven years. When I was younger, I indulged in a little traveling and I've seen a bit of the world. And Gretl shared my view. At least, she never expressed any desire to attend any of these ludicrous balls, where she had danced as a girl. If we needed diversion, we traveled to Vienna and went to the opera, the Burgtheater, and if we felt like more frivolous fun, we tried a vaudeville show. But I now sometimes thought that we had done too little traveling.

The annual Ball of the White Rose, which took place eleven days before the planned academy, was always somewhat better than the other public functions. It was usually attended by the highest officials as well as several young aristocrats. This time, in order to heighten the brilliance, they even announced the presence of a cabinet member and several government functionaries. We, including Cella, received an invitation to this ball. For once, I was untrue to myself. Gretl and I had an argument about it. She said we had never mingled much since our wedding, and she had been quite willing to go along with my aloofness. Why should we make an exception to this good rule now that we were both too old and the child too young, especially in such a difficult time? It was precisely in a time like this, I replied, that I found it necessary to socialize and emerge from our not particularly splendid isolation, which was only due to an unsociable haughtiness. We also ought to give up our comfortable seclusion for the sake of Cella and her future. A public life involved social obligations that Cella could not learn early enough.

As I went through these arguments, I was assailed by an old suspicion that I thought I had shaken off years ago in the course of our long marriage. Gretl had certainly suffered a thing or two from her family by marrying me. Even her relationships with her next of kin had gradually ceased, although I personally got on very well with those people. I had taken great care not to limit Gretl's freedom, much less draw her over to my side. The cooling-off was due not to her family (although her parents were no longer alive), but to my wife. Goodness knows, I suspected, perhaps some old frozen shame had thawed out in her, what with everything that was going on. Although not a very open person, Gretl is unbelievably intuitive. She promptly sensed what I was feeling, and she smiled at me with her beautiful, helpless eyes.

"As you like, Hans," she said, adding, "don't you always get your way?"

I was offended by these additional words. But Gretl placed her hand on mine. I pulled myself together. "I want both of you to be very beautiful. Cella is no longer a child. I would like to be proud of you and her. Please indulge me and buy yourselves two first-class evening gowns in Vienna, and all the paraphernalia. Incidentally, think about the academy too. And this time, money is no object. My career is on the ascent, thank goodness, somewhat late, but still . . ."

"You see," Gretl smiled, "you always get your way, you tyrant."

And that same day, the two of them went to the city. At

Krupnik, a conservative but highly esteemed fashion house, they bought two evening gowns, a black one for Gretl, a cream-colored one for Cella.

The gowns were beautiful. Cella and Gretl were beautiful. And I could really be proud when the three of us entered the White Rose. The long theater auditorium, as cold and sober as the soul of the province, was completely decked out with red-white-and-red flags, ribbons, garlands, paper lanterns. I was delighted by these dear, vivid colors of Austria, despite the tasteless decoration. On the stage, where normally the guest performance of the Viennese theaters took place, two orchestras spelled one another: the military band of the infantry regiment stationed in Eisenstadt and a jazz band in white tuxedoes, vibrating and gesticulating tirelessly according to renowned patterns. The dancing had begun long ago. On the estrades flanking the dance floor, most of the tables were already occupied. The group seemed less provincial than usual. A large number of Viennese must have come in. The government minister who was patron of the ball would not be showing up. The reason would be made clear soon enough. On my tuxedo lapel, I wore the small chain with miniatures of my numerous wartime medals and ribbons. I freely confess that this chain with these gold links (one has few opportunities to wear them) pleasantly enhances my self-esteem; it not only relaxes me, but also gives me an odd sense of fulfillment, as if I were bigger and more rugged than I am. However, I found it undignified of other veterans, who had likewise brought out their medals, to be sporting carnival hats of gaudy paper—the insignia of a lamentable and conventional sense of humor.

The caterer, Herr Alois Mulminger, came over and exuberantly kissed the hands of my ladies.

"Upon my soul . . . what a joy . . . I must say," he stammered blissfully as if discovering friends whom he had believed dead. Yet we had not met Herr Mulminger more than five times in our whole lives. He did not look anything like a restaurateur—this slender man, who had more gold teeth in his mouth than any normal mortal. As he steered us to a free table, his golden mouth did not stop moving.

"Dear Herr Doctor, how are you, how are you? . . . Not bad, not bad . . . People like us too . . . A restaurateur is a public barometer, I always say. The purest radio weather report. A low-pressure area in the west and an uneven distribution of air pressure over the Alps. I'm the first to feel it. . . . Just yesterday I was saying to my better half: How come we never get to see the Herr Doctor, upon my soul, and the dear Frau Doctor, as young and beautiful as a twenty-year-old, and the Fräulein, so tall, completely grown up, I must really congratulate you. . . . And we keep hearing such lovely things about the Herr Doctor. We understand one another. Our hearts are in the right place." He again shook my hand with profound sentiment. We had reached the table. While Mulminger poured out his honeyed speech, his emotionless gaze of a commander-in-chief took in the drinking guests, the new arrivals at the entrances, the waiters, the dancers, and the band.

The military band was playing a waltz. Memories surfaced in me. I took Gretl by the arm and led her down to the dance floor. She danced with her eyes shut. That was why she did not see that I soon felt dizzy, and my heart pounded wildly. It was only under such a major strain that I noticed there was something wrong with me. But I did not want to show any weakness or present myself with my guard down, not today. And so I danced until the waltz was over. Everything kept spinning around me for a while, and in these surging circles, I saw Myslivec, who greeted me pompously. But he did not come over. Either he had a bad conscience, or, in my numb state, I had not thanked him warmly enough for driving me, and he was both sensitive and rancorous.

Later I quietly danced a slow foxtrot with Cella. During this leisurely motion, my heart did not let out a peep. Cella drifted tall, still, earnest, as if she were dancing with just anyone, and not her father. The cloud of a slight, but rigorous, activity lay on Cella's forehead. And once again, as on that November day, when she had played Bach and then kissed me, I was pierced by that ineffable sense of farewell. This girl is an alien soul, a free, autonomous creature, granted to you by a decree of nature, so that with her victory she may leave you far behind.

Upon our return to the table, we found Gretl with Nagy and Styxi, who, brooking no resistance, pulled us along. In the adjacent room, there was a nicely decked-out table. Seated around it was an elegant company, Styxi's friends, several gentlemen and two young ladies. There was no wine from Burgenland or Lower Austria on the table; instead, I saw several empty bottles of champagne, Röderer Cabinett. Since it was doubtful that such treasures could be found in Herr Mulminger's stock, one could only assume that the prince had had them brought from the cellars of the Residence. Zsoltan Nagy filled our glasses so eagerly, as if it were his treat. He was already quite excited. His smooth cheeks were glowing, and his always impeccably groomed hair was slightly tousled. However, Nagy was one of those rare people who remain attractive even when they are not in form. Raising his glass, he introduced us. "Ladies and gentlemen, these are no ordinary people whom we are bringing to you. Bodenheim is my oldest friend; I won't say how long I've known him. Fate bound us together and tore us apart again—that is, it tore me away, not him, for I am disloyal and he is loyal—"

"Hush up, Nagy," I said, but he did not hush up.

"Ladies and gentlemen, look at him. Do you notice something? My friend is a courageous man. If there were more such men in Austria, then . . . Or are you only an occasional hero, Bodenheim?"

A foxtrot bawled into the room, putting an end to his tipsy nonsense. The prince asked Gretl to dance. Zsoltan went to dance with Cella, who, incidentally, was wearing his jade on her neckline. I gazed after them. He and Cella were almost equally tall and looked strangely harmonious together. And yet Nagy is three months my senior.

The evening, apropos, was truly lovely. We drank a lot,

Gretl even too much; champagne is her great passion. But Cella pushed the glass away when she realized that the wine was going to her head. I noticed that little movement. It gave me food for thought. My heart was warmed by the way this small company treated my two ladies. I could sense the great affection they aroused. Everyone had already heard about Cella's talents. The two young women looked at the child with curious admiration. In their souls, these idlers could not imagine what it is like when a creature is chosen from among thousands. They kept talking about the academy with lofty expectation.

There would be nothing else to report about this successful festivity if two dramatic moments had not made it noteworthy for me. The first, fleeting moment concerned me alone.

Gretl had danced almost every number with Nagy, and then all at once, she wanted to dance with me. I was a bit frightened, for I remembered my earlier palpitations. That was the reason I winked at her.

"I would not dare compete with Zsoltan. He is your honorary escort. You do not need me."

Perhaps these words I employed to beg off came out differently than they were meant. In any case, Gretl, excited by the champagne, blushed a deep red, and her right hand cramped up.

"I want to dance with *you,* Hans."

I remained in my chair, irresolute. Then Cella nudged me, and eying her mother in female complicity, she whispered, "Go ahead, Bulbul, dance."

It was the turn of the military band, and luckily they were not playing a waltz, but a yearning tango. Yet no sooner had we executed the first steps than Gretl halted in the throng.

"Why are you so pale?" she asked, and her own face was strangely bloated and bewildered.

"Am I pale? Really? I feel wonderful."

"Do you know what you are, Hans?"

"At the moment, I am a dreadful traffic obstruction," I said, for couples were bumping into us on all sides.

But Gretl held me tight and would not budge from the spot.

"You're a miracle, Hans. The best man in the world, a wonderful human being. Thank you."

I caressed her arm and gently steered her out of the crush. "Don't drink any more, Gretl," I said. But she sobbed, "Don't be stupid! God, are you stupid, a smart man like you."

Outside I had to wait at least ten minutes until she had wiped away the traces of her tears.

When we came back to the *chambre séparée*, we found Styxi all alone. Standing erect at the table, in his full overlifesize stature and spongy tenderness, he was giving a speech. His drilling eyes were relentlessly fixed on the absent audience, in which we were not included, for his eyes did not move toward us. Yet he did not seem at all drunk; he appeared to be off on a flight of fancy, in profound concentration.

"Austria," he said rigorously, "that is the true Third Reich, the Third Reich of music, you do understand, do you not? Haydn, Mozart, Beethoven, Schubert, Johann Strauss, yes, I must absolutely insist on Johann Strauss, those are the kings. . . . And so on . . . An elected monarchy, of course . . . And a corporative state . . . Corporative state, that is a musical score arranged in a hierarchy, you do understand. At the top, the flutes, the other woodwinds, the horns, then the brasses, the percussion instruments, the string quartet, if you please . . ."

Part of the company returned from the dance floor. So did Cella. Styxi gestured angrily, as if waving off an inconvenience. But his rigid, lordly gaze did not budge an inch from its target.

"Each newborn child is given his voice, his part, in which absolutely nothing, I repeat, absolutely nothing can be revised. In this connection, I would like to implore the conductors and the virtuosi. . . . The Church is the pedal point, if you please, you do understand, to which the whole is harmonized. . . . I suggest an extended A flat and a descant. . . . Austria is written in A flat major, if I am not mistaken."

Beyond Styxi's bizarre political address and the laughter and chatter of the others, I noticed that Mulminger, Nagy, and

Myslivec had just entered the room. They were whispering intensely to one another. Several others crowded in after them, wearing paper caps on their heads, and their faces were sheepish or hungry for sensation. I immediately felt that something significant had happened. Slowly I walked over to the group, which had halted irresolutely at the door.

"Is there a festive surprise tonight?" I asked.

"Indeed there is, domine," Myslivec sang in a Slavic cadence, "these are historic hours." And he pensively sighed, "Oh my goodness!"

But Alois Mulminger opened his golden mouth and, as if apologizing, reported, "On the radio, Herr Doctor . . . Oh, my . . . Our Herr Chancellor has gone to Berchtesgaden."

"To Berchtesgaden, to . . ." I said, and did not utter the name that I will never utter. At that moment, everything was clear, I knew everything. We had to get home! Pack our things! Tonight! And get out of this doomed country! We three! But unfortunately, this lucid impulse lasted only for a moment, and then it was wiped away by anger, disgust, impotent depression. I looked at Zsoltan Nagy, who was lighting a cigarette in vast indifference. Without quite meaning to do so, I asked a thoroughly stupid, unnecessary question: "What do you think, Nagy, will the academy take place?"

He smiled, and many golden sparks flashed in his eyes, whose color could not be determined. "Of course it will take place. Why should our academy not take place?"

Mulminger's mind had likewise refocused on his business. "Herr Doctor"—he winked—"please, please, do not forget, Ash Wednesday, an elegant herring feast, Herr Doctor."

And I truly did not forget those two phrases: "Ash Wednesday" and "herring feast."

The academy was to take place in any event. However, it was rescheduled for the twelfth of March. By then, the disquiet and insecurity prevailing throughout the country would no doubt be gone. Nagy was willing to take an oath on it. His motto was: Everything passes, and the worst passes very quickly. And one day he said to me—and these were his exact words: "You know, Bodenheim, I'm not very educated and I'm no intellectual or anything, but I have a flair, a sixth sense, it is a little gambling knack, that's all. . . . I can feel success and the successful in advance, I'm like a greyhound, I smell a certain pungent perfume, very pleasant. . . . You can put your mind at ease, Cella's got what it takes. She will always be dealt a good hand."

Terrified, I begged him not to challenge the gods. Otherwise, however—to state it frankly—Cella and the academy were the farthest things from my mind during those agitated weeks.

I had gone to the city in order to deliver my 1,507 signatures to Lieutenant-Colonel Dagobert Grollmüller. The knight of the Order of Maria Theresa received me in his home, the shabbiest rented room that one could imagine. The building stood in the eighth precinct, fairly far up, in an area known for its down-and-out ex-officials, its indigent widows of officers and court councilors, and all sorts of shamefaced paupers. I gazed about Grollmüller's room, unable to conceal my embarrassment. Truly, a classic old-time barracks room, the sort that used to be tenanted by Austro-Hungarian lieutenants "without private means." Not even the officer's boy was missing. But this "boy" was an old man with a paralyzed leg, who announced me with "yessirs" and "nosirs." He wore the white jacket of a waiter. The brass bed was covered with two brown "horse-puke" blankets. The wall at its head sported a cheap color portrait of Emperor Franz Joseph, hundreds of thousands of which were mass-produced in the old days. To the right and left of the old Kaiser, there were two smaller photographs: one of his successor and one of the current pretender to the crown. They were adorned with personal dedications. Those were the only things decorating the walls, aside from a small crucifix and two framed, cabinet-sized portraits of women. The walls in the room of the former lieutenant had at least been richly enlivened by sultry illustrations from *The Musket* and *La Vie parisienne.* But this room looked dreary and hopeless. Hopeless? No! It looked as if he were about to march off to war. The office desk at the window bore neat heaps of files, which were sorted and trussed, as if they were to be carried off today. On the table in the center of the room, one could see a pair of military binoculars, a freshly oiled army pistol, and, next to it, several cartons of ammunition. But in one corner, I sighted an officer's packed kitbag, an army reserve coat, strapped on according to regulations, and a thermos bottle. The room was bitterly cold. The stove was out.

Grollmüller, who looked old, shriveled, and slightly foolish in his shrunken coat, noticed my surprise.

"An old soldier like you," he said, "knows what it means to be prepared. Well, I am prepared in this miserable bivouac here; I have been prepared for days now. We are all prepared, and you are too." As if it were a matter of course, he had suddenly switched to the familiar form as in the old Austro-Hungarian army.

"Orders to march can arrive any moment now. Our cause is in fine fettle, very fine. Throughout Austria, they are waiting for the order: Get set! According to the dictates of logic, the government has no other choice. Would it rather submit to the gangsters from Berlin and Berchtesgaden? The government will summon its legal ruler, according to the dictates of logic."

Grollmüller's blue eyes and mummylike but firm features contained something that I can only describe as frozen resoluteness. Frozen in goodness knows how many winters of want and waiting. The slightest breath of any doubt, any qualm would not have been understood. Nor did I have any doubt. I felt only that tingling thrill of respect and almost painful flattery that I had experienced in my army days whenever a high superior deigned to address me personally. Grollmüller was now a high superior for me, more by his nature than by rank. I was in awe of his consistency, his staunch will, his unswerving faith in a *summum bonum* that would never bring him any practical benefits, whether money or power. And I was also in awe of this wretched little cubbyhole, which was so cold that it numbed your fingers. Grollmüller produced a bottle of slivovitz from an otherwise empty closet. Obviously, this source of inner heat had not yet fallen victim to the preparatory packing. The lieutenant-colonel filled three snifters and called his old orderly. "Maniuk! Come and get what's coming to you!"

The stiff-legged old man skillfully clicked his heels and took off with his treasure, to which I hoped he laid claim several times a day.

But now Grollmüller, brooking no interruptions, described the situation (I was feeling slightly dizzy), and he clearly and openly expounded the plan of a military defense of our fatherland against the "gangsters from Berlin and Berchtesgaden." He kept using the word "logical," which moved me deeply, even though his bold trains of thought sounded more fanatic than logical. In the midst of his exposition, he stood up and proclaimed in a rousing tone, "Over in Berchtesgaden, the Antichrist is sitting, the great dragon. And no other power in the world can free us from the dragon except the predestined dragon slayer, the St. George of the House of Austria. Nor are you and I the only ones who know this. Our chancellor knows it too."

I had risen to my feet along with him. All at once, he pulled out his watch.

"I have two tickets to the great speech in Parliament today. I imagine you'll come along, if that's all right with you."

We still had time. Slowly we ambled down Josephstädter Strasse to the Greek temple of the old Reichstag. Vienna had changed considerably since my last visit. The subdued indifference, the lurking innocuity had given way to a dark humming. The whole city throbbed with this odd humming. Vienna too was breathlessly prepared, without, of course, knowing what it was prepared for; it yearningly waited for marching orders that would release it from this torturous twilight of various convictions, these nervewracking ricochets. Huge loudspeakers had been set up everywhere on the streets and squares, and throngs of people were eddying around them. From the nerve harp of these masses, the excitement intermittently evoked chromatic whimpers that sounded like the autumn wind in the country. Soon, the loudspeaker funnels would emit the reply that our chancellor would give to the dragon, that biggest nonentity of them all, swept to the top by zeros hoping to become powerful numbers. Grollmüller was extremely inventive in his hatred. The dragon, he said, was the pathological hybrid of a small-town fortuneteller and a sideshow barker, proud of his phony diction, who simultaneously functions as the "fence" for a gang of burglars.

"But today Vienna is the pivot of the world," he went on. "Pivot" is military jargon for the shaft of the gun barrel mounted on the carriage. Today Vienna was truly the pivot of the world. I felt it throughout my body as we took our places in the gallery of Parliament.

Someone tapped my shoulder. It was Pramer. Have I already mentioned Ferdinand Pramer in the course of my account? He was the third of my boyhood friends, the kindest and most innocent of all. Six feet tall by the age of thirteen and amazingly voluminous, he was known as the mammoth baby among us. Although he had one of the slowest minds in our class, he was someone I needed to lean on, perhaps because of his towering physique, which promised help and protection. Pramer was the most decent one of us. He literally suffered from intermittent courage in that he owned up to his misdemeanors, never lied or cheated like the rest of us, silently put up with unjust punishments, and occasionally even fought to defend weaker people. His fists had defended me several times. However, a worm lurked in Pramer's innate superiority. He was unable to complete anything. He would always make a wild start, but then, for no reason, he would abruptly plunge off before reaching the summit of his magnanimous feats. It was a sudden weariness, feebleness, collapse, that often assails large, fat people.

I can still see the boy jumping up at his school desk, his unshapely, childish face reddening all the way to the roots of his hair, his hands flailing as they tried to advocate some just cause—and all at once, unexpectedly, he would turn pasty and slack, tearfully pouting; apparently, the reason for his noble agitation had been whisked out of his mind. These pathological eruptions and disruptions might have been cause for concern about Pramer's future. But he had managed to fend for himself as an employee of the largest insurance company in Austria, and now he actually had a prestigious and well-paid position on its board of directors.

We had last met on a sad occasion, exactly one year earlier. I had come to his wife's funeral. Tears and sweat kept pouring incessantly down the poor wretch's smooth baby face, and he reeled like a wandering tower between his two sons at the edge of the grave. I can still remember that his bewildered sorrow commanded something like vague horror rather than pity.

Now, that anxiety-ridden giant eyed me reproachfully. We were standing in the narrow, winding corridor leading to the Parliament galleries. It was like one of the classical theaters of Vienna.

"How nasty of you," he said, "you're in town, and you don't even tell me. A fine friend you are."

"You're right, Pramer, it *is* nasty. But I come in so seldom. And lately, so much has been happening, alas."

"Where are you staying?"

"Staying? If it gets too late to go home, I'll spend the night at the Union Hotel on Nussdorfer Strasse."

"How awful, Bodenheim. I tell you, next time you're staying with me. Just drop me a line. Why else should I have a ministerial apartment, I'm a lonely old man, and it's much too big for me. My boys won't bother you, I hardly ever see them myself."

The murmuring all around us had turned into a roaring swell that shattered in the thunderous applause. Someone intoned the national anthem. Soon, we were all on our feet and the entire house was singing. I stood right next to Grollmüller, who stood frozen at attention but did not emit a sound. My heart—goodness knows why—was pounding in my throat, as in times gone by, when I had been overwhelmed by patriotic pomp and circumstance. The applause died out, the anthem ended. The government had occupied its bench. The chairman of the house opened the meeting, saluted the chancellor, and gave him the floor. And then the man who was entrusted with our fate in these catastrophic days mounted the rostrum.

He was relatively young, despite his salt-and-pepper hair. Rather tall and slender, he could be called handsome, with his narrow head and well-formed face. This was the first time I had ever laid eyes on him, and I felt drawn to him. His cheeks looked tanned, but their hue could not come from the winter sun; it could only result from excitement, enervation, anxiety, sleepless nights, and cigarettes. The pages of the manuscript in his hand trembled so conspicuously that all eyes clung to them. This small, white trembling was the only moving spot amid the overall immobility. At first, the trembling prevented me from listening. But the chancellor's voice was strong, calm, decisive, and its tone authoritative. Yet behind that resolute façade, I sensed something else, but was unsure what it was: something eroded or apathetic or shattered that tried to drown itself out with persuasive rhetoric. Did this man have doubts about his mission, about the possibility of victory? Or was he merely numbed by the tremendous responsibility of his decisions, of the words spoken here in this venerable temple, which had already witnessed so much history? If Austria fell, then Europe would crumble. Without Austria's freedom, the small nations could not maintain their freedom. This voice—somewhat too bombastic, too convulsive for an old-time Austrian with such a quiet attitude—this voice knew how far along it was and what depended on it. But we others did not know. This man was taking the words right out of our hearts, as never before. We clung to the unambiguous force of this masterful speech, which wiped out all the hidden fears and protests of reason. At last, clarity and firmness! No more bleak com-

promises, no ingratiations, no impotent attempts at reconciliation, no futile entreaties aimed at merciless cunning. Instead:
"Bis hierher und nicht weiter!" This far and no farther! And
when the chancellor's voice hurled those words into the room,
they were like a liberation, like the roaring air of a glacier after
years of lying in a musty basement. And they were answered
by long cheers from all of us.

There is no worse degradation for a nation or an individual
than being unable to fight, than being unarmed and helpless
and enduring the foul destiny inflicted by an enemy whose only
virtue is to be stronger and more unscrupulous than we. Ah,
what did I know, in my middle-class narrowness, about those
primal feelings of impotence, which I had only read about in
high school. To fight! A pensive smile hovered on Grollmüller's
face, which was the color of withered leaves. Nudging me, he
nodded his head. Now, "preparedness" was no longer a quirk.

When we came out into the street, it was already night. The
flags, red-white-and-red, undulated fantastically from the poles
and buildings into the dusty light of the arc lamps.

Red-white-red,
Living or dead.

The speech had ended with this old Austrian motto. Everyone had faith. Hundreds of thousands of people swept from
the Votive Church to the Opera. The trolleys were not running. But there was no mass pageantry, no torchlight parade,
no demonstration. The huge consensus was not disturbed by
any prearranged, artificial propaganda. The lurking daytime
hum had turned into a deep, satisfying roar. Amid these hundreds of thousands of people, I too was filled with a roaring
confidence; a relief, a profound sigh, ineffable. The old, merry
marches came crashing from the loudspeakers.

The crowd surged all the way to the outermost gates of the
castle. The center of the crowd swirled and eddied. It was the
chancellor surrounded by his friends, his enthusiastic support-

ers. Almost no policemen were in sight. Today, no one feared the white-stockings. The fervent vote of the people of Vienna had swept them from the streets. So it appeared. Nothing hostile was to be felt. The adversary had been perceptibly assailed by a huge weariness. The masses are governed by unknown constellations that change their emotions from one hour to the next. And only terror can stop these incomprehensible metamorphoses. We came right up to the castle gates. The air was flooded with spotlights. The chancellor and his men had reached the merlons over the gates and were letting these proudest moments of their lives surge past. Workers saluted them with clenched fists. Unity blended with reconciliation.

Grollmüller, holding my arm, motioned toward the gate and said very calmly, "Now it's starting. Our marching orders are coming. I was not mistaken about him."

"Perhaps we really are saved," I shouted into the huge roar.

"We will be saved at a certain moment, you know what I mean. First the decisive days will come, our days. Petitions will not help. Other weapons must be prepared. I will need you."

"That goes without saying, sir," I replied, straightening up a bit. "Why else am I here?"

We now stood right at the fence of the Imperial Garden and had a bit of free space in front of us. Moving to the side, Grollmüller spoke calmly and earnestly, in a commanding tone. "Second Lieutenant Bodenheim, you have been detailed to me personally. When will you be ready to begin your tour of duty?"

And I, a staid husband, father, lawyer, who had work and worries enough, who could not have been further removed from politics, who had nothing but a dreadful and splendid recollection of war and soldiering—I now replied without qualms, "I shall report the day after tomorrow, sir."

And I took my prompt concurrence as much for granted as his choice, which had fallen upon me, an unimportant civilian, not to mention a member of our people. . . .

"Bulbul, I've been studying Schumann's *Carnaval.* It fits in with the season. Professor Scherber says it's insolent of me, and he's scolding terribly. But Uncle Zsoltan says it's all right."

Cella sat on her mother's bed. It was just about the crack of dawn. Her long, beautiful chestnut hair, of which all three of us were proud, streamed, unbound, over her still so childlike shoulders. Gretl was tidying my suitcase, which I had packed as sloppily as always.

"Uncle Zsoltan," I said, "what does he know about music? What a joke."

Cella seemed dissatisfied with my putdown of Nagy.

"He? Why, he's as musical as a Gypsy."

"As a Gypsy perhaps. But he's never studied anything, that rascal."

"It's funny," said Cella, becoming very pensive, "Uncle Zsoltan can play anything you want from memory: Puccini and Wagner and all the latest hits. You just have to order him."

"From memory, yes! But he probably can't read music to save himself!"

Cella gaped at me in amazement. "But don't you find that wonderful, Bulbul? Anyone can learn how to read music and play a score. Lots of people manage to do that. But from memory? Just by hearing something? Don't you see?"

Although I was slightly annoyed, I did not care to deprive her of her enthusiasm for Nagy's seductive talents. So I held my tongue. But she suddenly asked, "Do you think the academy will really take place, Bulbul? I'm so excited, yet I'm so scared."

"It was unclear a couple of days ago. But now, child, after the great speech, I am dead certain that it will take place. And you mustn't be afraid. I will be back in plenty of time, and then you'll play your program for us two or three times."

Gretl was refolding my uniform, the new one, whose purchase I had concealed from her.

"Why this, Bodenheim?" she inquired.

"We may need it, in the near future."

"Do you have to get mixed up in it, Hans?"

"I am not getting mixed up. I am only defending myself. And that is something everyone should do."

"Everyone? Oh, God, Hans, what do you know about them?"

"Nagy, for instance—"

"Nagy says explicitly that you shouldn't touch them with a ten-foot pole. Nowadays, a man like you should avoid making waves."

"Aha! Don't make waves, don't get pushy, don't start anything—I said those very same things—and remain as meek and invisible as possible—and be trodden and slaughtered. . . ."

"I was only repeating what Zsoltan says."

"Zsoltan, Zsoltan, a sublime paragon, your Zsoltan. I guess I'm just not as smart as Zsoltan. Or as homeless and rootless. I have something to defend, he does not."

Gretl placed my box of war decorations atop my now meticulously packed uniform, and she closed the suitcase.

"Wouldn't it be better," she said, "to emigrate in such times?"

Her words instantly put me at ease. I laughed. "You're acting as if I'm traveling to America, at the very least."

The carillon of the Haydn Church began. Eight o'clock! Goodness, my bus was leaving in ten minutes. I quickly hugged Gretl and Cella. They walked me to the door. But suddenly, at the threshold, I felt an unmotivated anxiety. I gazed into the bright faces of my wife, my child. Why did they both look so strangely bewildered? Only then did I say good-bye, really good-bye, hugging and kissing them over and over, Cella and Gretl and Cella.

"I'll be back by Sunday at the very latest. And if it's at all possible, I'll spend a little time at home in the evening."

Cella's hair was redolent with chamomile and childhood. This scent haunted me throughout the bus ride. Why did it fill my soul with melancholy?

Chapter 6

The Plaster Heads

I was actually sitting at Pramer's table.

My old friend had not exaggerated. He had a lordly apartment with gigantic rooms; it was located in the oldest part of the inner city, on one of the hushed side streets between Freyung and Wipplingerstrasse.

After some wavering, I had decided to accept Pramer's invitation. I reckoned—I was not sure why—on a tour of duty lasting eight or nine days in the city, during which time I would be completely at the disposal of Grollmüller and our cause. The academy was scheduled to take place right after that, and I would have to return home for Cella's sake. Nor would my work permit any longer absence; indeed, even this interruption would, presumably, put everything at sixes and sevens.

The Union Hotel was not a cozy place to spend the night. The bleakness it had to offer, with its damp, ripped, flowery wallpaper, its creaking bed, and its consumptive illumination, could not even be called cheap. Since I am an incurable creature of habit, I had remained loyal to the Union since my student days. Now, I was delighted to be rid of that oppressive place. And yet, I do not enjoy laying claim to hospitality. A guest is always a subordinate person, subordinate to the home that receives him. He feels the troublesome obligation of constant gratitude, while the happy and generous host can comfortably yield to his hospitable beneficence. 'Tis better to give than to receive, goodness knows. Particularly when the recipient is dependent on the giver. The guest is all too readily and morosely suspected of playing his hallowed role purely for the sake of thrift. For the most ordinary things in life, one must be either gifted enough or dull-minded enough to overcome their embarrassing ambivalence. For instance, one must have a great sense of freedom and a great scorn of other people to be a useful parasite.

However, I felt no such qualms about Pramer and myself. He was obviously delighted that I would be spending a few days in his home. A bed, a bath, and a meal had been luxuriously prepared—especially the meal. Pramer, who did not have to stint, and did not stint, appeared more than delighted by the opportunity to extend and enjoy his own festive hospitality. I knew this old weakness of his. After all, I so well remembered the uncontrolled greed with which the fat little boy used to scrutinize the sandwiches of schoolmates during morning recess. In the course of decades, the human mind and soul undergo the most incredible transformations, so that a man scarcely recognizes himself in the earlier phases of his life. The only things that remain unchanged from the maternal breast to the grave are the primal drives, the intrinsic habits, good and bad, which form the most shameful continuity—our sole character, as it were—the chain of our uninterrupted breaches of loyalty. Pramer had always been voracious. Since, of all the deadly sins, gluttony is perhaps the one most alien to me, I had always gladly given him part of my school lunch without having to work up much virtue. Now, Pramer was the soul of generosity, paying me back with interest and compound interest for what he had once consumed. As he did so, those familiar cadging eyes breathlessly followed the proffered dishes, while his lips tirelessly relished them in advance.

The table was set for four. But Pramer and I faced one another by ourselves. His sons, Otto and Harry, evinced neither respect nor punctuality toward the paternal meals. Pramer mumbled some resigned comment, from which I gleaned that he had failed to make any headway with his offspring. I now understood why he had invited me: the isolation of a fifty-year-old man who lived comfortably but had neither the strength nor the spirit to remain alone. Goodness, a daily visit to your café is enough. After supper at home, a man likes to enjoy some wine, a cigar, and peaceful conversation. My friend Pramer was very good-natured, a highly impractical quality that had little to do with goodness, but all the more with weakness.

Although I had nothing to hide, I did not immediately reveal the purpose of my trip to the city. My host seemed utterly indifferent to the throttling events of the times. I was doubly surprised. It was well known that Pramer had been close to the Social Democratic Party just a few years ago and, if I am not mistaken, he had been active as a trustee at some major organization. At that time, of course, he had not yet become a leading figure in the insurance business, and his income had been modest.

So we talked about the things that settled men talk about if they once went to school together but now see little of one another: vanished memories, grotesque teachers who died long ago, and very mediocre schoolmates who have not yet died, although they give fewer and fewer signs of life from one year to the next. Zsoltan Nagy, the most unusual emissary of our modest class, played the largest role in our conversation.

Finally, Otto, Pramer's younger son, showed up for dessert. He was a veritable hulk of fat, like his father; however, his unstructured corpulence gave an impression of overlifesize indolence, but certainly not of a good nature. Otto muttered some sort of excuse, held out his slack, pudgy hand and plopped into a chair, making the entire room quiver. The father was quite obviously afraid of this abundant likeness of

his, for he asked Otto a few almost humble questions, as if to
ingratiate himself, and the son replied with vague growls.

Harry, the elder brother, who burst into the room when we
were drinking our coffee, was an entirely different matter.
Harry was not his father's likeness at all; he did not take after
him in any way. He was short, thickset, lively, with a shiny
black moustache and a hint of a modish Vandyke. In his tempestuous haste, this very model of a charming Viennese resembled a man who never quite gets it right and therefore has to
keep jumping onto the moving train. He amiably ran his hand
over his father's bald head and clicked his heels in front of me;
his entire face was beaming.

"A thousand pardons . . . Just stopping in between two important meetings . . . I wanted to say hello. . . . Wanted to
listen to you for a while. . . . Then I'll be going off again. . . .
Hard day today, alas. . . ."

Like Myslivec, Harry's diction bristled with all sorts of ironic
fustian, but *his* bombast seemed more than the mere rhetoric
of an insatiable politeness that gilded the lily. Pramer gazed at
his elder boy with anxious admiration. Harry had already made
his way up to an envied position as secretary in the Industrialists Association.

I could sense that this anxiety-ridden father wanted his guest
to find grace and honor in the eyes of his difficult sons. Perhaps
that was why he asked me to speak about myself and the plans
that had brought me to the city. For once, I had young people
in front of me, something that happened so rarely. I overcame
my inner resistance, which had grown because of Otto and
Harry, and I began to talk about what was virtually stifling me
in these fateful days, about Austria's great counterthrust, the
levée en masse, and the savior whom providence was holding
in readiness. Nor did I neglect appealing for active assistance
from the younger generation in the guise of Pramer's two sons.

"Marvelous. Simply wonderful," said Harry, beaming at me
in admiration, "but may I humbly take the liberty of focusing
your worthy attention more closely on this younger genera-

tion, to which your humble servant has the honor of belong-ing. We are a rather strange generation."

"We were young too and not even that long ago, isn't that so, Pramer?" I looked at the worried giant of a father, who blinked at us with tiny, watery eyes. "And you probably recall that for us, youth was the time of disinterested ideals and a repugnance toward any sort of opportunism."

I was seeking help, so that my words might, as it were, stave off unpleasant revelations.

"Brilliant," beamed Harry, bowing tersely to his father and to me. "I would not dream of denying the existence of ideals in the present generation, to which I have the honor of be-longing—"

"Ideals," Pramer sighed profoundly. Harry ignored the interruption.

"One must simply distinguish between ideals and those pre-historic illusions of which our reprehensible predecessors are not to be exonerated. Let us, for instance, take the most pres-tigious ideal of our highly venerable forerunners: money! 'Money is power' was the motto of our most recent history. But today we know that power is money. Yes, power is prop-erty, culture, a higher standard of living, and therefore the true goal of life, a goal that is free of illusions. Power is even high society. People who are too haughty to shake hands with a genius of jurisprudence writhe in ecstatic convulsions before the upstarts of power. That is why the new generation is en-tirely devoted to the acquisition of power. However, small po-litical territories like ours are quite naturally always excluded from power. That is why our generation, which scorns all ar-chaic sentimentality, is striving for a large political territory, which will bring it the leadership of Europe and thereby a more intense feeling of life, to a degree as yet unknown."

"My goodness," I blurted out, folding my hands in terror, "this delinquent morality is certainly free of illusion. But is there no such thing as love of one's homeland, loyalty to the past, hatred of the lowest baseness, incorruptibility, higher aspirations, is there no such thing as a self that loves itself and that seeks its own perfection?"

"Please understand me." Harry smiled. "I personally do not much care for this tavern morality, because as Papa's son I am genetically handicapped and not typical. But the world is fed up with that weepy sense of 'self.' Much too fed up. I was alive during the delightful earlier period. Nothing but great minds and staggering personalities that were bound to make one feel small. But now the fad consists of lining up in single file, shoulder to shoulder, and merrily prattling in chorus. Life is so much easier without an individual 'self.' "

"And what is death like without a 'self'?"

"Death? Why that's the biggest hit of all. Dying is the easiest thing in the world. For only a highly individualized self can really die. That is why the generation to which I have the honor of belonging is so bent on dying, as if it were a barrel of laughs. You and Papa can see that this solves one of mankind's oldest problems almost perfectly."

Closing my eyes, I leaned back and listened, not without surprise, to how soft and tired my voice sounded: "I have no sons, but I do have a daughter, Cella; she is about to turn sixteen. Fate has given her a great, I may say a tremendous, talent. Music, Pramer, you know . . . This girl Cella also belongs to the younger generation, but she is not at all interested in lining up with anyone. She sits at the piano all day long, practicing and practicing Bach, Beethoven, Mozart, Schubert. If a bar doesn't come out right, if she can't get a tiny mistake out of her fingers, then she suffers and gets as mad as a wet hen. Her only dream is perfection: refining and improving her musical self by means of hard work. I see this daily and have to hold her back lest she make herself ill. This child, gentlemen, would be unable to understand a younger generation that would rather grab hold of a gigantic locomotive in order to be hauled to a more intense feeling of life without straining themselves. Cella loves her hard work; her lessons with Scherber

are her greatest fun; she would not care to have anything for
nothing, you may take my word."

Pramer triumphantly banged his cupped hand on the table.
"Bravo, Bodenheim. Just tell them, give it to them, those
goddamn boys. Now you can see what kinds of personalities
still come forth from the younger generation. This whole philosophy is nothing but a base pretext used by good-for-
nothings."

"Not at all," beamed Harry, clicking his heels under the
table. "We simply have to congratulate Herr Doctor Bodenheim for having such a wonderful daughter."

Pramer egged me on again. "Just tell them, Bodenheim, give
it to them."

But Otto, the fat colossus, who had not yet spoken a word,
pulled a newspaper from his pocket and began to read.

During the next few days, I was completely occupied by
Grollmüller and the Iron Soldiers Ring, so that I usually did
not come home until late at night. And poor Pramer, who had
hoped for a loyal table companion, got the short end of the
stick. I briefly ran into Otto and Harry only twice more.

One of the most important tasks that Grollmüller entrusted
me with was to induce the embittered labor force to join our
side and accept the idea of a general resistance. My target was
the so-called Republican Defense Corps, which had been disbanded after the brief, ill–starred Civil War in 1935; according
to rumor, however, the Corps had buried a portion of its
weapons. But the official bridges that the government was
starting to build in its dire plight were not sufficient to get
through to the elite unit of the Social Democrats. The brilliant
leaders of the "Red past" had to be won over to our great
cause, for they were the only ones whom the workers trusted
in spite of their defeat. One of these brilliant leaders was R,
whom Pramer knew very well. I was counting on that.

I had not forgotten that day. It was the eighth of March when Jacques Emanuel Weil came to visit me at Pramer's home. Despite his massive build, he sat on the very edge of the chair without removing his fur coat or his gloves.

"When the chancellor gives his speech at Innsbruck," he began, "he will announce a plebiscite."

"How do you know, Herr von Weil?"

"From the very best source. The white-stockings."

"That is certainly the best source. They know the government's decisions even before the government knows them." Ignoring my remarks, Weil continued, "This dangerous plebiscite is bound to have crucial consequences. It will bring either final salvation or final doom. I personally believe it will be doom."

I gaped at him in dismay. He waved me off with his leather-gloved hand, which looked like an artificial hand.

"Please make allowances for the fact that I have a pessimistic nature, in unglorious contrast to you, Doctor Bodenheim."

"And what do you plan to do?"

"For our people, it would be wisest to leave this country, indeed not wait another day."

"And where do you intend to go?"

"I am going nowhere; I am remaining."

"Remaining, without faith?"

Weil now looked at me for the first time, with his shy, fleeting eyes, which seemed to be ashamed of themselves as if they were something illicitly naked.

"Listen, Bodenheim," he said, "I have not forgotten our conversation in the Castle Park. It actually had a very powerful effect on me—I mean your firm view in all these matters. We are accused of being homeless materialists and profiteering nomads, with no relationship to the earth that nourishes us. I consider that one of those half-truths or half-lies on which mankind is choking today, and which are far more dangerous than whole lies or whole truths. In any case, it is documented that my own family lived in Styria as far back as the twelfth century and moved to Burgenland, that is, close by, during the

Counter-Reformation, under Ferdinand II. Accordingly, when it comes to being a native son, I have every right in the world to call myself a genuine Austrian. Indeed, I have even more right than Herr Myslivec and other expert patrons of traditional native culture. But that is not crucial. The crucial thing for me was our conversation. You convinced me. Thus, I will not follow the example set by the Gypsies of Sankt Margarethen. Instead, I will 'fight,' as you phrased it. This is a relatively easy decision for me since I am unmarried and, fortunately, bear no responsibility toward children."

While speaking these words, Jacques Emanuel Weil solemnly and ceremoniously peeled off his right glove, exposing a strangely tender, milky hand, a sensitive and highly protected entity, which reached into his breast pocket and produced two thick, well-bound packages. Money, a very great deal of money.

"This is two hundred thousand in cash," he said, almost apologetically and without waiting for me to ask him anything. "Originally, I wanted to go to the chancellor himself, in order to make this sum available to him for his propagandizing efforts during the next few days. But then I reconsidered. In the hands of the government, this money would most likely not be employed for the purpose that I regard as the only one with any prospects of success, namely, armed resistance. This, as I have been told, would buy around sixty heavy machine guns, which will be delivered without further ado and as swiftly as possible from the Skoda supplies. If the various combat units of our patriotic population can be armed in time, then I see a glimmer of hope—mind you, only a glimmer. The enemy may flinch at unleashing a new Spain in the middle of Europe for the sake of his own nationalism. He also knows very well that the white-stockings are numerically weak here and fairly scattered. At the same time, the army, the rural constabulary, and the police would be free to guard our borders. That is why, as I have said, I view arming the population as a vague chance. However, this plan can work effectively only in the name of

the legitimate, time-tested idea that reconciles all partisan con-
flicts. Your wife, dear Bodenheim, has told me about your
present activities. And so I have come to you to put in my
pennies, which, mind you, add up to a nice handsome sum—
no more modest than I myself."

We immediately took Weil's magnificent automobile to the
office of the Iron Soldiers Ring. A bright morning sun poured
springlike into the two tiny rooms of this office, which was not
much larger than Grollmüller's home. Today, the tiny rooms
were thronged by many veterans, especially gray-haired ones.
They had come from all over the country to receive their battle
orders. Eyes like mine, blinded by partisan passion, could easily believe that our cause was on the verge of victory, for the
reports, offers, words of encouragement, and particularly curious questions were piling up on the desks. We lost far too
much precious time answering superfluous letters. Dagobert
Grollmüller accepted Jacques Emanuel Weil's contribution with
majestic equanimity, as if it were a natural tribute of wealth
to righteous necessity.

"You are doing the correct thing, Baron," said Grollmüller,
"by giving the money to us rather than to the government. In
no way do I doubt the good faith and determination of our
government. On the contrary. But its hands have been tied ever
since it signed a pact with the archenemy at Berchtesgaden.
When the time is right, *we* shall lead the national uprising at
the orders of His Majesty. The preparations are being made
punctually, as you can see. A confidential agent of the Czech
nation has promised us a huge delivery of weapons for this
Saturday. On the whole, we cannot complain about assistance
from the capitalists."

Grollmüller's last comment was true to some extent. Only
yesterday, a banker, a sugar manufacturer, and a textile maker,
all three of them belonging to *our* people, had promised finan-
cial help. Of course, the powerful Industrialists Association, in
which Harry Pramer had his envied little position in the sec-
retariat, was shrouding its head in vagueness.

Grollmüller and his colleagues, whom I had joined, were living in constant euphoria. No intoxication is more dangerous, more deceptive, than the one induced by work. We had no chance to eat or sleep. I had the ominous sensation that my aging head was growing from hour to hour, as if bloated by weariness and probably also extreme tension. Vienna had been turned to gold by an unduly radiant early March. In the parks, premature buds were already emerging from the brown joints of the bushes.

Encouraged by the Pact of Berchtesgaden, suburban white-stockings had broken into the inner city. At first, they were sly and timid, like profaners entering a sanctuary. But then they grew more and more insolent and aggressive. They marched through the streets in groups, gangs, and swarms, clustering here and there, breaking into irksome songs or chanting slogans that seemed to come not from human mouths but from the rhythmic gasping of a gigantic machine. Sometimes they were opposed by groups of outraged people, and they engaged in Homeric battles of invective. As a rule, the white-stockings would eventually retreat. We mistook their withdrawals for fear and cowardice, but they were actually following carefully laid tactical plans. Since I seldom returned home before dawn, I noticed few of these disturbances.

I noticed nothing, I thought of nothing but the growing flood of our agendas, the endless correspondence, the numbing sequence of meetings and negotiations in which we had to participate. Even Cella had vanished from my consciousness in the furious torrent of these times.

The Ides of March had begun. On a Friday. It was the Friday of my life. I have no notes, but, ignoring the rules of terseness, I must make a strenuous effort to conjure up every event and every emotion of that blackest of all my days. (Alas, the world still does not realize that this has long been *its* blackest day, too, and will be that for a long time.)

After several hours of very inadequate sleep, I awoke around nine A.M. The mendacious bombast of that premature March sun practically blew up the large guest room I was staying in. It took a great effort to gather my feelings. I soon realized that they were extremely bitter, unhappy, anxious feelings. Am I ill, I wondered. No, I as an individual was not ill. It sounds crazy, but I cannot express it any more lucidly. It was not I who was ill, but the world around me and in me, and I myself was only the affected organ, the center, the neuralgic point of this disease, as the phrase goes today.

Pramer entered my room, his overflowing body wrapped in a black kimono with an embroidered gold dragon. A Mongolian shaman, a fairy-tale executioner. The good man offered an ill-omened spectacle. His small eyes seemed glued together. He pursed his lips and clicked his tongue, as if bidding his own sensory indolence to enjoy itself.

"What weather we have today, what weather."

And his lips savored the word "weather," as if it were a very special young wine. He placed a letter on my bedspread. I recognized Cella's large, vertical script. She had had an adult handwriting for roughly a year now.

"Again it's been delayed or maybe canceled altogether, dearest Bulbul," she wrote. "Although I am quite glad, I feel very sorry all the same. I've been practicing six hours a day. It's good you weren't here, Bulbul, you would have scolded me constantly. Uncle Zsoltan is gone, too. He's not living with Prince Styxi anymore. He had to move to Vienna, it was very urgent. When are you coming home? The two of us are very lonely, it's not nice. Love and kisses from your loving daughter, Cella."

Folding the letter into a tiny square, I made up my mind to desert, even though I did not fully realize the paradox. I wanted to go to Scherber without delay. Herr Professor, I heard myself shouting, don't lose another moment! Go straight to the American consulate! Make all the arrangements for yourself and Cella before it's too late. . . . I would accompany the old man

to the door of the American consulate to make sure he did not
stray; by then it would be past ten, and I could just barely
catch the bus on Schwarzenbergplatz. Home! To Gretl and
Cella! Use the time! Get our passports in order! I must have
dunked my head in cold water at least ten times to pull myself
together.

I then actually did go to Scherber's apartment on Mondscheingasse. He had gone out of town two weeks ago; the but-
ler showed me a wire announcing the professor's return that
afternoon. Damn it all, I had known that Scherber was away:
after all, Cella had not been going to Vienna for her lessons.
Carrying out my decision, I trotted slowly toward the bus
station. The bus was still empty. What about my baggage?!
And Pramer?! So what, I'll just write Pramer a long thank-you
note explaining everything, and tomorrow I'll send someone to
get my valise. I paced up and down in front of the bus several
times, like an overpunctual traveler. But then I inconspicuously
moved away as if concealing something, and I strolled down
Ringstrasse, along the grand hotels, all the way to the opera.
I was driven by a very specific, vehement curiosity. I turned
into Kärntnerstrasse. And indeed, the ominous travel agency
of the Third Reich, the citadel of the enemy, resembled a mau-
soleum after a sumptuous interment. Deep inside the room,
the huge portrait of the pasty-faced dragon with the poignant
forelock was almost choked by nosegays. And in front of the
picture, a thick trail of flowers ran all the way to the entrance,
right into the display window. A crowd thronged outside the
agency, mostly women, petty-bourgeois, but also ladies in fur
coats, staring through the glass with languishing shrews' eyes.
This main artery of the city was clogged. A large squad of
indifferent policemen stood on the side, leaving the crowd alone
as it kept crying, "Heil Hitler!" An airplane circled in the sky.
A flurry of small white leaflets timidly drifted to the earth. I
picked up the leaflet: "Vote for a free and independent Austria!" Many of the people bent down toward this snow. An
overlifesize voice approached on a truck that carried a gigantic

loudspeaker. The invisible hollow voice, similar to that of a primordial deity, hurled its beseeching sound fragments across the throng: "Vote! Plebescite! Sunday!" Barely understandable, these words plopped like stones into the foamy flood of Heils. What was going on? I grabbed my forehead. I awoke. I left for work.

Our office was strangely deserted today. Nevertheless, one could barely get across the waiting room. It was stuffed with piles of crates. Three orderlies—elderly unemployed men whom we had hired—and the building superintendent were dragging the crates, one after another, into the basement. The concierge, a scraggy woman, stood there reproachfully. Grollmüller personally supervised the operation. Weapons, munitions? I gave him an inquiring look. He, more wan than usual, was helping the orderlies. He offered no explanation. All at once, he turned to me, an elderly man, breathless from his strenuous work, and gave me an order: "Call up. All the men you can reach in town. Follow our list precisely. First the active ones, then the reserve. Everyone is to be stationed downstairs in front of the building at two-thirty P.M. In uniforms, with decorations. Everyone is to pass the orders along to his people, relay system, understand? Those who have already been notified are checked off in red."

With the list in front of me, I began telephoning. Not a very elegant task. But I felt as if I were lying with a machine gun, letting the cartridge belt whisk by. And again I was overwhelmed by that dangerous and deceptive intoxication of work, which helps us to cope with anything and yet plunges us into the abyss. Soon the sweat was pouring down my forehead. I was seized with the numbing ambition to keep each call down to one single minute. It was not yet two P.M., and, since eleven A.M., I had already transmitted Grollmüller's orders to more than one hundred former officers.

Then I staggered to my feet. A sudden dizziness knocked me against the lieutenant-colonel. He clutched me and callously shoved me toward the door.

"Fine, and now you'll drive to General Dudenovich and notify him that everything is going smoothly."

I arrived fifteen minutes late, since, following orders, I had changed into my uniform after visiting the venerable ghost. In front of our agency building, I found a troop of twelve men in worn-out uniforms. All in all, we had notified at least two hundred men, not counting the relay system that I had demanded during each and every call. Yesterday, we had seemed to be at the hub of a dynamic movement; but today, not more than twelve men had obeyed the earnest order. Twelve apostles, bowed and threadbare and gray, as apostles are usually depicted. There were three staff officers, two captains, and seven reserve lieutenants, all of them looking quite wretched. Grollmüller did not display the slightest touch of anger or disappointment. He asked the men to line up in the lobby. Then he stood in front of us and told us to regard ourselves as a detachment of the old Imperial-Royal Army, which would play a major role at a crucial moment. We would now immediately march to the seat of government at Ballhausplatz and inform the Herr Federal Chancellor of the unshakable will of the old army.

Grollmüller motioned me over to his side. In his impeccable uniform, which looked as if it had just come fresh from the military tailor, he looked like a new man: taller than usual, more erect, and incredibly ageless. Previously, he had gone about in disguise, like a fairy-tale prince. We marched off.

On this Friday, the streets kept changing from hour to hour. Now, toward three P.M., the hubbub had vanished, and the patriots seemed triumphant. Troops of adolescents with red-white-and-red flags were marching everywhere, singing, and shouting, "Austria!" At the chancellery, the sentry was striding to and fro. I looked up at the balcony of the mansion. "Imperial and Royal Ministry of Foreign Affairs" passed through my mind, and "House and State Archives," and it dawned on me that almost twenty years had passed since I had been part of a hollow-eyed crowd on this very square, a crowd that had invincibly laid siege to the building. I remembered the short man—a Baron Burian, a Hungarian count, I think—stepping out on the balcony and trying to begin a speech in his washed-out ministerial voice. He did not get far. It was not the din, but the tremendous naked pressure of these ten thousand starving people that throttled his voice, forcing him to withdraw, bewildered, like a booed actor, with a tormented face. Were they the same masses loitering in the streets today, waiting for their cue to consolidate? I thought of the chorus on the opera stage. Today they are Egyptians, tomorrow Druids, the next day German knights or the sansculottes of 1789. But one always recognizes them despite their varying costumes, the same badly paid supernumeraries with their potbellies, potato noses, and plebeian knock-knees or bandy legs. Whenever history has another premiere, the chorus always shows up, the populace, and it is always the same, whatever its political costume.

Passing the sentry, the fourteen of us, under Grollmüller's command, marched through the portal of the chancellery. The concierge held out his arms to ward us off. Grollmüller scornfully handed him a letter bearing the signature of Austria's federal chancellor. The gold-braided concierge looked like an exhausted supervisor, floundering in utter confusion, uselessly throwing himself against the growing chaos, exerting himself beyond the call of duty.

"All these gentlemen?" he asked with an offended yet utterly resigned glance toward the gateway arch. Grollmüller ordered the two eldest staff officers and myself to follow him. The others were to wait for us downstairs until we returned with positive news.

We ascended the grand stairway to the second floor, where the magnificent, historic rooms and the chancellor's offices were located. There was a hectic coming and going, almost in double time. High-ranking officials dashed by, their faces beet-red, stewed in the mysterious steambath of the still concealed events. Grollmüller accosted one, then another, waving his letter. He received either no answers or frenetic ones, as if he had startled a somnambulist on the edge of a roof. We finally wound up in a lofty waiting room, which smelled of wet clothes. (Why? It had not rained or snowed for days.) Mountainous heaps of overcoats lay on tables, chairs, and even the bare floors.

The tall, white French doors to the adjacent room kept opening, and out came crimson or gaunt apparitions, sweating profusely. Forming groups, they instantly looked for a corner where they could whisper and gesticulate. I felt that we four men, in uniforms and decorations that were no longer part of real life, were a superfluous, nay, ludicrous obstacle, embarrassing remnants of a grand but long-perished era. What luck, I thought, that none of our wretched war invalids has come along, no blind man, no trembling man, no man with artificial limbs. Perhaps Grollmüller had similar thoughts to overcome. He stood there, frozen at attention, while the deep holes of his mummified cheeks grew darker and darker.

We waited. Jammed into the center of the room, we waited, not stirring, not speaking, surrounded by whispers from all corners. And after we had been waiting for almost an hour, something happened that, in contrast to us, sharply belonged to real life. Nothing actually happened, except that suddenly there were two strangers here who were indescribably different from everyone else.

Perhaps it was this difference that made the two strangers look like twins. Both men wore the same dashingly belted trenchcoats as a kind of transitional coat between mufti and military. Both men had ears that stuck way out from their heads. Both men had the same facial coloring, the piglet pink of a baby's bottom that has been exposed for a long time. Their pear-shaped skulls were shorn all the way to the crowns. But on top, something was sticking up that resembled the colorless down of a young bird. And when they turned their backs, we were astonished to see that both of them had the same scarlet hill-and-dale necks covered with crater landscapes of faded boils.

In their tones and words and at every step, the twins emanated a numbing self-confidence that was as unknown in our climes as the horses of the conquistadors among the Aztecs. The effect was like that of death rays upon the whisperers, who abruptly broke off. Turning gray and fading, rubbing their hands in a winterly way, two courageous men—presumably ministers or section heads seeking to collaborate—came over to the twins, who sparkled and crackled like a high-voltage system. With an obsequiousness that was ashamed of itself, the two courageous men ushered the two highly explosive envoys through the French doors. No sooner had they vanished than a high-ranking general of the Austrian army emerged from the same French doors. He was one of the beet-red men. With long strides, Grollmüller went over and stood before him. His voice resounded. "Sir, general, old friend, may I—"

The general broke in while his rigid gaze slowly focused. "Grollmüller, old friend, you too."

"Sir, may I recall our telephone conversation of two days ago. You promised—"

"Two days ago—" the general gaped, as if that call had taken place decades earlier.

"The federal chancellor, with whom you have been conferring, is willing to receive me and the delegates. . . ."

"What federal chancellor?"

"What federal chancellor? What do you mean?"

"I mean . . . Go home, dear Grollmüller. All of you. And put those rags away where the moths can eat them as soon as possible. Those rags will not be very popular during the next few years."

"You mean—?"

"I mean . . . It's over . . . finished, the boat's leaving! So let us go, Grollmüller, old comrade."

He ran his hand over Grollmüller's Maria Theresa cross, lightly touched his cap, and let it be. He ignored our salute.

We descended slowly to the other ten veterans, who were waiting below, deathly pale and exhausted. We formed a tight, speechless squad.

"It is over, gentlemen," said Grollmüller, "over. The government has failed. I can do nothing more. Thank you, gentlemen."

And when no one stirred, he yelled at us like a drill sergeant yelling at dumbfounded soldiers: "Company dismissed!"

Grollmüller then marched off, his long legs taking long strides. I hurried after him, I caught up with him. "Is everything really lost?"

I panted as I ran alongside him. He did not answer. It was not until we reached Herrengasse that he turned to me as if I were an irksome petitioner. "Herr Doctor Bodenheim, you are slow-witted. It is finished. Finished."

And he raised his emaciated head and, with astonishing sharpness, he whistled the old signal, "Finish," into the twilight air.

I sat in the Café Rebhuhn. I drank four black coffees. I heard the voice of the departing chancellor on the radio. His voice no longer sounded bombastically confident, it trembled and gasped. I noted a few sentences spoken by that heart-wrenching voice:

"Since we do not, at any price, wish to shed the blood of our brothers, even in this earnest hour, we have ordered our army to retreat without resistance in case the Germans march in."

And then, after taking a long breath, "And so I take my leave in this hour with German words and a wish from the bottom of my heart: *Gott schütze Österreich!* God protect Austria."

I sat and drank my fifth black coffee. My pulse was racing. But, exhausted and uncomprehending, my head sank down almost to the marble tabletop. The voice on the radio yielded to a hollow silence. This silence was a gasping dread. This

silence was the fate of the man who had spoken. Then came a
solemn funeral march, to fill out the chasm between two eras,
before a new voice began, presumably the voice of the twins.
This music, by Haydn, blended with Haydn's old imperial anthem. Not only did the patrons of the coffeehouse vanish one
by one, but so did the waiters, except for the hoary, gouty
maitre d', who nodded at me knowingly.

I found St. Stephen's Square bizarrely dead. All the people
probably had their ears glued to radios. The evening was rather
cold, the sky cloudless. The arc lamps seemed dimmer than
normal. The black monster of the cathedral cowered as if trying to make itself less vulnerable to attack. The spire tapered
off into invisibility. A few stars glittered over the spire. When
does one see stars above the misty glare of a city? I dreamed
that Saturn was in the ascendant, with Libra in conjunction.
Pisces had set. Those were empty words, sheer nonsense, for I
understood none of it. But I firmly believed that we human
beings do not weave our fate; our life is too intricate, a rope
consisting of billions of threads. Why should the stars, celestial
Loreleis, not plait this braid? Who observes all these tiny laws,
these crazy series? Recently I had encountered an amazingly
high number of redheads within half an hour; and whenever a
hunchback crosses my path, I am certain that he will not be
the only one. All these tiny phenomena probably have their
astral significance, a positive one and a destructive one. The
choking effort, the impotent aspiration to untangle the thousand threads of chance, is called superstition by blockheads. I
will untangle nothing. Why, I did not even fully grasp what
had happened. However, as if awakening from a narcotic, I
slowly felt a tide of fortune descending upon the city of Vienna. I felt this tide throwing me aside and sweeping others to
the surface.

The tableau already began to change at the corner of Der
Graben. Many clusters of people were standing there, shouting, flailing their arms. Suddenly cars whizzed by at disastrous

speeds. Men loomed from the cars, hollering incomprehensible words into the empty air.

It was like a signal. The groups dissolved. People dashed toward one another, yelling like madmen. Friends embraced, breathless. Women sobbed jubilantly. Amid the roaring flood of voices, one could hear such cries: "I always said so, he won't abandon us. . . . No, he's not abandoning us. . . . Did you know he's taking the government over personally? . . . Goodness, he himself . . . Congratulations, Toni! . . . Now you'll make it. . . . Everyone, I tell you, everyone, no one'll stay in the dirt. . . . The plebiscite, and you guys believed he'd tolerate that swindle. . . . You just don't know him. . . . He won't put up with crap."

He? Who was that terrible He who drove people crazy? I leaned slackly against a building wall. Next to me, several others were leaning; they gaped like dying fish at the small crowd, which kept growing by the second. I was terrified by them— my own mirror images. All at once, the mob was completed, the operatic chorus of a great premiere of history. And now it broke out, the bawling that consisted of only two notes: "Sieg-Heil! Sieg-Heil! Sieg-Heil!" Like the braying of an automatic, mountain-sized donkey! Like a paleolithic war whoop, mechanized in the industrial age.

The human flood swept us, whether enthusiastic or hostile, into Kärntnerstrasse. But the victorious party did not seem to overestimate the number of its supporters. Long rows of buses and trucks came rattling up, spewing hundreds of white-stockings into the throng. Many were already wearing swastika armbands. They were young boys, mostly teenagers, transported from nearby small towns like Mödling, Baden, Bruck, Eisenstadt, Fischamend, Sanktpölten, and thrown into the conquered metropolis. "There are the corset bones," I heard someone say—a Prussian term, completely foreign to Viennese ears. This neo-German language haze now settled down, strangling the graceful dialect of our homeland. The victors pushed the throng senselessly, chaotically in all directions. This was known as "public order." Several swung rifles, clubs, steel rods. Their smooth or downy boyish faces burned with a somnambular intoxication, caused by a more vehement wine than the dear wine of our homeland.

No revenge is headier than that wreaked on the old values by a repressed sense of inferiority. Not only had the party of youth broken the resistance of the oldsters, but the small town had conquered the big city. The mob without history had conquered the spirit of history; sports had conquered science; the illiterate soul of this morning had conquered the arrogance of a culture acquired in the course of centuries; the jungle horde drive had conquered the scrupulous conscience of the free personality.

The odd thing was, however, that not only adolescents and hysterical women writhed in the bloody cloud of mass intoxication. I saw men like myself, elderly and old, by no means belonging to the victors, yet emitting dervishlike sounds and flailing their arms like clipped wings. Yet the most incomprehensible thing of all was I myself. In front of that travel agency, the throng, surging to and fro, was overwhelmed by a religious hush. Someone was giving a speech in long, sultry sounds, like a possessed shaman. Women suddenly fell to their knees, stretching their arms to the heavens and worshiping the dragon. Next to me, an old crone, who probably did not even know what was going on, broke into quaking sobs.

Then it happened. I was seized unawares, beyond all reason, by the depth of planetary life. I was swept away. I cannot understand it, nor can I conceal it. For several seconds, I *identified* with my *mortal enemy*. I became my mortal enemy. I understood everything, I was a drunken white-stocking. The enthusiasm that was bound to shatter my life flared up in my breast too.

The plunge from those seconds of communion with my mortal enemy was like a brain concussion. I was choked by nausea. If I, an absolute opponent, who was utterly "immune," had been forced to undergo that unspeakable experience, what could I expect of all the others who, after all, stood in the middle, between me and the mortal enemy? At that instant, my exile began. All around me was an alien land, more icy than Greenland. The familiar streets, squares, buildings died for me. From now on, every step I took was a forbidden step in the middle of a prohibited Mecca.

I began to run. The medals on my chest clattered. Damn uniform. Breathless, I reached Schwarzenbergplatz. The bus to Eisenstadt was not running. Like all the others, it had been chartered to drive the victorious populace to the city. I hurried along Prinz-Eugen-Strasse to the southern railroad terminal. All trains to Burgenland were out of service. Snotnoses with swastika armbands were demanding ID cards from travelers. I saw them arresting a man in a bulky fur coat. I walked over to the taxi stand. No cabdriver was willing to travel that far on this night.

At the railroad station, I drank two cognacs, a kirsch, and an allasch. I was almost the only patron. I dozed off.

The waiters allowed me to sleep until closing time, one A.M. I staggered to my feet. Home to Pramer. Of course! But it was not such a matter of course. Pramer's apartment was no longer located in my old Vienna; it was now in the middle of the new, foreign, lurking, prohibited Mecca. I knew that Pramer would be up, that he would be waiting for me, very embarrassed. And what about Otto and Harry? They too would be at home. Harry presumably "between two meetings." The speeches of the new rulers would certainly be shooting from the radio, and also that Horst Wessel song, in which the march step of ogres enters into an amazing union with the sentimentality of suicidal chambermaids. I played with the house key in my pocket.

The stars of this night were still in the cold sky. A sharp wind was blowing. Groups of white-stockings marched through the streets, no longer in a disbanded order as just a few hours earlier, but in rank and file. One could sense an alien drill. The boots banged insultingly on the asphalt. Were Austrian youths

tramping like that? The pride of our regiments was once that
light, springy step, swinging even in a parade; but not that
deadly, stiff-kneed hammering without music.

Just before reaching Pramer's building, I about-faced. I was
afraid of the strangers in whose home I was living. I felt drawn
to Ballhausplatz, I do not know why. As if a final resistance
were still awake there, a stifled fire, glimmering, hot enough
to warm my numb hands. All the lofty windows of the chancellery were lit. The new government—or that which considered itself such—was working through the night. Wraiths of
transition were humbly hanging on the telephone earpieces in
order to receive orders from the dragon's lair. The dragon's
seed was sprouting all around, to the horror of many weaklings who had flirted with the powers that be. I imagined the
piglet-pink faces of the trenchcoat twins, belaboring Metternich's Empire furniture with their whips. Icy-gray privy councilors were smiling in appreciation. What could they do? Their
pensions were at stake. Outside the portal, the sentry of the
guard battalion had been withdrawn. A detachment of policemen was loitering there, likewise adorned with the desecrated
cross. Cars came zooming up, slamming on their brakes, making their axles groan. This was the new life-style of "dynamism." Hurried men with briefcases kept getting out of the
cars. Their faces expressed their profound astonishment at the
roles in which they had been cast by the events of this night.
These hurried men dashed through the gates. No porter asked
them what they wished or held them up.

I too was allowed to enter unobstructed. I stared up the
magnificent grand stairway as if the deus ex machina would
finally have to appear at the top and revoke everything. The
wide purple runner glowed so warmly. The deus ex machina
did not appear. However, what came next was not unworthy
of an Aeschylus. At first, a company of fairly slumlike figures
in filthy boots recklessly tramped down the hallowed carpet of
the quiet diplomatic steps. The boys were wearing some kind
of provisional semimilitary party uniforms. "SS," everyone

murmured respectfully all around, an abbreviation that was supposed to designate a very specific part of the horde, for "Aryan" meant "barbarian."

The very first hour was already teeming with such abbreviations. The dragon men had borrowed this practice from an ancient mysticism of letters, developed by the Jewish Cabbala. The compulsion to imitate the enemy, consciously or unconsciously, is one of the infernal urges of human life.

The raucous, laughing horde hopping down the staircase consisted of six or seven adolescents. But they were only a vanguard, which kept looking back, yelling orders and scornful jokes. After a while, a tiny row of beadles showed up at the top landing and began descending in a macabre single file.

The employees in high Austrian agencies always wear an abraded black—grieving widowers of a grand idea that lay on its deathbed for decades. They do not wear livery as in other countries, much less heavy gold chains as in France. Moreover, no matter what their age, they always seem to be ill-humored septuagenarians. In this hour of a true Walpurgis Night, the beadles, who climbed down the stairs at an oppressively slow speed, were a dreadfully tragic sight to behold. For each one of these old men carried a burden that was far beyond his strength: heavy white plaster busts, which they pressed to their shabby black chests with their trembling arms. As they lurched along, commanded by the hollering horde, lugging their burdens toward the interior courtyard, I recognized the individual plaster heads that had been stolen from the consoles of the ceremonial rooms. I and all the other spectators in the entrance watched the agitating cortege, which lacked only the accompaniment of a muffled roll of drums. Upon reaching the courtyard, the old men in black had to line up.

The leader of the horde was wearing a saber. Drawing his weapon, he strode over to the row of men and snarled: "Attention! Stand at attention! Eyes left! In the name of the German people, I hereby pronounce the death sentence on Franz Joseph of Hapsburg! Attention!"

He lowered the saber. With a tortured gesture, the beadle at the left end of the file tilted his head and dropped the bust on the pavement. It shattered with a loud crunch. In this manner, the old Kaiser, who was present in triplicate, was executed three times. Next, his fate was shared by his successor, who had once exalted me; then, the previous chancellor, who had been cravenly assassinated by the white-stockings; and finally, the unfortunate last chancellor. After each and every one of these executions, the horde burst into a triumphant howl and the two brief sawing sounds of their "Sieg-Heil!" The gapers joined the hollering each time. It could not hurt.

$\mathcal{I}$ stepped out into the nocturnal square. I was weeping. I wept not for those executions but for myself, my foolishness, my negligence, the loss of irreplaceable time to save Cella and Gretl and myself. I dashed through narrow side streets. I heard my medals clattering.

Chapter 7

Dances of Death

I knew it.

Pramer was standing outside his apartment door, waiting for me. His anxious, gigantic body was, incomprehensibly, wrapped in a brown raincoat, and a far too tiny hunter's cap was perched atop his pallid face. My suitcase was leaning against the half-open door. He had probably packed it himself.

"Bodenheim," he clucked, as I came up the last few steps. "For hours now . . . What do you say to this whole business?"

I said nothing. But he timidly nodded toward the illuminated crack of the door and whispered, "Otto. Would you have imagined that Otto is in the eighty-ninth standard? Otto will be the death of me."

"I don't know what that is, the eighty-ninth standard."

"Be glad you don't. Otto is a big cheese there, a Storm-troop leader."

When I heard that title, that snotty rank used by boys playing soldiers, I thought of Otto, that colossus with his dismal jowls, and I burst out laughing. Pramer was terrified, he held up his hand defensively. "Quiet, for God's sake. Otto is working with his friends."

"What about Harry?" I asked, still laughing.

"Harry is being delegated to the Labor Front. He secured his position a year ago."

"What about you, Pramer?"

"Goodness gracious, now I'm dependent on the boys. My golden twilight years; I was so greatly looking forward to my retirement, Lord only knows. The boys can destroy me. You know, people used to think I was a Red, which is completely untrue, of course, completely—why, it's totally contrary to my temperament, I was just simply a wee bit idealistic, you know how I am. But if anyone feels like it, if they sniff around a little, if they really want to take me to a concentration camp. Please don't think me a scoundrel, Bodenheim. Will you forgive my conduct?"

"What conduct should I forgive?"

"You see, it's absolutely not my fault. A guest is sacred to me, especially you, since we're old friends and went to school together, almost like brothers, all the things we did . . . So many years, the world was so wonderful back then. . . . But Otto feels that it is simply impossible for . . . Now that . . . You as . . . He cannot afford to let you remain here, he says. . . . Bodenheim, I feel horrible."

We had been standing in the darkness for a long time, because the staircase light had gone out. Only the crack of illumination from the apartment vestibule showed me that the sweat was pouring down Pramer's face.

I was astonished at how cold this crass treatment left me. My mood was almost good.

"Don't carry on, Pramer," I laughed, "I already wanted to take French leave several times today. You've facilitated the matter and made my decision for me. Farewell. Have a good life, under these circumstances."

He shut the door behind him very softly. Profound darkness. His voice whispered sharply, "What do you think I am? I won't leave you alone. I'll take you to the hotel, of course."

I groped for my suitcase. But Pramer had already seized it and would not let go.

"This is my concern, Bodenheim. Why, just imagine . . . At least, do me the honor of allowing me to carry your valise."

After we had walked a bit through the fresh night air, I said: "Okay, Pramer, now help me find a cab that will take me to Eisenstadt."

Startled, he placed the suitcase on the ground. "But you can't. . . . I totally forgot to tell you. . . . Your wife called me. . . . Around eleven. . . . She's been warned. . . . You are not to come home for the time being."

"Who warned Gretl?"

"I don't know for sure. But according to her hints it was—"

"Zsoltan Nagy?"

"No, Myslivec, definitely Myslivec. Myslivec is going to be a big cheese, by the way."

"No doubt, since he is a true-blue German and all."

"Don't take it so hard, old friend," said Pramer, dragging the suitcase behind me. "One shouldn't take anything hard. At our age, one must start coming to terms. What else can happen to us? Here today, gone tomorrow. One night you jerk off, the next day you go on pension. That's a law of nature, I'm not responsible. It'll pass quickly. Main thing that the boys— well, that's none of your concern. Believe me, their bark is worse than their bite, and they may be barking up the wrong tree. The city's big, nobody knows you, you can stay in the hotel for a couple of days, relax, and once the first storm has died down, you can go home to your dear missus, I kiss her hand, and your darling little girl, she's so talented. . . ."

He talked a blue streak. Remaining silent, I let him carry the valise, which he put down from time to time in order to rest. We had left his place way past three A.M. We made very slow headway. Troops of yowling white-stockings were still marching through the city. Pramer made long detours to avoid the gatherings, so that we did not reach the Hotel Union until much later and only very circuitously.

"Naturally, I'll keep an eye out for you," Pramer promised upon leaving, as if no gulf had opened between us; and he added, "But you know, it's better if you don't ring me up. Those bastards are listening in on all phone calls."

The night clerk took me to one of those melancholy rooms that I was already acquainted with. This time, no dog roses bloomed on the torn wallpaper in the glow of the weak bulbs; instead, violet grapes spread out, surrounding me with a monotonous grape harvest. I paced to and fro endlessly between the cliffs of sharp-edged furniture in this hole. Then I opened the window in order to let out the spirits of my predecessors, the smell of mouthwash, dirty laundry, burned hair, and stale sleep. In the blackness of the night, the sky already held an inkling of the fragrant dawn. I took the necessary things from my valise. My slippers were wrapped in old newspapers. I smoothed out these pages. I read: *"Bis hierher und nicht weiter!* This far and no farther! Our freedom is beyond question!"

I kept gazing endlessly at the letters of these banner headlines. And they were not just a few short days old; they were decades old, and older than the battle reports, long ago and far away, of the world war; they were older than anything I had ever read in a newspaper. This far and no farther? Farther and farther, incalculably farther! And nothing will bring back the day on which those words were spoken, words that had filled me with such deep faith that I had left Cella and Gretl alone. No experience of the past twenty-four hours could hold a candle to my painful horror inspired by last week's newspaper. Our high-spirited yesterday gaped at me with the glassy eyes of a corpse; and I had lost, frivolously, without thinking of my near and dear.

I lay down in a hard, clammy bed. I sank into a deluge of sleep.

𝒢 was not excessively surprised that slender and lacy railroad bridges and viaducts curved through the lofty space of the baroque ballroom. The trains kept thundering back and forth incessantly—not so much trains, but torpedo-shaped electric railcars. I was not even surprised that Cella, at the grand piano, was outthundering the thunder of the cars with the tremendous basses of the Bach passacaglia. I felt proud to the very roots of my hair, but I had never doubted that it would be "child's play" for her to carry the day at this academy, which would now take place despite everything. Wielding a small baton, Styxi stood in the midst of the indescribably select audience, conducting it. But somewhere, high above, I noticed Nagy. He wore a uniform, a stationmaster's uniform with a red flatcap, and he was waving red-white-and-red flags with both hands and signaling to the wild trains, which, despite their tremendous power, seemed like toys. But his signals were suspicious, for the more he waved his little flags, the louder the thunder boomed. I realized that Zsoltan Nagy had been not only my enemy from the very beginning, but also my child's enemy. He wanted to destroy Cella's career with his insidious signals. I tried to figure out the fastest way of climbing up to the gallery of the ballroom in order to pounce on Nagy. But then I was seized in an iron grip by the leather hands of Weil, who was among the guests. "Don't do anything foolish." He had to shout into my ear because of the din. "We mustn't do anything. We are to vanish from the surface of the earth." At that instant, Cella could no longer be heard; only the thunder existed, which, instead of starting and stopping, lay upon me like an immense mattress woven out of steel bass notes.

I leaped from my bed right into the thunder, which did not yield.

The German bomber squadrons were passing unremittingly across the tiny fragment of sky revealed by the hotel window. The dragon had sent out his aluminum vultures even though we had been beaten without a fight, and no weapon had been raised against him in our strangled country. They did not have to drop any bombs. The city was crushed by the very roar of the propellers in the indignant sea of air.

I lay down again. I began to think very hard. It was obvious that we had to leave this country, Cella, Gretl, and I. Even if

Gretl was not one of us, the accursed, Cella was nevertheless my child and therefore equally cursed. In Cella I had been entrusted with the most divine thing in the world, a blessing. I could not let her perish here. But what could I do to get across the border quickly and safely? In my unforgivable recklessness, I had given no thought to the future; instead, I had seriously compromised myself with the petition and my activities during the past few days. I would have to stay hidden for a while until the conquerors got over their anger. Like Pramer, I was ridiculous enough to believe that everything would calm down in a few days, allowing me to return to my family; we would then be able to settle our household affairs with all due deliberation and move to another country. But where? And with what, since nobody was allowed to take money abroad? And who would help us? I reviewed the names of all my friends and acquaintances.

There was only one person who could really help. He was a star in his field. His name was known around the globe. And he loved Cella and thought the world of her: Scherber! Nobody was as independent as Scherber or could do as much, not even the old Prince Esterhazy. If the white-stockings were afraid of anyone, it was the international celebrities, who could harm them abroad. And Scherber was certain to have made all his preparations.

I sent for the hotel clerk. His name was Rosenbaum, he was slightly stunted, and he was crazy about music. I had known him for more than twenty years. He gazed at me with his dark eyes, which seemed lubricated with shrewd melancholy. "You're lucky, Herr Doctor," he sighed, "those guys were here right before you came, and they put all the guests through the wringer."

"Police?" I asked.

"Police? The police would be fine. A lot worse."

"Listen, Rosenbaum. I want to telephone my wife. Could you please put me through to Eisenstadt?"

"Impossible. The operators are only allowing local calls. They're expecting "*him*" today."

That "him" contained an unreproducible expression of scorn, horror, and fear. I asked Rosenbaum to telephone Professor Scherber and find out when I could visit him. After a while, he came back, saying that Professor Scherber was not picking up. I thought out loud: "Why is my name Bodenheim, Ground-Home? It's like a mockery. For those are the two things I no longer have: the ground under my feet and a home."

"What can you do," said the clerk. "My name is Rosenbaum, Rose Tree, and I haven't noticed too many roses in my life."

The mattress of steel-woven thunder lay upon me day and night, countless hours. The booming lulled me to sleep—that lullaby of the apocalyptic dragon. From time to time, Rosenbaum came and told me about things that were happening to our people: looting, arson, murder. He ordered me not to leave my room. But on the third day, I could endure it no longer and I got dressed. I attached the small chain of war decorations to the lapel of my topcoat, as a jest. When I stole past the hotel desk, I saw that Rosenbaum had been replaced by an adolescent who, instead of the badge of his profession, two crossed keys, was flaunting an ostentatious swastika.

And once again I hurried through an utterly transformed city. The revolution, with its abatement of a bloody tax, this rebellion against the most resolute nonresistance, had ended. Only a few plundered shops testified with their smashed windows and suspicious names to the cheap victory of the white-stockings. There were two kinds of people in the streets: a colorless mass, flowing to work, grayer, more depressed, more hopeless than ever; and a number of uniformed figures weaving singly or in small groups into the crowd, apparently in order to keep an eye on the people and terrify them. Those figures—I will not deny that some of them were tall and impressive—instructed me about the form of modern tyranny, which is not so much a domination of an individual, a clique, a class, as a

serried despotism of opportunists culled from all ranks of society. In this age of numbers and masses, nothing has less
power than numbers and masses. It suffices if the select minority of opportunists are convinced down to the innermost
recesses of their hearts that there are only two possibilities for
them: the uninterrupted triumph of their power or the martyr-
dom of vendetta, but they cannot endure being peacefully replaced by a new regime. This awareness of mortal danger turns
an opportunistic minority of the guardians of the nation into
cynical, violent maniacs. There are snake venoms that instantly paralyze the nerve center. I felt something of the sort
when I watched those men, a few of them splendid, striding
through the crowd as if the oft-cited Community of the People
were a bothersome mud.

I suffered from very weird feelings. I hugged the buildings to
avoid drawing notice. Now and then, I entered a dark lobby
in order to muster new nervous energy against the unfathomable hatred that lay upon the streets like the stench of fire. And
yet, despite everything, in my heart of hearts, I did not yet
know what had happened. Something inside me was numbed,
aghast, incredulous, and incapable of swift action.

Mondscheingasse was far away. But despite the great distance, I did not dare take the trolley. Long-familiar things suddenly became the worst possible dangers at every step of the
way. I turned at the corner of Josephstädter Strasse. Actually,
it was not I but my legs that swerved from my route, carrying
me to the building where Grollmüller had lived in constant
"preparedness" in his naked room. The concierge's door was
open. The petty-bourgeois smell of lard, roasted onions, and
unaired beds swept toward me. This smell seemed strangely
triumphant. Maniuk, Grollmüller's gray orderly, sat on a chair
in the middle of the room; he was a broken man, as pale as
death.

I learned that last night at three A.M., a horde of white-
stockings had broken into the room of the Knight of Maria
Theresa in order to arrest him. Grollmüller had reached for

his service revolver. Seriously wounded, he had been brought to the prison hospital around dawn. He lay there now, at death's door. And Maniuk was not allowed to be with him now, Maniuk, the only person whom the lieutenant-colonel had—Maniuk, who once, at the Battle of Ravaruska, had carried Captain Grollmüller, with a bullet in his lungs, from the front lines. So he has fallen in action after all, I thought. Maniuk was crying unabashedly. Between his knees, he held the officer's kitbag with the attached thermos bottle and rolled-up coat. However, an imperious woman stood at the gas range, stirring the pots emphatically. It was the janitor's wife, and she supervised everything, no doubt. She was proud and inflated, the goddess of victory for this day and this city. And she had no sympathy for the crushed orderly. No. Stirring and strutting, she preached a sermon to the orderly, his dying master *in contumaciam,* and me.

Go on, Grollmüller, go on, Iron Soldiers Ring, I no longer think about you, I have given you all up. I have given you up, Austria, and you, the last three months and the forty-nine years of my life before that. Gone and never was! I felt as if the curative powers of my mind were pouring together to close the wound and undo its infliction. My suffering was over. To my great surprise, I was filled with a beneficent indifference to all past events. Had those mental healing powers that I now felt operating been granted only to our people, forever expelled and forever gaining a new foothold? Were we given those powers so that our souls would not be overwhelmed by sorrow for any earthly homeland, so that we would not be diverted from the unfathomable mission of the wandering Jew, wandering across this planet, which is itself a wanderer?

I no longer walked, I wandered through the old streets of this newborn foreign land. I still recognized all of them, the familiar friends and neighbors of my life since childhood. I had always greeted them again and again with the joy of secret co-ownership, and they had returned my greetings, almost imperceptibly, but with faith and benevolence. Ah, there you are,

you huge city hall, you steel-gray playfulness with your Gothic
tracery, pointed-arch windows, and filigree towers. When I
was a student, your clock made me hurry every morning. And
across the street, there you are, Burgtheater, the theater of the
royal court, you belonged to me, too, in my young days, when
I climbed the steps of the fourth gallery, with a sweetly pounding heart, and then peered down with awesome vertigo into a
shaft of golden rapture, from which the verse-scanning voices
of priests soared up to me personally. Now I did not greet
those familiar neighbors. Nor did the frozen faces of the buildings seem to recognize me; they gazed past me, the way Myslivec would now look past me if we ran into one another. It
was no mirage: the old imperial architecture, as cowardly and
opportunistic as the people who administrated it, had changed
its conviction.

At this time, I was filled with a great, roaring optimism—I
do not know why, or how. All my optimism focused on the
name Scherber. Remember that during the past few days,
Scherber had always been at the center of my thoughts, which
had been torn back and forth: he was the only person who
could save us, especially Cella, from destruction. But now it
was no longer a possibility that I was eying, it was complete
certainty. In my youth, I had, alas, been a hopeless dreamer,
nursing all sorts of pleasant illusions. But later, I went to a
great deal of trouble to mold myself into something of a real-
ist—or at least, so I hope. But now the former dreamer inside
me was breaking out again with twofold strength. Eagerly
dashing along, looking neither right nor left, I saw Scherber
before me incarnate in a vision. The small professor stood amid
mountains of baggage. His unkempt gray hair was surmounted
by a top hat, its dusty felt exposed by a ruthless sunbeam. He
wore his greasy velvet jacket as usual, and his feet, contrasting
harshly with his top hat, were thrust into thick, wool-lined
slippers, the kind used by palsied old men. The worn-out pince-
nez was not perched on his nose, it dangled from a black string
on his chest, for Scherber kept leaping to and fro impatiently,

touching his baggage. I saw all this in my thoughts. I also saw the line of his students thronging at a respectful distance—a hazy wall in which no face was recognizable. But all at once, Scherber put on his pince-nez and thrust his forefinger toward the crowd of students. "Cella Bodenheim," he cried in the irritated tone of a schoolmaster, "Cella is coming with me, no two ways about it. You're coming with me."

I was just passing the small post office on Nibelungengasse. Entering it, I sent Gretl a wire: "You and Cella come immediately to Scherber." As a cautionary measure, I did not sign it, and I gave the clerk a false name. My hopes became daring. I was an attorney. Scherber would be able to use me. Did he not have contracts to annul and to sign? Did not a scatter-brained expert like him need a hardworking quartermaster, correspondence clerk, and secretary? An international celebrity like him? And in a new country and a new life? My English was imperfect, of course, but I felt I could at least write a tolerable letter. In this way, I would not only work off the fees for Cella's lessons, but also make all sorts of connections and, with God's help, perhaps build up a new career in America. Men less musical than I had found niches for themselves in the world of music and concerts. I wanted to work, day and night, to earn however little the three of us needed to live. My day-dreams did not strike me as illusions. I had committed no crime. My activities as a war veteran for the Kaiser could not be grounds for preventing my emigration. I felt confident, even adventurous as I turned into Mondscheingasse.

I looked up. I halted in my tracks. Not only my feet but my entire body came to a standstill. There, some two hundred feet in front of me, I sighted a mute gathering. This was no political assembly about to burst into a Sieg-Heil. At such moments, one can sense, one can sniff the purpose and dangers of a mob. Some misfortune had occurred, a simple, unpolitical, ordinary, human misfortune.

Cold flashes cut through me. For an instant, I closed my eyes. And in that instant, one of the very few childhood mem-

ories that I cannot forget welled up in me. It was a terrible
memory. My good mother was holding my hand, for I could
not have been more than four years old. Every Friday, she
would spend a few hours in the city, shopping for certain things
that could not be purchased as cheaply in the countryside. It
was spring, and we were walking down Schönbrunner Strasse,
a long street, to one of the stores she had come for. I can still
remember the house with the mute throng in front of it, just
like the one outside Scherber's house now. My good mother's
hand convulsively squeezed mine. She yanked me off the sidewalk and onto the roadway. We made a wide detour around
the gathering.

"What's going on there, Mama?" I asked.

She whispered to me in a horrified voice, "Don't look, Hans!"

But I did look back, gazing and gazing with greedy horror
to discover the forbidden thing. I recall the shrill female voice
and the words spoken right in back of us: "The privy councilor's maid . . . Well, his wife . . ." And through a gap in the
crowd, I saw something, perhaps a female body, lying face
down. I saw disheveled hair. And a pool of blood spreading
out from the hair, and all the people wordlessly staring down
at the blood. My mother ran her hand, in the brown kid glove
(oh, the lost smell of my mother's gloves, which were cleaned
so often with benzine!)—my mother ran her hand over my
eyes, covering them with kindly darkness. For a child should
not be exposed to the sight of terrible death.

Now, no one kept my eyes shut. I saw something lying on
the sidewalk. I saw glowing splashes of blood far out into the
roadway. The lying thing was covered with coarse sackcloth,
so that the human shape underneath was barely outlined.
Scherber—I knew it right away, I did not have the slightest
doubt. He had jumped out the window like the unforgotten
maid in my childhood.

In order to keep the area clear, two policemen stood in front
of the small heap of death under the sackcloth. With weighty
indifference, they gazed across the heads of the spectators and

into the distance. During those days, Vienna's renowned guardians of the law all had the same look of sarcastic apathy in their eyes. Between the two policemen, a little old lady kept moving back and forth, chattering a blue streak. On the one hand, she was vividly reporting the tragic event and its background to the two representatives of the authorities; on the other hand, she was giving an impressive performance to the gathered audience, not unaware that she was shining with her thespian gifts. Scherber's concierge differed from Grollmüller's in every way but one: both had the inflated feeling of exaltation that imbues a powerless caste when it is suddenly elevated to public power. Everyone lived in a building. Every building in Vienna had a concierge. Every concierge—a few had already assumed the title of "block warden"—decided on the political reputation of every tenant in the building, for it was the concierge and no one else whom the victorious Party consulted for information about the favorable attitudes of big and little people. This hard-boiled concierge kept running at the mouth, nor was she put off by the corpse at her feet. She was in the midst of her delivery when I came over.

" 'You know, Frau Kulka,' he says to me yesterday, 'I think I'll have to kill myself.' So I says to him, I says, 'Why do you have to kill yourself, Herr Professor, an old man like you, you can wait it out.' So he says, 'I have to kill myself because the city's too noisy for me now, and my ears are so sensitive to false notes.' 'Goodness gracious,' says I, 'what about your students, Herr Professor, you listen to them until nine at night with your sensitive ears, and what a racket they make—that's why the government councilor on the fourth floor, a very fine gentleman, moved out.' So he says, 'Maybe you're right, Frau Kulka, then I'll just have to kill myself because I'm a Jew.' So I say, 'Gracious me, that *is* awful if someone's a Jew, and a scandal. The Jews came just a few years ago with nothing but dirty shirts on their backs and they got rich off of our property, which belongs to *us* and not *them,* that's pretty obvious, with department stores and everything.' So he says, 'Frau Kulka, you noticed that when I moved into the building I had nothing but a dirty shirt on my back.' So I says to him, 'Herr Professor, you're different, you're a gentleman, everyone in the building says so, but the men on the radio, they must know the truth. And you know what, Herr Professor, just rely on our führer. He cares about people, just like the old Kaiser.' So he says, 'Good night, Frau Kulka, pleasant dreams,' and he gives me a tip, just like at New Year's. And this morning, three men from the Party went up to the fifth floor to wish Fräulein Macak happy birthday, and he thought they were coming to arrest him, and so . . ."

At the climax of her dramatic scene, the old woman was interrupted. An ambulance came howling up. When it screeched to a halt, the silence was sepulchral. People stood with gaping eyes that had suddenly filled with the indescribable horror of their own lives. With casual movements, as if we were irksome flies, the policemen ordered us to step back. A physician in a white smock barely raised the sackcloth at the head of the small heap of death and instantly dropped it again. I saw nothing. It all took place virtually by rote. The attendants had already whisked the shrouded corpse upon a stretcher and shoved it into the ambulance. The engine was already switched on. The ambulance was already driving away. Someone had already brought a tub of sand and begun strewing the sand with a crunching shovel. The bloody traces were already disappearing under the yellow sand. In these days, good old Vienna had acquired a remarkable routine in clearing away the bodies of suicides. On the faces of the gapers, the indescribable horror at human life melted, giving way to the commonplace apathy that makes life bearable in the first place. The onlookers began to scatter.

I pressed my hand against my stomach. I felt very sick. And yet I had seen countless mangled corpses in the war. And yet just a few short days ago, I had been prepared for new bloody fighting. All at once, someone stood in front of me, staring at me with a waxen face. I recognized Scherber's friend Lateiner, the critic. His wreath of white hair bristled in the wind. Why does this man never wear a hat, I wondered and, oddly enough, not without anger. Lateiner's head was too heavy for his slack neck. It was almost resting on his left shoulder. "That fool," he hissed, "that fool . . . If *I* had done it or *you* . . . But he already had his affidavit for America in his pocket. And he would have obtained one for me too, an affidavit."

It was the first time that my as yet untutored ears had heard this magic word, this magic thing craved by so many hundreds of people. And while the streets filled with the Sieg-Heil yells of the victors, people in darkened rooms and corridors were conspiratorially whispering: "Affidavit . . . Affidavit . . ."

"Forget Scherber," I wired Gretl. "Wait." Actually, I could not hit on anything better to wire. After Scherber's death, all roads seemed blocked. What friends were left to advise us, help us? I bought an afternoon newspaper. It swept against me like the stench of sulfur. The very first page featured a foul attack on the princely House of Esterhazy, and the second page an even fouler attack on the firm of S. Weil & Sons and its owners. Apparently, Prince Styxi and Jacques Emanuel needed help even more urgently than I. All at once, the face of the new desk clerk at the Hotel Union flashed through my mind. Would I even be able, I wondered, to return to my room with the violet wine grapes? Might the triumphant young man not report me and hand me over to the Party thugs, who were rooting and grubbing through the city, looking for people more innocent than I? What should I do? Where could I hide and spend the night? Only one faint hope remained: Nagy! There were probably few situations that Nagy, the lighthearted man, was not capable of mastering—unlike myself! But how was I to locate Zsoltan in this metropolis, in this transformed Mecca of a new faith, where it was ineffably painful for me to cross the threshold of a post office or restaurant? It was only at this point that I was overwhelmed by a decision that, inexcusably,

incomprehensibly, had not yet occurred to me and that now
relieved some of my tension. (I have, incidentally, spoken to
many other refugees, who behaved no differently during those
first few days of mental chaos.) The thought of leaving my
family without saying good-bye, without conferring with them,
was too absurd to be obvious. I counted up my cash. It came
to ninety-three schillings, more than enough to get me across
the border to a neighboring country, assuming that the border
was open for our people and that the old laws were still in
effect. I wondered in which direction I should take the train:
east, south, or west. Western Terminal was closest, for I was
standing by the Goethe Monument in the Imperial Garden.
The West spelled salvation. I dashed across Ringstrasse to the
large taxi stand outside the coffeehouse.

The cabbies were loafing in the afternoon sun. I hailed one
of them. Nobody stirred. They seemed not to notice me. Suddenly, I was flanked by two burly types. They wore leather
jackets and puttees. Such faces had never been seen here before
in broad daylight: flattened noses, pockmarks, protuberances
on their foreheads, and red paws dangling from their sleeves.
They looked like assassins, informers for the criminal investigation department.

"Are you one, too? Yes or no?" I was asked by the leather-
jacket on the left.

"One what?" I replied, amazed at my own calm.

"You don't even have to ask," the right leather-jacket
instructed the left one, pointing to the chain of my decorations.
"If he wasn't one of them, he wouldn't be wearing his little
ribbon as an alibi."

"Take a good look at the ribbon," I said, "and let me go."

The paws grabbed me right and left and shoved me forward.
The leather-jacket on the left guffawed.

"There's no more unemployment. Now we're gonna be
working. My good sir—"

"What do you want? Where are you taking me?"

"Not far, my good sir. Better not make a fuss. Do you have any valuables on you?"

"Only this little ribbon," I said, reaching for the chain.

"That's worthless today," said the left leather-jacket, reaching into my pocket and taking my silver cigarette case.

"Why are you doing that?"

"Why, my good sir?" said the right-hand man, exposing his Party pin. "Why? He was cremated on the eleventh."

Nagy's quip flashed into my mind: a part-time hero! Oh, how easy so-called heroism had been in a world in which friend and foe obeyed the same rules of honor. Try being a hero now, wedged in between two thugs, who are responsible to no one for your life. You have to gather all your mental strength to maintain the little composure without which you cannot live. The leather-jacket on the left handed me a nail brush, a rag, and a piece of sand soap. I did not ask why, but I had to pay ten schillings for these items, and I realized what their purpose was by the time we reached the corner of the imperial stables on Babenbergerstrasse. There on the square, which is left free by the traffic, something was happening that appeared to be lots of fun. The performers of this little farce were about a dozen people, mostly men and three elegantly dressed women. More than half, as I instantly saw, were our people. The rest were notorious Austrian patriots whom the laughing mob around them had caught on the street, just like myself. There was a very fat, short-necked man, with torrents of sweat pouring down his padded cheeks. He looked like a desperate morgue official. Next to him knelt a small, pale man, whom they jeeringly addressed as "Count." A genteel old lady in a widow's veil with a white furbelow was working with her right hand, while her left hand tightly clutched a lorgnette in front of her eyes, a dissonant gesture that filled the spectators with endless glee.

The leather-jackets ordered me to kneel down next to this lady. Our job was to use the nail brush, rag, and sand soap to clean away a large propaganda slogan scrawled in red oil paint on the sidewalk. The inscription said: "Austria forever." On the morning of its last day, the government had inscribed those words here and in several other places in the city. I was ordered to eradicate the "r" in Austria. The delightful humor of the comedy that so profusely entertained the golden hearts of our audience came from the utter unsuitability of our tools. Streams of turpentine might have made a dent in the blood-red oil paint. But as we scrubbed away on the tremendous letters with our little nail brushes and our weak suds, our efforts were ludicrous.

White-stockings, leather-jackets, and suede-jackets formed a circle around us. Some held sticks, with which they prodded the laborers. The ringleader, who may have been eighteen years old, had a large violet birthmark on his right cheek. From time to time, to the joy of the gapers, he kept repeating, "You're not working hard enough. Where'd you ever learn how to work? If you keep on like that, you won't get home till three A.M. I've got time."

At my right, one of our people was kneeling, a young man with an unpleasant clerical face. Whenever the ringleader delivered his comments, the young man began to scrub wildly and eagerly, nodding as if to inform our tormentors passionately of his concurrence and readiness. At first, the sight of this boy made me choke more than anything else did. Otherwise—I cannot phrase it any differently—I was ruled by a tense apathy. As I casually scrubbed back and forth across my red "r," my eyes wandered and I observed sharply. One of our people was an old man whom the white-stockings must have yanked from his prayers in the synagogue, for he was wearing a prayer shawl with black and white stripes; they would not allow him to remove it from his shoulders. He was so old and feeble that he almost stretched out on the ground, his white-bearded head raised very slightly, his hand barely hinting at wiping motions. This collapsed old man was the main source of the comical pleasure. Now and then, the leather-jackets poked him lightly with their sticks and howled, "Don't try none of your gold-bricking, you Elder of Zion."

There was a sputter of laughter. The old man remained silent. And I saw the faces of the spectators. These were not oppressed people with minds unhinged by the intoxication of victory. They were respectable philistines from the neighborhood: grocers, tobacconists, restaurateurs, waiters, salesmen, and harmless passersby. Their faces did not mirror the loathsome reality; they appeared to be watching a harlequinade, standing in front of a showbooth, as if it were all just theater. It may sound exaggerated, but what I saw in the faces of these guilty bystanders was a degenerate innocence.

How difficult it is for me to record that scene, although far more dreadful things are happening every day, indeed every hour. Originally, I wanted to omit that event, for, in my opinion, degradation should be forgotten, not preserved. However, for my sake, I cannot ignore what happened. I will try, as far as possible, to reawaken my feelings sincerely, record them in black and white.

First of all, I sensed that all of us who were kneeling, sitting, crouching, lying, kept growing uglier by the minute, increasingly pitiful, less and less likable. This was no ordinary ugliness, no ordinary process of becoming ugly; it was a mysterious sinking into a state of lowness. Debasement makes you base. That is a law of the soul. The object of persistent cruelty ultimately justifies the cruelty. That is one of the harshest facts of life, but it must be faced. One would have to be the son of God to remain a beautiful human being even when scourged, spit at, and crowned with thorns. Yes, we, the dishonored, we the violated, were base, ugly, despicable, extinguished. I felt dirty to my very marrow. And yet, it would be a terrible lie if I now wrote that I hated my humiliators. Never has my soul been further removed from feelings of hatred, of anger, or vengeance. Does one hate a fire, an earthquake, a typhus epidemic? Nothing was more devoid of personality, hence responsibility, than those adolescents in white stockings, in windbreakers, or leather jackets. Hatred, too, needs points of contact in order to be discharged. I was filled with nothing but the dirty feeling of baseness, from which I had to free myself.

The old lady in the widow's veil and lorgnette collapsed.

"Holy Mother of God," she exclaimed rather loudly.

The eighteen-year-old with the birthmark heard her and crowed, "Your Holy Mother of God is nothing but a Jewish slut."

Now no one laughed. He then added, "Well, it's true, isn't it?"

I got to my feet, held out both hands to the woman, and pulled her up. I felt that by helping this frail person, I was also helping the old man in the prayer shawl.

"Please go home, Madame, so that you won't fall ill. I'll do your job for you."

I spoke loudly and unselfconsciously, not aware of any courage on my part. I must have had a mild fit of abstraction.

"Who's giving orders here; who does the kike think he is?" yelled the boy with the birthmark, and the white-stockings, windbreakers, and leather-jackets were already strutting toward me.

"Get down," growled the ringleader, "get down. You hear me. Are you gonna get down or not?"

I remained standing. I felt infinitely light and no longer base. A splendid indifference was playing in my muscles. I spoke calmly, but loudly enough for the spectators to hear me too. My hand lay on my gold chain.

"You stupid snotnose . . . I was fighting at the front before you were even born."

My words were followed by an ambiguous silence. Then came a whirlwind of sticks, arms, shouts. I waited, indifferent. A heavy hand fell on my shoulder. It was a huge policeman, six feet four inches tall, who suddenly joined in. A friendly face winked at me imperceptibly.

"No sir, no sir," the policeman growled, "we don't tolerate mutiny. Come along."

My persecutors were stopped short. They did not know what to do. One of them shouted, "Fine, go ahead. Arrest him, lock him up, Dachau . . ."

The huge policeman put his arm around my hips and pushed me along. Some of the ragtag and bobtail came along, shouting national slogans from time to time.

At the police station, I had to present my identification card. Next to the official on duty sat a sarcastic dwarf in plain clothes, his jacket sporting a huge swastika that would have been more suitable for a giant. The dwarf glanced at my card, then perused a long list of names. Suddenly, he gulped with delight and ogled me benevolently. "Herr Doctor Bodenheim. How nice of you to honor us with your presence. We have been expecting you, Herr Bodenheim."

Chapter 8

A Prince, A Priest, A Plunderer

I was brought to "Liesl." This friendly, girlish nickname is used by the boarders of the huge police prison on Elisabethpromenade next to the Danube Canal. It is an enormous, fortresslike building which, along with many of its architectural siblings of the 1870s and '80s, was built in that playful iron–gray Gothic style that bears Tinkertoy witness to the false dignity, culture-vulture prosperity, and richly decorated dishonesty of the era of the upper bourgeoisie. At my age, of course, I belonged to those who prefer the lies masked by these tried-and-true paragons of style to the naked truth that followed. For this truth endorses with the coldness of a dog's muzzle the collapse of all that is human. This truth is nothing but a trick of the devil, who loves disguising ethical bankruptcy as a logical profit. Despite its lavish Gothic exterior, Liesl's interior is nothing but a dismal, old-fashioned prison with long, lightless corridors and airless courtyards, all filled with the characteristic stench of such hells, blending the vapors of stale urine, iodoformed spittoons, dusty files, sourish legumes, fermenting masses of sodden bread, and the aroma of human misery in every size, shape, and form. Of course, during the days whose quivering curve I tried to follow here, Liesl, like her sister on Rossauer Lände (not to mention the "Gray House" on Alserstrasse), was a rather welcome domicile, which, under the aegis of the lawful police, offered many victims of persecution an escape from torture and murder. I, too, was saved by the kindhearted policeman, who transferred me to prison from the hands of the white-stockings and windbreakers. Despite everything, however, it *was* an illegal detention. Austrian law, which I, as an attorney, know inside and out, has no article allowing "protective custody" (to supply a name for the matter) such as was now inflicted on me. If a person is arrested anywhere in the world, he has the unconditional right to know the grounds for his arrest and to be taken before a judge within twenty-four hours. When I, still a callow beginner in the world of rightlessness, called attention to these benefits of the law, the gray-haired officer who was processing me responded with a soft, inscrutable smile. "Herr Doctor," he said, unusually polite, "you will have no cause for complaint. I am housing you decently, in the Burgenland cell, with several gentlemen. . . . Unfortunately, we are sold out three times over."

I really was placed in a "Burgenland cell," where I found two acquaintances.

Entering a prison cell as a prisoner is one of those few solemn and terrible moments of life, akin, say, to the first day of school, a serious operation, or the baptism of fire in war. Retrospectively, one is not ungrateful to life for the dubious pleasure of such moments, since they spell a proud wealth of spiritual experience, which raises them far beyond the more pleasant wastelands of normal living. During the year of my forensic practice, I had seen several cells like the one in whose dishwater penumbra I was now standing. Six paces long, four paces wide—in peaceful times, it was probably meant for three inmates. Indeed, three beds were strapped to the wall, two on the long side, one on the short side under the small barred window. But it was very difficult moving in the narrow space, because there were two flabby straw mattresses on the ground, meant for the extra tenants. There were five of us. So one can imagine that I, as a newcomer, was not exactly welcomed with joy. Nevertheless, this cell was considered one of the finest apartments in the building, for in other rooms, the occupants were penned in by the dozens. To my astonishment, however, I instantly noticed that, in contrast to more modern rooming houses, this one still had the infamous bucket for calls of nature, that is, for friendly common use by at least five people.

The guard's key grated behind me, just as in hundreds of suspense novels I had read as a young man. This guard—incidentally, like the rest of the personnel—acted friendly and obliging toward the innocents in protective custody; they virtually shrugged at the cruel way of the world, which they had to serve even if they did not agree with it. Not a single one of the prison officers neglected to address me as "Herr Doctor." Here, the truth was revealed. The white-stockings pumped into the capital may have taken over the streets, but Austria's resistance was far from broken inside the houses, offices, and institutions.

The first man I recognized in the cell was my Burgenland neighbor, Franz Stich. Herr Stich, a native of Bohemia, sixty years old, with bushy eyebrows and a gray moustache, had once been a foreman or overseer in a textile factory; during the Social-Democratic era, he had held the office of town councilor. I knew him very casually. We had last met at the beginning of February in the Castle Park, strolling for a brief half hour and conversing anxiously. I liked Herr Stich; he was very down to earth. He was the epitome of those devout Social Democrats for whom the world had collapsed several years ago—the world whose future they had figured out in a very rudimentary way. Childishly worshiping a scientific approach made up of worn illusions, they believed that nothing could halt the ascent of laboring humanity to a reasonable system. They poignantly called themselves materialists because, with their innocent German efficiency, they believed that the tricky material (rays, currents, waves) of which this life is brewed can be sorted and regulated. But they were materialists only to the extent that, with the social envy of all little people, they wanted to strike a blow at the dreaming spirit owned by independent sons of the middle class. In a reality of unpredictable shifts and dodges, these people were convinced by their unerring sense of hard facts and proved to be the visionaries of a linear, fairy tale–like progression from chaos and evil to usefulness and goodness. They had good hearts. They were the last people whose life goals were not just power over others, but also happiness for the greater number. At least, that was what they claimed. And people have a certain share of what they claim. (Harry Pramer, in contrast, had spoken of a "grand political dream" as the goal of his life.) Herr Franz Stich was one of those visionaries. And his eyes gazed at me with a hurting sadness. "Last time," he said, "we breathed better air, Herr Doctor."

"Herr Stich, the outside air is no better now," I replied, merely in order to say something.

At this point, an overlifesize figure rose from the straw sack at the window wall and trudged toward me, reeling slightly. He was my second acquaintance here. To my amazement, I saw Prince Ernst.

"You?" I cried, seizing his soft, flabby hand. "How did you get here, Prince?"

As was his habit, he focused his eyes unswervingly on my left ear and murmured absentmindedly, "How did I . . . How . . . Oh, but that's completely uninteresting."

"And since when," I continued my inquiry, "and how is this possible? Does Nagy know about your arrest?"

"Nagy?" asked Styxi, as if not recalling the name. "Oh, yes, Nagy, damn him! I feel sorry about our academy. My quartet sounds, if I may say so myself, truly marvelous. And your Fräulein Cella would have been sensational. We rehearsed only last Tuesday."

The third man joined us. He was a short, robust redhead

with small, blinking eyes. One could tell he was a priest merely
by his black jacket, with which he wore hiking knickers and
half hose. His collar had been removed upon his arrival here,
like our shirt collars, ties, and shoelaces. This is customary in
all prisons in order to deprive the inmates of any instrument
of suicide. Human society, which does nothing to guarantee
the life of free men, does all it can in prisons and madhouses
to protect the lives of the lost against themselves. That is one
of society's mindless contradictions. The redhead's freckled
peasant hand squeezed mine vigorously. His handshake radiated a good, calming strength.

"I am Father Felix of Parnsdorf," he introduced himself. I
told him my name and profession, whereupon he winked at
me. "Don't take it too hard, Herr Doctor. The main thing is
we're still alive for now. We're nicely sheltered here and we
get along famously. Herr Stich, don't make such a sour face to
welcome our new friend. Everything is in order."

Father Felix's name seemed appropriate. His large-pored face
with its rather thick stubble beamed felicitously, although there
was nothing in the circumstances to justify it. He motioned to
the fourth inmate, who stood at the folding table next to the
ominous bucket, rolling cigarettes with magician's speed—an
activity thoroughly condemned by prison regulations. His body
was that of a tailor, his blue-black hair was parted down the
middle, he had two dissimilar eyes, one of which remained
open and wary, while the other squinted craftily, and there
was a large gap in his upper row of teeth. He wore a striped
prison suit, not because he had to, but, as he claimed, because
he had "requested and received it," in order to protect his "civilian clothes," which the government would not replace if he
wore them out in Liesl. He deferentially wiped his blunt fingers
on his uniform before shaking my hand.

"My name is Hipfinger, Herr Doctor. I'm not a political
prisoner like these fine gentlemen. Just a simple looter."

"Hipfinger, Hipfinger," the Father admonished him, "you'd

like that, wouldn't you? Nowadays, looting is a political act."
Hipfinger's open eye looked offended.

"Father, I don't know what you mean. Just because I may
have peeked into a safe when I was a kid." And he sighed
mendaciously. "An unemployed man . . ."

"You are forgiven, my son," Father Felix laughed, "because
you're doing a good job for us. Really, Herr Doctor," he said
to me, "Hipfinger is a treasure. Where would we be without
Hipfinger?"

His praise was well-founded, as I soon learned myself. Hipfinger, an esteemed expert on and steady customer at Liesl,
enjoyed a preferential position in the establishment. Now that
several hundred political prisoners of all sorts had entered the
prison since Black Friday, the overworked guards could not
take care of everything. So they drafted minions of the law,
old acquaintances like Hipfinger, who were familiar with the
prison, to perform the most diverse tasks. They kept summon-
ing him to do some kind of work, to clean the cells and corridors, but mainly to assist with food distribution. While the
rest of us were stuck in our cell's cube of air, this career criminal moved freely throughout the building. Father Felix had
not exaggerated. Hipfinger was indeed a treasure. He played
the role of telephone, newspaper, radio, tobacco smuggler, and
Santa Claus in one person. He was a true philanthropist, rejecting any gratuities from us with great professional pride, for
he was virtually the host here, and we the poor orphans. I have
never found a more assiduous, more cunning jack-of-all-trades,
even among the former military orderlies. Goodness only
knows why we four—a prince, a priest, a town councilor, and
a lawyer—were so solidly in Hipfinger's good graces that he
outdid himself making our stay endurable. Perhaps he wanted
to convince us solid citizens that there were worse places than
a prison cell and worse people than a veteran safecracker. Or
perhaps it was a kind of paternal compassion that he felt toward people like us, who struck him as failures in the struggle

of life because of our class and professions. No matter! We
gave Hipfinger a little money, and he brought us cold cuts and
bottles of beer, cheese and cigarettes from the canteen. He even
got me a second blanket. In this way, we avoided the dreadful
lentil soup into which the prison kitchen threw a rancid blob
of margarine, and which tasted like warm slops. Hipfinger, in
contrast, lapped up this soup with attentive satisfaction. Liesl,
he explained, was not a penitentiary, but only a police station,
and Liesl's soup was delicious compared with other soups. For
example, at the Stein Penitentiary, the soup was laced with
sodium carbonate to keep the inmates from dreaming about
women. And indeed, this chemical ingredient had an amazing
effect.

Hipfinger was full of such arcane behind-bars tidbits. You
would forget your own fate for minutes at a time whenever the
husky voice of this marginal man strung together his glosses
and anecdotes. Every time the guard hauled him out of the
cell, we waited impatiently for his return, the way the inhabitants of a snowed-in mountain nest may wait for the postman.
And he always came back with a pile of mail, which he zest-
fully unpacked. He told us about events within the new regime
and unpreventable things that were about to happen. He listed
the names of the new potentates, some of whom he knew from
the slum taverns. To each name, he appended, "He belongs in
Liesl, not you gentlemen." One of them, he said, had shot a
poor jeweler, the other had cheated a nightclub waiter of several thousand. "I'm not like that," Hipfinger exclaimed indig-
nantly. "That's why they won't make me mayor." He knew
what had happened to yesterday's VIPs, he knew which of
them had been killed, which were languishing in the grip of
the German Secret State Police, and which unprincipled lack-
eys were dangling sweatily, waiting to be graciously accepted
by the victors. He knew which notables had been delivered to
Liesl just an hour ago, and in which cells they were penned
up. He also knew who would be lucky enough to be released

during the next few days. He knew which of the guards was bribable or the very opposite, a lousy bastard. He knew what we did not want to believe: that the Party had issued a strict secret order that the families of political prisoners were not to be informed of their whereabouts. The letters we wrote were taken, but not delivered.

In short, Hipfinger knew more than I can enumerate here. He was the one who taught us the difficult and intricate art of secret prison messages, at which he was a past master. He knew how to write dense telegrams on pieces of cigarette paper the size of a fingernail and smuggle them into the outside world. It was thanks to him that Gretl very soon learned of my whereabouts and was able to work on my behalf. At certain times, Liesl was transformed into a haunted house. Dull knocks drummed all around us. Hipfinger deciphered them nonchalantly, never really listening to them. The prison communication network functioned efficiently. In this way, important news was brought to the inmates. Of course, we inexperienced and awkward political prisoners never plugged into this circuit.

Hipfinger seemed to nurture a special affection for me. From the start, he treated me like a difficult child who requires greater care. At three o'clock that first day, the cell door was yanked open. A judiciary soldier shouted: "The Aryans—report for walking!" Styxi, Stich, and Father Felix slowly trudged off without looking at me. Hipfinger remained and tried to keep me company, since the new penal regulations prohibited me from getting fresh air. I impatiently sent him out. I wanted to be alone, if only for half an hour. I hated my cellmates with the full hatred of my body, which needed room, with my lungs, which wanted to breathe freely, with my modesty, which was long unused to such physical closeness. During my brief solitude, I ran up and down like a lunatic. I collapsed on the straw mattress. I ran up and down again. The first night of my imprisonment refused to come.

The first night came. Father Felix had virtually forced his wallside bed on me. He said he was accustomed to sleeping on the ground, and we could take turns, after all. Styxi lay on the bed underneath the window, Stich on the bed next to the door. The priest lay down on the straw sack next to Stich, but Hipfinger kept as respectful a distance as possible from us, for he was a stickler for wide berths. I slept in the middle bed. Or rather, I did not sleep. My ears, so nervous and hypersensitive, alas, detected my companions drifting off. First, the prince began to snore. It was the snoring of a great gentleman, in a slow andante rhythm, full of unflappable self-assurance, drawn from the innocent thoughtlessness of a soul that is not accustomed to having peers. Next, Hipfinger followed him into sleep. He did not snore, but he sounded as if he were hastily blowing on soup, and then the noise turned into the quick rustling of mice, revealing unsatisfied greed and an eternal search for food.

Each sleeper's rhythmic breathing seemed to expose his character. Herr Stich, for example, irregularly emitted pettybourgeois yowls and whimpering sobs as if, in his profound slumber, he were lamenting the collapse of his statistically corroborated ideals. Only the priest breathed soundlessly. I was thankful to him for that and admired the discipline of the Catholic Church, which rules even the unconscious and vegetative impulses of an ordained man.

I, however, lay hopelessly awake. The tormenting secret of insomnia is not that the victim is unable to lose his alertness, his consciousness; rather, he must endure a hundred times more alertness and consciousness than ever during the day. Following the priest's example, I tried not to move on my narrow sack. I felt as if a whole wagonload of coal had been dumped on top of me. Contrary to regulations, our cell was dark. Styxi, who could not sleep with the light on, had managed, with the help of bribes and Hipfinger, to have the bulb in its grated cage put out at night. (This, incidentally, was one of numerous privileges that we owed to Styxi's presence.)

I tried to gather my thoughts. However, my overalertness did not make my mind any sharper. It kept drifting away from the subject. And this subject was I, not Cella and Gretl, but my own misfortune, which had trapped me; for I had passively allowed four irreplaceable days to elapse since Friday. I kept preparing my defense. After all, I was an attorney. As a veteran in my field, I would never have dreamed that they could lock someone up without an investigation, a trial, and a lawful verdict. I weighed my rights and their abrogation in terms of the new conditions. I still had not realized that the dragon did not acknowledge justice and injustice; he was concerned purely with whether something helped or hurt his cause. However, the summation that I drafted was repeatedly crisscrossed by and interwoven with a breathless torrent of images.

Finally, my convulsive alertness began to relax a bit. It was already very late, or rather, very early. I sensed something caressing my senses like a dear hand. Then a whisper from the next bed struck my ear. It was an almost childishly groping sound, with which Herr Stich was trying to find out whether Father Felix was asleep.

"Father . . . Father . . ." he whispered twice in a barely audible voice.

"I am listening." These words coming from the straw mattress were soft and toneless yet clear and audible, as if no sleep had confused the senses of the man who was replying. I thought: Felix probably showed the same toneless calm in the confessional when he spoke to his flock. Not breathing, I listened to the dialogue that developed, with long pauses, in the muffled voices of the two men.

"Forgive me, Father," the former town councilor began, "I don't want to bother you or annoy you, I swear. But don't you tell children about God and so on? That God has a son and what not? And that the Holy Ghost is a dove? Isn't that so?"

"Just pour out your heart, Herr Stich."

"Please forgive me, Father, but do you believe all that? Please don't be angry."

"I am not angry, even though the question is an insult."

"So you do believe it, Father. Oh, well, believing isn't knowing."

"Very true, Herr Stich. For one doesn't have to believe something just because one knows it."

"Please, Father, you also say that God, the Almighty, is good. I have never seen a powerful person who was good. When I had some power, I wasn't good either, I was conceited, and I told people where to get off if I felt like it."

"Herr Stich, our Good Lord in heaven is not a town councilor."

"Father, our Good Lord doesn't exist. And heaven doesn't exist, it's the ice-cold cosmos, which astronomers are so familiar with. All I want to know, Father, is what you base your assumption on that our Good Lord has such a good heart."

"I am listening, Herr Stich, for you want to tell me something else."

A very long pause ensued, implying that Stich wanted to break off his inquisition of the priest. Minutes wore by before he resumed in a soft yet altered voice, "Yes, I want to tell you about Maria, Father. She's my child, you see, my little girl, my ray of sunshine, as they say. But my ray of sunshine has TB—that's what the doctors call tuberculosis. She was a war baby, Father, born in 1918, nursed on watery milk and cornbread. Maybe it was our fault too, God knows. Maybe we weren't paying enough attention, my missus and me. But you can't tell the girl's sick, not in the least. She looks so fresh, I tell you, such a nice little figure, as tender and nimble as . . . A beauty, I swear, I'm not saying so because I'm her dad, everyone says so. And she's got such a fine character, Father. Why, she'd sacrifice her life for her mom and me. Heavens, if your Good Lord were as good as my daughter, then . . . Yes, then the girl—she's twenty now—she wouldn't have suffered

such tortures since the age of eleven, fever every day and choking fits and pneumothorax and so forth."

I could hear Felix get up and then sit down on Stich's bed.
He had probably taken hold of Stich's hand. His words came
over to me, clear and toneless: "You know, Herr Stich, there
are very learned and astonishing answers to all these things,
for poor, wretched mankind has been asking itself these questions ever since it learned how to speak. I also have colleagues,
who have those irrefutable answers ready for all sad cases and
they dish them out by the spoonful. I'm not putting down my
colleagues; they have a much harder time than some people
realize. But I personally don't like consolation from a tin can.
You are right, Herr Stich. Strive against God as bitterly as you
can. That's not a bad approach. I do it myself, and not just
once a day, for the Good Lord is truly dreadful."

"That's pure blasphemy," Stich broke in, louder than before.
"Claiming he created us, the Good Lord, *us*—can you imagine!
But just listen to a few things about the goodness of mankind,
Father. Seven or eight years ago, I got the girl into the Alland
Sanatorium. I don't have anything, and during the time when
other men in my position managed to acquire something, I was
stupid, because anyone who tries to be decent in our time is
stupid. I couldn't send the child to Davos or Arosa, where she
might have been cured. But Alland is quite good for the bad
months, and that was how we got Maria through the dangerous period every year. And now listen carefully, Father. In
February 1934, when your people came to power after the
Civil War, the new director or administrator of Alland summoned the girl and told her: Dear Maria Stich, I'm dreadfully
sorry, but unfortunately your father is one of the Red bigwigs,
and now we're having a change of shift, and I need space for
our people, and your medical diagnosis is excellent, and you
can go home."

"And what happened then?" asked Father Felix, his voice
still soft, but no longer toneless.

"I ran around from pillar to post, and finally I came to the dean of St. Stephen's Cathedral; he comes from the same area I do. And he got the girl a much better place in a wonderful sanatorium, five thousand feet high in the Stubai Alps in the Tyrol. And that's where Maria is now, because it's March. That is, she was still there on Sunday when they searched my home and took me along."

After a while, Father Felix said, "I can see your dear child, Herr Stich, in the flesh. When I am again permitted to read the holy mass, I will insert a quiet prayer for Maria."

"Even though it won't help. But it certainly can't hurt, Father. Now the Nazis are in power. We're really going to experience the goodness of your Almighty. I'm curious to see what he does."

"He has a hard time with us. People all pray against one another."

"No conversations, please," Styxi's voice grumbled. They lapsed into silence. No one snored now. But I pulled out Cella's photograph, which I always had with me. My hand clutched it in the darkness. I felt helpless.

We were awoken at six A.M. Taking off his jacket and shirt, Hipfinger promptly made the beds and straightened out the cell. I could not help admiring the energetic play of his muscles. What an excellent worker this burglar was and what an obliging temperament he had. He served us with mute devotion, asking no gratitude. Presumably, he saw his reward in the social elevation of sharing a cell as one among equals, with a genuine prince and an ordained priest. All people have the same motives, and in his heart of hearts, in the core of his sincerity, even the most hardened Bolshevik knows about high and low. Snobbery is not a bourgeois disease, it runs straight through all levels of human society, for it is based on the irrepressible yearning of each individual to be recognized as worthy among those recognized as worthy. Nowhere, of course, is this urge stronger than in the classes that are regarded as low. If envy, as we are told, is the father of all revolutions, then snobbery, that pathological yearning for recognition by the recognized, is the mother of all revolutions. For if one wipes out the recognized, who do not wish to recognize one, then one replaces them. However, we recognized Hipfinger not only as an equal but as a superior. This visibly imbued him with satisfaction, and he did not slacken in his efforts for us.

While in normal times, the regulations of Liesl prescribed that the inmates had to clean themselves every morning in a special washroom, we political prisoners were not allowed to leave our cells. Hipfinger was called out and brought us a small, battered tin basin, in which we took turns washing. However, our magician had conjured up a white towel and piece of soap for each and every one of us. Then the thing that I had feared the day before happened, and for the sake of completeness, I will not leave it out. Prince Ernst was the first to use the bucket. He acted solemn and unembarrassed. He eyed us pensively, severely, asking all sorts of questions and receiving answers. I was reminded of the baroque kings who sat on their chamber stool during their levee while the royal household, frozen in their bows, listened to the royal utterances, which were accompanied by the latest ode from the poet laureate. What I greatly liked about the young prince was that he could be thrown into jail but not robbed of his sovereign freedom. He had the unassailable self-confidence of African big game, about which he occasionally told witless hunting stories. Granted, Styxi was not free of snobbish traits. They were aimed, understandably, at the only class that was above him and unattainable by him: the class of genius. Once, when our factotum happened to be out, Styxi said that if Beethoven or Bruckner or Richard Strauss had been sharing the cell with us, then he, Styxi, would gladly have been Beethoven's Hipfinger. And, at this sublime thought, Styxi's rigid black eyes shone with a fire that was rare for them.

Now it was the priest's turn. He smiled, raising his coarse hands, turning his palms toward us, and said, "Please turn your backs, gentlemen, while I play musical chairs." The municipal councilor, in contrast, had a hard time answering a call of nature. He suffered from constipation, which was part of his kind but narrow nature. His inadequate efforts went on for quite a while. And they elicited his wild curses, something that one usually did not hear from him. Yet oddly enough, his fury was vented not against the white-stockings, who had robbed him of everything and imprisoned him. Instead, he fulminated against the previous regime, from which he had endured only a relatively mild blow; after all, he had lost nothing but a modest political office. The old Social Democrat was so thoroughly dominated by his hatred, which had grown and developed for decades, that he could not take on a new hatred. He almost appeared to be applauding the white-stockings for getting rid of his old enemies along with him.

With the perfect gesture of a lackey, Hipfinger invited me to take my predecessor's place. I begged off. With all my heart, I hoped to schedule this necessary matter for those hours in which the "Aryans," that is, my cellmates, all went strolling in the prison yard. After the embarrassing procedure had been carried out expediently, Hipfinger received from the hands of the guard that which was known as "coffee" in the kitchen of Liesl. He poured this undefinable concoction into our mess tins, which reminded me of my military time.

Thus the day began, and it was followed by many, many others, all of them indistinguishable. Since the situation is what shapes man, and not vice versa, we probably behaved like typical prisoners. Every cellmate kept a wall calendar of misfortune, inscribing rows of small strokes, each signifying a day of his incarceration. We lay or sat around or paced up and down the possible four yards, our heads between our shoulders, our hands clenched in our trouser pockets. What were we doing? We were waiting. I already knew from my army time that waiting by no means spells leisure; it is a tense occupation, indeed, a very hard labor. But what was the chore of waiting in the barracks yard or in the trenches—a virile activity in fresh air— compared with the overpowering load of waiting in the gray shaft of a cell? Human beings do most of their work in space. They dig, they build into space. But waiting is a labor that takes place only in time. Waiting means carrying off time, shovelful by shovelful. Every human being has a specific pile of time inside him, which he has to carry off. Perhaps in our cell, I had the biggest pile of time and Hipfinger the smallest. Trudging back and forth, we had a useless thought on every shovelful of time. For instance, this one repeatedly: Footsteps outside . . . The court's officer is about to enter and take me to the investigating judge. I have absolutely nothing to fear. No one can prove that I performed any illegal political activity, for, as it now turns out, several of the victors also belonged to the Iron Ring. They will give me a warning and release me. I will no longer have to hide then; I can prepare our emigration with Gretl and Cella in peace and quiet.

The footsteps clattered past. But new ones kept arriving all the time, triggering such reflections. I do not know whether the same thing happened in other cells; but in ours, we exchanged our stories only allusively and incoherently. At least, that was so during the first week. I said next to nothing about my circumstances and learned nothing more from the others. I only knew about Stich's great paternal anxieties from the nocturnal conversation on which I had eavesdropped. Nevertheless, Stich was the first at whom I aimed my nervous intolerance, which resulted from our close confinement. One day, Hipfinger, worried as always about our morale, spirited up a set of indecent photographs. With bogus fear, he concealed them from the priest, who merely cast an indifferent glance at them. Herr Stich, however, the father of poor, lovely Maria, immersed himself in them, thoroughly scrutinizing these pornographic images of the very cheapest slum taste. God only knows why I was so infuriated by that trivial nonsense—I am no sanctimonious bigot. But I was irked by the eyeglasses that Stich took off and polished in order to see better. I grabbed the whole disgusting lot of pictures and hurled them into the bucket. Herr Stich did not speak to me for the next few days,

and the overall mood was sultry and oppressive. It lifted only
on the day that Styxi was permitted by the prison administration to receive a valise containing clothing, linen, chocolate,
and toiletries. When the prince opened the valise, we were all
as excited as children. The entire contents were fraternally divided, even though the shirts and sweaters of the overlifesized
prince dangled way over our fingertips. On this occasion, I
tried to get Styxi to talk, since he acted utterly apathetic about
what was happening to him.

"Tell me, Prince, were you arrested in the Residence? And
why *you* in particular?"

"Because I'm the youngest. They would have loved to drag
my father off to Vienna."

"And what does this madness mean? Have you any explanation?"

"Perhaps your petition, dear boy. Perhaps a denunciation."

"Denunciation? Is there anyone you suspect?"

"Oh, yes. Our landmark fellow. Just what was his name? A
janitor's name."

"Myslivec. I can't believe it. Myslivec is a teacher's pet, an
opportunist. But I don't think he's capable of denouncing
someone."

"In politics, everyone is capable of anything. And the fellow's quite big now. In culture . . . kul-chur."

He repeated that derisive pronunciation several times.

"And Nagy has slipped off," I said. "He's smart, all right. I
wonder what he's doing now?"

"Trading horses," Styxi answered drily.

"No worse than selling hearing aids."

"The water hasn't been created that Nagy could not swim
in," said the prince, turning away.

I believe I have already revealed that I had asked Hipfinger
to establish contact between myself and the outside world. But
twelve days had already worn by since the looter's colleague,
who had been released from Liesl, had gone to Pramer to bring
him the note containing my cry for help. The reader may be

surprised that I had turned to that fat coward who sighed under the strict hand of his son Otto. But was there anyone else I could turn to in Vienna? The labor of waiting grew more burdensome from day to day. My thoughts grew blacker and blacker.

Hipfinger swore that he had been notified by his unquestionably reliable communication service that Herr Director Pramer had meticulously carried out my request and informed Gretl of my whereabouts. At the same time, Hipfinger put a flea in my ear, which doubled the hard labor of my waiting. People were saying, he reported, that the race protectors had devised a very cunning piece of diabolism to break up happy mixed marriages. In cases like mine, the Christian wife was pressured by the most devious threats and lures to institute divorce proceedings immediately against her husband. The fact of racial difference was a sufficient ground for the court to declare against the husband and dissolve the marriage. As a reward for her betrayal, the wife received many privileges, especially the entire property of the ostracized husband, and the children were accepted into the so-called German folk community, thus saving their future.

Suddenly, I was no longer sure of Gretl: after seventeen years of the most intimate life together in which we had had no secrets from one another, or so I had believed. Was there any woman who could resist this truly devilish temptation to save home and homeland for herself and her child? The more or less repressed discord and misunderstandings of our marriage, the friction resulting from our different backgrounds grew in my memory minute by minute as I waited. On the night of the twelfth day, lying helplessly awake, almost paralyzed, at the mercy of the sleep noises of my companions, I was just on the verge of giving up on Gretl and Cella. Go and vanish happily from my existence, you dear wife, you beloved child, my pride and my supreme hope. Let my cursed life trickle away without a trace. What else can I expect, I, a prisoner of war of the faithless, who bow only to power and violence but never to any divine or human justice? There is only one road out of this prison, and it leads to a concentration camp surrounded by electrically charged barbed wire. There, a human being decays while still alive, if he is not lucky enough to be killed first. Release me, Gretl and Cella, leave me alone.

On the morning of the thirteenth day, just as we had taken our coffee and bread, the guard, winking kindly, brought me my suitcase from the Hotel Union. And I instantly recognized Gretl's hand, which had packed it, adding several important items. There were also books inside. And Tolstoy's *Resurrection* contained a letter, written on the thinnest tissue paper, which had eluded the eyes of the censor.

> *My dearest husband,*
>
> *Don't worry! We will soon get you out. Cella and I are now in Vienna in order to be near you. Zsoltan is behaving very decently on your behalf. He is the one who had these things sent to you. I felt awful that you couldn't change your linen for such a long time—I know how you are. I hope you're not giving in to any bad thoughts. You ought to know that your life is our life. I hug you with love.*
>
> Gretl

I held the scrap in my hand for a long time. My hand trembled.

Unfortunately, Herr Stich received some bad news that same day. He was taken to the warden's office to hear that his daughter Maria had been released from the sanatorium a week ago and was now at home in bed. The new rulers, who had their political prisoners cut off from any news of their families, never hesitated for an instant to keep them abreast of any cases of disease or death. They saw this as an educational spice of imprisonment. Upon returning to the cell, Stich collapsed face down on his straw sack and remained silent. Father Felix sat down next to him on the floor.

"This is no reason to despair, Herr Stich," he said. "Don't

overestimate the little bit of mountain air. And it's almost April now."

After a while, the town councilor turned and asked: "What's the weather like?"

Hipfinger reported accurately that there had been storms and snow for a long time. (A genuine winter had followed the mendacious hints of spring.) From this moment on, the poor father's fear was expressed in a dismal torpor that would not subside. He no longer abused the priest with atheistic platitudes as he had during that nocturnal conversation. With an admirable delicacy that I alone could fully understand, Father Felix remained inconspicuously in Stich's proximity. He uttered no grand pronouncements, the word "God" never passed his lips; but now and then, he offered a jest or a tale from his pastoral experiences, showing that seriously ill people, to whom he had already given the sacrament, had found their way back into life and were flourishing and thriving even today. Hipfinger had formed chess figures out of bread. We had drawn a chessboard ourselves. I asked Stich to play a game with me. He accepted, but his mind was elsewhere as he played. When twilight thickened (we followed the lengthening of days with the yearning of Greenlanders), Felix said to us, "Gentlemen, things can't go on like this. With great effort, I managed to get you to exercise half an hour a day. But that's not enough. The mind also needs a little gymnastics. I therefore suggest that each of us take his turn as an instructor for the others and either give a lecture about his field or simply tell us about something he's experienced in his life. Goodness knows we've all experienced enough recently."

The priest's idea was accepted—indeed, with visible enthusiasm by Styxi. And it was he who gave the first lecture the very next day, naturally on a musical subject. The rest of us barely understood it. Nevertheless, and even though the prince's talk lasted for almost two hours—he either overestimated or disregarded his audience's mental capacity—I found it very beneficial to hear obscure but grand words and to be liberated from my own gnawing mental pain. The lecturer spoke under the window, sitting on the bed, which Hipfinger had unstrapped. This place now became our rostrum. The prince never deigned to glance at us; he stared stiffly and rigidly at a corner of the room, just as he had done in his drunken state at the White Rose Ball. We were not present for him. He titled his talk—which I am far too ignorant to set down—The Holy Figure Four in Music. The gist of it was that the most important law of the musical world is based on the number four. In classical music, a melodic idea has four or eight measures, a sonata or symphony contains four movements. He supported this thesis with countless examples, singing them to us in a bristly voice. Hipfinger grinned from ear to ear. Then Styxi described the satanic process of dissolution that had invaded all branches of life since the previous century—first and foremost, the realm of music. The modern composers, obsessed by the devil, had long since destroyed the holy four in musical structure, paving the way for cynical disorderliness. And he concluded by stating that for decades now, the disintegration of this art, which was symbolic of the human soul, had been forewarning lucid minds about the victory of the white-stockings. Whether we understood him or not, the four of us outdid one another applauding him, and we were profoundly grateful to the speaker for liberating us from reality.

I then chose a topic: The Rights of the Individual and the Rights of the Community. Forgotten reminiscences of my student days floated to the surface. I worked on my piece for more than two days, and at my first lecture, I was overcome by those agitating thoughts that became so crucial for me later on.

Herr Stich talked about the development of labor unions in Austria. Dry as his subject was, he had a great success among us as a veteran speaker who knew how to achieve pungent effects. Afterwards, he collapsed again, subsiding into his torpor.

Nor did Hipfinger care to be outdone. He told a tale about the lootings in the Jewish neighborhood of Leopoldstadt.

The only person who had not yet taken his turn in the round of offerings was the priest. Having come up with the felicitous idea, he had allowed us to go first. Now, when it was his turn, he sat down on the lecture bed under the light hole, from which the final dirty flakes of twilight were drifting down. It was ice-cold, and we were all freezing miserably.

"You gentlemen have honored us with such excellent instruction in the areas of music, law, and political life," said Felix, "that a person like me is somewhat embarrassed. For years, I have been nothing but a country boy. Should I blurt out some wisdom from the seminary? It's been such a long, long time. I would rather follow in Herr Hipfinger's footsteps and tell you a personal story. Please do not expect any grand, suspenseful tale. It is not even fiction, it is dreadful truth, just as I experienced it, before I came here to Liesl. That was Tuesday evening. On Wednesday, Doctor Bodenheim arrived. . . ."

The faces of my companions were so green and emaciated that I was startled. Had imprisonment had such a dreadful effect on me too? The priest began. I do not dare record the story as he himself told it, in his way. His mind is not mine, and I fear I would falsify many things if I let him speak himself. His tone was so modest, so simple, and yet so firm and superior.

Chapter 9

The Priest's Tale of the Righted Cross

Father Ottakar Felix headed the parish in the tiny village of Parndorf, which is located in the north of Burgenland, between the forested Leitha Mountains and the reedy, swampy shores of huge Lake Neusiedl. With its ring-shaped marketplace, its goose pond, and its low thatched roofs crowned with stork nests, Parndorf is one of the drab church villages in this region, whose peculiar Eastern character mournfully contrasts with the charm of the overall Austrian landscape. I have been familiar with all those villages since my youth. The border between Eastern and Western Europe seems to cut through them very precisely. The only significance of Parndorf is that it lies on the main route between Vienna and Budapest, and the shiny cars of the Orient Express and the Arlberg Express zoom past its tiny station house—a sophisticated distinction granted to neither Eisenstadt nor the other main towns of Burgenland. The parish of this nest is under the patronage of the monastery of Maria Elend, which belongs to Rhenish fathers. It is not clear to me why Felix was transferred to the godforsaken ham-

let of Parndorf from the Viennese working-class suburb of Jed-
lersee, where he was priest at the main church. But since his
transfer took place in 1934, after the dismal battles between
government troops and socialist workers, I reason that he might
have compromised himself in the eyes of his superiors during
the bloody month of February and now had to endure a kind
of punitive exile. He offered no hints about it, and I felt a
justifiable reluctance to question him.

A small community of our people lived in Parndorf. There
were about ten families, totaling forty people altogether. Such
communities lived in all the tiny villages of my rather long and
narrow homeland—in Purbach, Forchtenau, Kobersdorf, in the
north up to Petronell and Kittsee, where Austria, Czechoslovakia, and Hungary collide, and in the south up to Rechnitz
on the border of the South Slavic kingdom. These communities
were normally made up of a few old families, who were related
by blood or marriage throughout the country. One finds the
same names everywhere: Fürst, Zopf, Perls, Knopf, Weiner,
Roth, Berger, Reissner, Balacz. In Eisenstadt, next to the Weil
family, the Fürsts were the most prestigious people among their
coreligionists, although in a very different way from the Weils.
They had never attained a great fortune; but since the seven-
teenth century, they had continually produced a line of rabbis
and scholars, who played an outstanding role in the strange
spiritual and intellectual history of the ghetto.

The Fürst family came from that same village, Parndorf, to
which an ungracious destiny had brought Father Felix. Aladar
Fürst lived there, a man in his thirties, who had married young,
and now had three children, of whom the youngest, a baby
boy, had been exactly three weeks old on Austria's Black Friday. Aladar Fürst must have been an eccentric and outsider,
for, as a doctor of philosophy, a graduate of the famous Hebrew Seminary in Breslau, he could think of nothing better to
do than return to the thatched roofs of his native village, bury
himself in the exquisite library that he had brought back from
Germany, and officiate as country rabbi for Parndorf and sev-

eral neighboring communities. He held services in a tiny house of prayer and gave religious instruction to Jewish children at the various elementary schools in the area.

Needless to say, the priest and the young rabbi ran into each other almost daily. And, given their mentalities and the delicate similarity and difference between their offices, it should also be needless to say that they did nothing but exchange greetings, until almost a year ago, on the occasion of a wedding feast to which Aladar Fürst had also been asked, they had their first long conversation. Next, Fürst called on the priest, and his visit was promptly reciprocated. Mutual invitations ensued, developing into a regular, albeit measured and not too frequent intercourse. I gleaned this from the way in which Felix spoke about their meetings. He and Fürst were separated not only by the restrictive power of their diverse faiths, but also by centuries of alienation, which could not easily be bridged. Nevertheless, Felix obviously liked Fürst. It was not just that Fürst was a well-read and well-educated intellectual—which Felix as a man of action appreciated less—but there was something that filled the priest with great astonishment. Whenever he spoke with a son of Jacob, he always expected the same liberal or orthodox banality—the marketable kind that always puts a limit on every conversation. Fürst, however, was strikingly different. He was extremely well-versed in the branches of Catholic theology (too much so, Felix must have thought—if I know him); he quoted St. Paul, St. Thomas, Bonaventure, and Newman more knowledgeably than an overworked village priest could do. However, Father Felix realized that far beyond this still gratuitous knowledge, Aladar Fürst had overcome his ancestral aversion toward Christ—a repugnance that was ancient and nonsensical although understandable, given the sufferings of his forebears. And indeed, Father Felix perceived that Fürst was heading down an unknown road, that he was struggling in earnest passion with the goal of his faith. Felix told us that a remark of the rabbi's had had a poignant impact on him. It was uttered during a conversation about the mission to convert the Jews. (The priest quickly glanced at me from his "lecture bed.")

"I don't know, Father," the rabbi had begun, "why the Church is so intent on converting the Jews. Can it suffice for her to win over perhaps two genuine believers among a thousand overambitious or feeble renegades? And then, what would happen if all the Jews in the world got baptized? Israel would vanish. And thus the only real witness to the divine revelation would vanish from the face of the earth. The Holy Scriptures would turn from a truth documented by our existence into a limp and empty myth like any Greek myth. Does the Church not see this danger? We belong together, Father, but we are not one. The Epistle to the Romans says, 'The community of Christ rests upon Israel.' I am convinced that the Church will survive as long as Israel survives, but that the Church must fall if Israel falls."

"And where do these thoughts of yours come from?" the priest asked.

"From our sufferings until today," the rabbi replied. "Do you believe that God would have allowed us to endure and survive uselessly for two thousand years?"

On Friday, May eleventh, at seven P.M., the priest was sitting in his room. One hour earlier, the radio had transmitted the cancellation of the plebescite and the chancellor's farewell address, and Felix was still sitting there, motionless. He wondered, inconclusively, how he ought to behave in this catastrophe that had broken in upon the poor country. Suddenly the door flew open, and Aladar Fürst stood in the room. He had not waited to be announced by the housekeeper. Fürst was wearing a solemn overcoat. It was already the sabbath, after all. His narrow face with its long lashes and short, black beard was several shades paler than usual. "Forgive me, Father," he started breathlessly, "for bursting in on you so informally. We had already begun celebrating."

"I can imagine that these events are disrupting the sabbath," the priest remarked, pushing over an armchair for his guest who, however, refused to sit down.

"I would like to ask your advice, Father. For you know, I myself, I didn't expect this, I'm really totally . . . Have you heard that Schoch is in the area; he's been here for more than a week. He's storm-troop leader of the SA. He's rounded up the whole gang—farmboys, laborers from the capsule factory, unemployed men—they're sitting in the tavern and threatening to kill all the Jews this very night."

"I'll go and see old Schoch right away," the priest said. "The boy is still afraid of him."

That wasn't true, and Felix knew it wasn't. Old Schoch was the richest farmer in the County of Rust and a good Catholic. He had suffered bad luck with his youngest boy, Peter. Before even reaching his sixteenth birthday, Peter had gotten a girl pregnant—a servant on his father's farm—and while that is no sin by country mores, he had also threatened both mother and child with violence and stolen all her savings from her suitcase. This matter was bruited about, and old Schoch was furious. He sent Peter to the forestry school in Leoben. But since the good-for-nothing had spent his six years of elementary school in first grade and still could not read or write, he flunked the entrance examination for forestry school (an examination that any lumberjack could pass) and was thrown out. Instead of reporting his defeat to his parents, he remained in that lively town, which he liked better than his home village and, wheedling huge amounts of money out of his father, allegedly for his studies, he squandered it all. In normal times, Peter's career would have come to a bad end; but in our day, he was saved by the "movement," which was handsomely subsidized by the Third Reich. In their farsighted wisdom, they secured such people, for a lack of literacy did not exclude a genius for ruthless violence. So the rich farmer's boy became an "illegal," who did not scorn the daily support of five schillings from the Party treasury: he spent it on his cigarette habit. A few daredevil misdeeds for the Party brought him some renown, and eventually, after spending a few months in prison, he moved up into the pantheon of martyrs who were released from shame and want after the day of Berchtesgaden. That was young Peter Schoch, whose very name could make Dr. Aladar Fürst turn white with horror.

Now, Fürst sat down after all. The priest handed him a small glass of slivovitz.

"One shouldn't think the worst right away," he said.

"Why not?" asked Fürst. "Perhaps one should. Listen, Father, one hour from now, a train is leaving for the Hungarian border. Shouldn't we, I mean . . . Please advise me. Of course, my poor wife only had a baby one week ago. What should I do, Father, please advise me, things look worse than dangerous."

And now Father Felix did something for which he will never forgive himself. Though he did not immediately specify what it was, I could sense it from his tone of voice. He obviously gave some very bad advice. But in a situation like that, who can know whether one's advice is good or bad?

"Do you really want to abandon everything, Herr Doctor Fürst?" he asked. "We don't even know the new regime yet. Who knows, perhaps in Austria it will all be different from what people expect. At least, wait a few days."

Aladar Fürst was almost relieved.

"Thank you for your advice. Perhaps you're right. It would have been very hard for me to leave our home; my family has been living here for ages, and I deliberately came back to Parndorf from the great, wide world. Perhaps . . ."

The priest saw him out into the starry night. "I'll look in on you tomorrow," he said when they parted.

But as he left, Fürst's last words were, "There is only one thing I fear, Father: our people may be too soft now, we may have lost the old strength and composure of our forebears in times of persecution."

The next morning, at nine o'clock, when the priest was won-

dering how far he could go in his Sunday sermon on the Gos-
pel, his musings were disrupted by dull noises and shouts,
which came through his closed window from the village square.
He dashed outside as he was, without a hat or coat. The square
was filled with a crowd even bigger than the usual one at the
weekly market. Looking forward to "fun," they had poured in
from everywhere—the villages in the bleak Parndorf heath and
even the small town of Neusiedl on the lake: grape growers,
farmhands, serving girls, workers from the nearby factories,
and a mob of people who had been cut off the relief rolls and
always thronged in for every rumpus. The nucleus of this
crowd was a detachment of white-stockings in rank and file,
now sporting arm bands and brown shirts. They were stationed outside the largest house in Parndorf. In their eyes, it
may have been inadmissible for the Fürst family to own this
splendid building, the only two-story structure in the area. But
after all, it was not Aladar Fürst's fault that an ancestor of his
had purchased this almost urban house over a century ago.
The entrance on the ground floor was flanked by two large
shops: Siegmund Kopf's bakery and the general store belonging
to Samuel Reissner's son. The proprietors, their wives, children, and staffs, were standing in a dense group outside the
main entrance; in their midst stood the young rabbi Aladar
Fürst, the only one who kept his head high and did not look
broken. Peter Schoch, clutching an automatic rifle, had taken
up his position opposite the trembling group; next to him stood
a short, squinting man with steel-rimmed glasses and a red
service cap. He was the stationmaster of Parndorf, Herr Ignaz
Inbichler. Peter Schoch, an extraordinarily handsome boy, was
just completing his address. "Fellow Germans, it is intolerable
for members of the German people to receive our daily bread
from the hands of a Jewish bake shop. In the name of the
German people, I hereby declare that the Kopf Bakery is
aryanized. It will now be run by our fellow German Leopold
Havranek. Sieg-Heil."
Peter Schoch spoke in a strained and proper German, with

the dialect peeping through all the many holes. The bellowing brownshirts echoed his "Sieg-Heil." But the crowd remained oddly silent, full of uninvolved curiosity, as it seemed. Now the squinting man with the steel-rimmed glasses and red service cap began to talk. He addressed the traumatized throng huddling outside the building door. "Ladies and gentleman, everything will proceed in an orderly fashion, we do not indulge in wild actions, everything will proceed according to orders, German means organized. We will not harm a single hair on your heads. You only have to sign a document that you are transferring your stuff of your own free will and volition and leaving German soil. Your deadline is four o'clock this afternoon, and it is irrevocable. If any occupant of this house is to be found here after five P.M., he will have no one but himself to blame for the unpleasant, indeed very unpleasant consequences. There are only two ways to solve the Jewish problem. In his infinite goodness, our führer is choosing the second way."

The priest instantly saw that the only thing he could achieve here would be to endanger his own person uselessly. He ran home and immediately telephoned the constabulary, the district commissioner's office, and finally the county government in Eisenstadt. The responses were all evasive or negative. They said that much as they regretted it, there was nothing they could do: the Party received its orders directly from Berlin. Father Felix then hurried over to a big landowner, borrowed his car, and raced to Eisenstadt half an hour later. There he ran about from pillar to post, eventually winding up at the Apostolic Administration of Burgenland, the head of the Church province, a Monsignor So-and-so. The prelate received him in a distinctly somber frame of mind. He said that since it pleased the supreme ecclesiastic office in Vienna to show confidence in the new regime, which, after all, according to the teachings, had to be of God, then he himself could only advise the curates throughout the country to remain completely nonpartisan. He knew precisely what was being planned today in most villages, but he urgently wished that there be no interference on behalf of Jews being expelled. These events were certainly condemnable, but in no way did they fall within the jurisdiction of the curates.

When the priest returned to the Parndorf square, the church clock was just striking three. The two trucks of the Moritz Weiner Trucking Company were standing outside Aladar Fürst's home.

Furniture, beds, wardrobes, tables, chairs were being hauled from the bakery, the store, and the front entrance and loaded on one of the trucks. Stationmaster Inbichler examined every item, for nothing was being released to the expelled Jews without his approval. He also put aside every object that he liked. The brownshirts, who had set their rifles up in pyramids, were lounging about and laughing. Schoch and his men were sitting in the tavern. The day was windless, and a strangely milky haze brooded over the village. Three more families had joined the group of deportees. Now there were more than twenty people. The priest was surprised that they darted to and fro, sedulous and panicky, performing hundreds of meaningless tasks and apparently having no plan. The children among them also stared at the hustle and bustle with eager excitement. They all looked like faded shadows being moved by an impalpable wind.

Father Felix entered the rabbi's home. His delicate wife, who came from Germany, had just barely recovered from giving birth. Breathlessly puttering about, she stood amid piles of laundry—sheets, tablecloths, and clothing—which she was trying to stuff into an overfilled basket. Her eyes were agape with feebleness and incomprehension. In the next room, one could hear the peaceful babble of children and the rebellious squawling of a baby. The priest found Aladar Fürst in front of his bookcases. Several hundred selected books were heaped up all around him. But he was holding a book, deeply absorbed in reading it, with the shimmer of a smile around his lips. The sight of this Jew reading amid the collapse of his world made a powerful impact on the priest. (He told us so himself.)

"Rabbi, Dr. Fürst," said the priest, "I gave you some bad advice, alas. Who could have known? Luckily, you have a Hungarian passport. Perhaps the Good Lord has better plans for you than for us. Perhaps He wishes to bring the nation in which He reveals Himself from the danger zone to safety."

Aladar Fürst gazed at the priest for a long, long time, and the priest was so moved and so calmed that he lent a hand and helped to carry down the chosen books.

One hour later, they were ready to travel. Inbichler had kept the best property of the deportees—the finest furniture, all the silver, all the women's jewelry, the cash and securities that he had gotten hold of, for each of the victims, including Fürst, was stripped and thoroughly searched. However, with a disparaging gesture, the stationmaster waved the rabbi's library through. Since everything had to "proceed in an orderly fashion," and "German" meant "organized," Inbichler filled out receipts for all the remaining objects and handed these documents to the unfortunates, thereby raising naked theft to the level of administrative legality. Peter Schoch, sitting next to the driver of the first truck, was already gesticulating furiously. The brownshirts punched and kicked the victims into the first truck, where they had to sit down on three long benches. Now the little children began to blubber heartrendingly. The crowd of spectators maintained a deathly hush, and their curious gazes did not reveal whether they condoned or condemned what was happening. Schoch's men were already starting up their motorcycles. At this point, Father Felix strode up to Ignaz Inbichler. "Herr Stationmaster," he said, drawing himself up, "I do not know whether and at whose official behest you are acting. But I must point out to you that if you are acting on your own behalf, you will be held responsible, some day, in one way or another. These families, as can be demonstrated, have been living in Parndorf for three centuries, and the people have never had any cause to complain about them. It may be different in the cities, but this is true here. You have terrified them profoundly; that is punishment enough; let it suffice, and wait for a lawful regulation of the matter."

The squinter with the steel-rimmed glasses sucked his cigarette voluptuously and blew a cloud of smoke into the priest's face. "Don't shove, Your Eminence," he purred, "everyone will get his chance. And the padres are next in line, I swear to you. But if you put in even one more good word for the kikes, then you can join them on the spot."

"That's exactly what I'll do," said the priest and leaped into the truck. The passengers stared at him blankly. He found room next to Frau Fürst. She held the baby in her arm while the father tried to calm down the second child, a tiny girl. The priest took the rabbi's eldest son, a four-year-old boy, on his lap and began joking with him. The engine started. It was followed by the engine in the other truck. Motorcycles howled behind them.

The motorcade drove past Neusiedl, down the highway that runs along the lake (it cannot be seen from there) and leads to the Hungarian border. Why they did not use the main road to the large border station at Hegyshalom remained Shoch's secret. No one said a word in the rattling trucks; only the children occasionally asked weepy questions. When the priest attempted to cheer up the deportees, they all listened with the strained and watery eyes of deaf-mutes. There were a few old people and sick people among them, for instance old Kopf, the baker's father. The trucks must have already passed the turn-off to the stone quarry of the free city of Rust when, with twilight, one of those thick, suffocating fogs rolled in from the lake—the kind of fog that the people of this area fear superstitiously. Schoch ordered the entire column to halt. The brownshirts dismounted from the motorcycles. A terse order: "Get out! Unload! The trucks, head back!"

In the witchlike steam, with the daylight oozing away, the storm troopers attacked the second truck. Dressers, sideboards, well-tended furniture, tableware, and kitchen utensils of all sorts crashed into the dirt of the road and shattered. Plaintive screams were heard from the women.

Felix grabbed Schoch by the wrists and bellowed at him, "What's the meaning of this? Are you crazy?"

The storm-troop leader punched the priest's chest, which sent him reeling. "Heel, padre! I'll get you soon!"

Now the rabbi's books followed the murdered furniture like fluttering birds. Aladar Fürst dashed over. But when the priest bent down to save at least one or two of the books, Fürst held him back.

"Why bother? It doesn't matter. If you lose, then you should lose everything, everything."

"Left of the road," Schoch commanded. "Forward march!"

And the hesitant victims, old and young, were driven out into the fields by the brownshirts. No one was allowed to remain. They showed no consideration for the old or the ill. If anyone died during this forced march, then so much the better. These people were outcasts, outlaws, not protected by any state power—quite the contrary. When could there be a permitted, a licensed manhunt in a civilized time, in the middle of Europe, if not here and now?! It got into the hunters' blood, with a fresh and cheery "Sic 'em!" They shook with laughter at their bogus game animals gasping and staggering along. The fog grew darker and darker. All at once, the priest felt that he was wading in icy water, ankle-deep, then knee-deep. They had wandered into the swamps by the lake near Mörbisch. Felix pulled up the four-year-old, whom he had been leading by the hand. He now carried him on his left arm, while his right arm supported the young mother, who could barely drag herself along with her baby.

At this juncture, the narrator paused. In his face with its large pores, the gray eyes gaped without seeing us. Taking advantage of the break, I asked, "When you were in the swamps of Mörbisch, Father, did you ask yourself why all this was happening?"

"I even had an answer, dear Doctor. Mankind must continuously punish itself—for the sin of lovelessness. Everything happening today is, to a certain extent, the imprint of the tremendous lovelessness that fills our world."

It was almost a miracle that relatively soon after taking this "shortcut," they managed to escape the swamps and get back to the road. And it was an even greater miracle that no one had been harmed or gone astray. When night fell, it grew bitter cold, and the fog scattered. Over there, they could see the lights of Mörbisch. Everyone broke into a run. The border, which they were all longing to reach, lay beyond the final houses of Mörbisch. Their homeland, which just yesterday had been taken for granted as the abode of intimate life, had now become a hell, which no one cared to look back on.

The night was very dark. An icy wind came blasting. The flag of the conquerors was already fluttering over the Austrian customs house. However, when the border guards, who had not yet been replaced, saw the SA with their victims, they dropped out of sight. The road to the Hungarian customs house, not even a hundred paces away, was clear. Aladar Fürst gathered the ID cards of the victims. Some of these documents, including his, were Hungarian passports since, after the peace treaties of St. Germain and Trianon, for various reasons, many inhabitants of Burgenland had kept their old Hungarian citizenship. The rabbi, carrying the pile of documents, went over to the Hungarian side. The priest accompanied him. Peter Schoch followed, whistling in delight, almost jigging along.

The customs official in the office did not even glance at the passports. "Do the gentlemen have permission from the Royal Hungarian consulate general in Vienna?"

Aladar Fürst's lips turned white. "What sort of permission, for God's sake?"

"According to the decree issued at twelve noon today of this month, no one can cross the border without permission from the consulate general."

"Why, that's impossible," Fürst stammered, "we knew noth-

ing about it, and we couldn't have applied for permission any-
way. They only gave us a six-hour deadline."

"That's none of my concern, if you please."

Schoch strode over and slammed down the documents that
the deportees had personally signed, stating that they were
leaving their homeland of their own free will and volition.

"Get your commanding officer," said the priest, and his tone
was such that the customs man stood up and obeyed unpro-
testingly.

Some ten minutes later he returned, accompanied by a slender man with salt-and-pepper hair; one could tell that he had
served in the Austro-Hungarian army. He fidgeted nervously
with the passports, while the priest tore into him, unconcerned
about his own fate. "I am a witness, Major, that just a few
hours ago, these people were robbed of everything they had
and driven across the swamp to the Hungarian border—worse
than animals. Dr. Fürst is a Hungarian citizen, and so are several of the others, as you can see from their passports. Among
civilized people, there is no legal decree that can allow anyone
to turn back these refugees."

"Now, now, Father," said the officer, gazing at Felix with
dark, bitter eyes. He then added with a sigh, "Difficult, very
difficult . . ."

"We're such a tiny number," pleaded Fürst, "most of us have
relatives in Sopron. We will not be a burden to the state."

The major brooded for a while with a wrinkled brow. Then
he made up his mind. "Go back across the border and wait!
I'll call up the district chief in Sopron."

There was a vacant area in front of the Austrian customs
house. To the left, a path ran toward the reedy banks of the
lake; to the right, the path vanished into a terrain densely covered with grape vines. In the vacant area, the brownshirts had
created an illuminated stage with the headlights of their motorcycles. They rounded up the elderly men in the glow of the
headlights and, following the renowned example of the concentration camps, they amused themselves by making these frail

oldsters do rapid knee bends: "Up, down, one, two!" After a
while, old Kopf collapsed with heart spasms. Kicks were supposed to help him back on his feet. The priest was on the verge
of joining the victims and taking part in their humiliation. But
he knew only too well that his deed would have no other effect
than to arouse the silly laughter of the brownshirts, who were
flushed with victory. That night, he was haunted by a single
thought. In our cell, he told us what it was: "These happy
people have to sin, but these unhappy ones can atone." Spectators were clustering about, people from Mörbisch and Hungarian border guards. The latter did not conceal their anger
and repugnance. The priest saw a junior officer spit and elbow
the next man. "If I went through anything like that," he said,
"I'd kill myself and my whole family on the spot."

Within half an hour, the district chief arrived in a car. Sopron—or Ödenburg, as it is known in German—the capital of
the German-Hungarian Province, was only a few miles from
the border. The administrative head was a fat, friendly man,
with the springy elegance that many overweight people like to
display. He had a red face and white moustache, and he was
sweating despite the terrible cold. After gathering everyone
around him, he thrust his fists into his hips in order to fully
bring out his ebullient shape, and he rocked up and down like
a horseman. "What kind of headaches are you people giving
me? I can't subvert legal decrees, I'm only an executive authority. I'm responsible to the Ministry of the Interior. Hungary is a constitutional state, and our policy is Christian. But
ultra posse nemo teneatur. I cannot establish a precedent. And
why should I? If I let you people across the border today, then
others will come tomorrow and cite this case. Tomorrow and
the day after and for a whole year. What a predicament we'd
be in, you must realize that. Hungary is a country whose arms
and legs have been cut off, and it has almost half a million
Jewish citizens, and it's got countless unemployed—this is all
we need. You catch my drift. So just go back home nicely, all
of you together. I personally regret it."

"Before these people here go home," said Peter Schoch into the silence, "we'll mow them all down." And everyone knew that his words were no empty threat. Aladar Fürst calmly tried to point out that there was no way they could let babies, children, a woman who had just given birth, and a large number of sick old people spend the night outdoors, indeed in no-man's-land. For a place that is neither one country nor the other is truly no-man's-land. He did not beg, he spoke mildly, like someone who knows precisely what lies ahead for him. The priest, however, begged and implored the high official in Christ's name at least to shelter the deportees for one night on his side of the border; for they would not be received in Mör-bisch or in any other Austrian village, even forgetting Schoch's threat. The district chief fervently rocked up and down, wiping off his sweat. "But Father, why are you making the matter even more difficult for me? Do you believe that I am not a human being and that I am not suffering now? Once and for all, the government has closed the border. I am truly sorry."

By way of comfort, he had his chauffeur hand the women and children some food that he had brought from Sopron. Was it perhaps intrinsic to his character that this food consisted mostly of the cheap candy that is hawked by pretzel vendors? The women took it with their lifeless hands but did not taste it. The major chewed his moustache and stared fixedly at his boot tips. The district chief then asked him and the priest to come off to the side. They walked up and down between the customs houses.

"I've had an idea," the district chief began. "Perhaps there is a way out. But I cannot know anything about it, do you understand, Major?"

And now he laid out his plan. The major could allow the group to cross the border only seemingly. But then, during the night, he would smuggle them back into Austria, preferably across the lake. This would satisfy the demands of both humanity and the law.

The major halted and drew himself up.

"Sir, you need only wink, and I will bend the law in this case. But I myself am a husband and father, and I will not allow women and children to be simply mowed down."

"By all means, old boy, it was just an idea." The district chief smiled and got into his car without heeding the raised hands of the priest.

The darkness had grown a bit lighter. A very pale quarter moon had risen, seeming to intensify the cold. In the nearby vineyards, the moon shone on a vintner's cabin, which served as a shelter against bad weather during the grape harvest. That was where Aladar Fürst took his exhausted wife and infants. The priest again carried the four-year-old boy, who slept in his arms. Meanwhile, the major had distributed straw mattresses, blankets, bread, and coffee from the Hungarian border barracks. He also ordered his men to pitch two tents for the deportees, one for the men, the other for the women. The brownshirts gazed very malevolently at these preparations on their own soil, but were presumably too embarrassed to interfere. The priest resisted the temptation to go to Mörbisch and ask for shelter in the presbytery. He was a hardened man, and a sleepless night would be no great strain on him. He had obtained a bottle of milk from the major for Fürst's children. As he approached the vintner's cabin with this gift, a sharp command suddenly resounded from the vacant area.

"Guard instruction! All the men fall in!"

The shadows, which had just stretched out to sleep, reeled to their feet and gathered in the light of the motorcycles. Aladar Fürst was the last to come. While the others whimpered softly, he gazed gently and imperturbably. Peter Schoch solemnly stomped over. The brownshirts laughed uproariously: the main attraction was beginning. Schoch held a large wooden swastika in his hand. It looked like a wretched grave cross that he had taken from the Mörbisch churchyard, nailing small pieces of wood on it in order to transform it into the victorious symbol. Brandishing the crooked cross, he headed straight toward Fürst and shouted at him; "Kike! You're the rabbi, ain't ya?"

No answer.

"You're a rabbi with peikes and rokelores and on shabbes you kiss the Ark of the Covenant, don't ya?"

No answer.

"If you're not gonna talk, then you're gonna kiss this, you dirty kike, and the padre is gonna sing kyrie eleison."

Aladar Fürst took the swastika and stepped back. But now something utterly unexpected happened. The priest said to us in the cell, and I quote, "A rabbi did what I, a priest, should have done. He righted the wronged cross."

Fürst acted with half-closed eyes, as in a dream, and not even with quick movements. He broke off, one after another, each piece of wood that had turned the cross into a swastika. A deathly hush. No one stopped him. For a long time, Schoch and his men seemed at a loss. Then suddenly, someone yelled, "You kike! Can't you hear?! Hungary's calling you. Run!"

And indeed, Aladar Fürst whirled around and began dashing toward Hungary in wild leaps. He was running for his life. In vain. A shot rang out. Then another. The brownshirts pounced on the felled man, trampling him with hobnailed boots as if trying to stamp him into the earth. Across the border, Hungarian commands resounded. With lowered bayonets, the border guards marched toward the killers, shaking with rage and ready to fight. The major was in the lead, releasing the safety device on his pistol. Schoch and his men discarded their victim, hopped on their motorcycles, and took off, leaving a foul trail of gas. The wounded man was carried to the Hungarian customs house and placed on a trestle. He was unconscious. The major summoned a physician, who arrived soon. He found two shots in the lungs. The poor man also had several broken ribs and serious contusions. The priest was tending to Frau Fürst, who was so traumatized that she had lost her power of speech. With gaping eyes, she crouched next to her husband, desperately and soundlessly moving her lips. The baby's sharp, thin bawling cut through the room. The mother could not give him her breast. Toward morning, Aladar Fürst died. Before the end, he opened his eyes, wide. They were looking for the priest. Their expression was calm, remote, and not uncontent.

By dying, Fürst saved the greater part of his congregation. The major flouted the law, imperiling his own livelihood by allowing them all to cross the border. The old, the sick, the women, the children were permitted to go to Sopron. Five men in their prime stayed behind. The major advised them to head north. He had gotten word that the Czechoslovakian border was open near Bratislava. They would have to find some kind of transportation on the other side of the lake.

"What about you, father?" we all asked in unison.

"I—"

At that moment, the door of the cell flew open, and a guard shouted, "Prince Ernst Esterhazy, report to the processing office for release!"

"Tell me about it tomorrow," said Styxi with the disparaging gesture of a grand seigneur. "I have no time now."

"For God's sake," laughed Hipfinger, "guys like us don' wanna be out in the cold in winter. But a real prince . . ."

Father Felix admonished him, "Don't do anything foolish, your highness, just get away from here as fast as you can. Someone has interceded on your behalf. The opportunity won't knock twice."

"I've gotten quite accustomed to the place," the prince declared sternly. "I'm in no hurry. First I want to hear the rest of your story, Father."

"If you pack your belongings in the meantime."

"I leave my things to you gentlemen, as friendly mementos. Let me leave this place just as I entered it. I bequeath the table clock to Hipfinger. Did you get back home, Father—I mean to Parndorf?"

"Heavens, no. My dear old housekeeper came all the way to

Mörbisch to warn me. My house had been searched, ransacked, my den sealed off. But on Sunday, I somehow made it to Kittsee."

"And did you find the Czech border open?"

"But gentlemen," the priest smiled, "what would I be doing here? That is a devil of a border. You see, it's where Austria, Hungary, and Slovakia meet in the so-called three-country corner, and there is a certain area there, a no-man's-land, and the great Danube flows through it. And all sorts of things took place in that area. For instance, there is a stone dam on the river, but that is not *one* story, it is twenty stories, and I have talked long enough as it is, and our good guard is waiting, your highness."

"Father," Styxi insisted adamantly, "I can endure neither music nor a story without a real ending. Where were you nabbed?"

"Well, I did something very stupid. At a certain point, I was at my wit's end, so I went to a fellow priest. He was sitting in his vaulted medieval chamber like Dr. Faust, taking a drop of Dutch courage, and when he saw me, he mistook me for the Secret Police. He stood up and murmured with a lowered head, like a catacomb Christian, 'I am ready.' And indeed, two Prussians were waiting outside the presbytery, and they knew my name and they took me along right away. That was late Monday night, and on Tuesday, I arrived at Liesl which, after all, is a fortune in misfortune. But you are now rid of this misfortune, your highness. Hurry up! What are you waiting for?"

"I am accustomed to setting my own tempo," said Styxi, adding, "I am actually sorry."

Meanwhile, Hipfinger had piled up the last few things from Styxi's valise on the folding table. With relentless honesty, this expert in petty larceny insisted on duly distributing each item to those of us who remained. He tenderly raised the silver clock to his ear and whispered with the full awe of a connoisseur, "This was bought at Hiess at the Kohlmarkt, and it costs—

Holy Mary, Mother of God—at least four hundred. I shouldn't pawn the clock, I ought to start a new life and rent a villa to house it."

Oddly enough, there was a harmonica among the prince's belongings. Herr Stich asked if he could have it. The dignified town councilor then instantly began to walk to and fro as he wistfully produced yammering chords. His eyes were filled with bright tears. The guard grumbled that he had no more time to wait for the highborn gentleman.

Eying us sternly, Styxi shook each man's hand. Mine last. "As soon as I get home, Bodenheim," he said, "I will attend to your Cella right away. We will concertize together. The girl has a marvelous character. Her touch—all my respect. Like an old lion, and yet she's a child, still sucking lollipops. She has to go out into the world, out of that mousehole."

"Yes, help us, your highness," I stuttered, my throat constricting. "I may never be set free again, there are enough such cases. But Cella . . . Nagy is working for her too."

"Nagy," asked Styxi, raising his head and perking up his ears, then pausing as if to inform me about a prickly matter concerning Zsoltan. But he said nothing.

Chapter 10

Jacques Emanuel Weil's Tale of the Raft on the River

I was certain that he would come.

At my arrival, the instant I was told about the "Burgenland cell," I knew that he would eventually be committed to Liesl.

I was probably thinking of the violent newspaper attack against the Weil firm, which I had only just read on the street. However, a great deal of time wore by after Styxi's release, and I had to endure many unspeakably uniform days and nights before the man whom I was secretly awaiting stepped through the iron cell door.

Meanwhile, all sorts of things had happened. At times, good old Liesl appeared to be sold out not only thrice over, but four or five times. We got new people. Occasionally, seven inmates were breathing in our gray cube of air. Luckily, however, the newcomers vanished quickly, and we four companions, Felix, Stich, Hipfinger, and I, remained alone again, which always created a festive feeling. Among the changing and highly forgettable types who joined us, I was especially bothered by a repulsive man with a weepy, fretful voice, who never gave us a moment's peace. His name was Goldbaum, and he owned a silk-goods store on Mariahilfer Strasse. He would victimize each of us in turn, grabbing his new prey by the coat and tormenting him with long yammering speeches, like the following: "Tell me, sir, why *me*? I am a knight of the Order of Franz Joseph, I subscribed my entire fortune in war bonds, I was wiped out, I rebuilt from scratch, I was wiped out again in the inflation, I rebuilt from scratch once again—by the sweat of my brow, I can tell you. The bank failed, the Depression came, I got through it, with losses, but I got through it, not only the immense taxes, I kept paying out money, more and more, for the government, for charities, for Jewish causes, they came every day, I stinted myself of food, as God is my witness, but I donated and donated, and I always emphasized our social prestige, my daughter Adele frequents not only the Ehrenreich home, but the best Christian society, I can tell you, including the aristocracy, and my son George, a double doctor *sub auspiciis,* his professors say he's a genius, he flirts a little with the left, what can you do, a young man, but so solid, and I visited the Salzburg festival every summer, with my whole family, it cost a bundle, but man does have higher needs, if only to hear Toscanini, and now, tell me, what now, after all the ups and downs of my life, after all my worries and sleepless nights, I believed and I was a patriot, and what now? When I get out of prison—God willing—I'll be a marked man and innocent and plundered, the business world is a battlefield, and a sixty-eight-year-old man with hardening of the arteries and a double hernia, what's to become of me? At best, I'll emigrate, God willing! But where to?"

Another newcomer, Herr Zweymerker, apparently a worker, was the exact opposite of Herr Goldbaum. He literally did not say a word to us. Truculently obsessed with order and cleanliness, he kept polishing his shoes and his suit half the day, and spent the rest of the time perched on his straw mattress with his head lowered and his legs drawn up. Perhaps he scorned us for being bourgeois, perhaps he was hiding his pain, the memory of a difficult experience, perhaps he was crazy. Throughout those weeks, incidentally, I came to learn that one almost never encounters a normal case of mental health. Even Father Felix had his quirks, his "boiling point." Hipfinger hated the mute Zweymerker from the bottom of his heart. He tore into him scornfully whenever and however he could. The loathing that some members of the lower classes feel toward one another can only be compared to the anti-Semitism that one encounters not infrequently among our people. It is a helpless hatred rooted in social self-knowledge, a snobbish hatred. But Hipfinger was known to be a snob. He gazed worshipfully upwards. Styxi's timepiece was more than a costly present, it was an emblem of social success. Luckily, Zweymerker was released two days later.

Unfortunately, a far greater cause of my vexation than those transients was good Herr Stich. I knew all about his personal sufferings, which were somewhat akin to my own, I knew that he was well-meaning and of mediocre intelligence. I also realized that he had fallen victim to a kind of imprisonment psychosis—the priest and Hipfinger pointed it out to me often enough. And yet, I could not help it, I frequently trembled with loathing, my egoistic defensiveness was boundlessly increased by our desperately cramped life. My bête noire was Styxi's bequest, that accursed harmonica. Stich yowled on that instrument almost nonstop. With nervewracking obstinacy, he finally managed to patch together three pieces that he reiterated incessantly: "O du lieber Augustin," the "Marseillaise," and "Vienna, You Alone." Even though I myself, as we know, am not very musical, I *am* Cella's father, after all, and thus accustomed to harmonious sounds; music was sacred for me, and the mere existence of that moaning mouth organ drove me crazy. I pleaded, I begged for mercy, I cursed and threatened. In vain. The priest tried to calm me down; he pointed out that this was how an unhappy man finds refuge from his thoughts.

None of this helped me. I pitied only myself. I was choked by
a diabolical compulsion to listen to that wretched screeching.
I was unable to shut it out. Nor did Herr Stich, even when
arduously using the bucket, fail to squeeze out the "Marseillaise" any less arduously on the harmonica. Then, one morning, I did something rotten, flouting all camaraderie, which is
a hundred times more mandatory in prison than in war. I
lodged a complaint; I reported Herr Stich as a troublemaker.
They confiscated his harmonica as prohibited contraband. The
old man, whose nerves were shattered, burst into tears and
could not be placated. He was not even comforted by Hipfinger's assurance that he had a recorder in view, which he could
get for the Herr Town Councilor very cheaply. Stich did not
listen; instead, he glared at me with wild, venemous eyes. "You
took my child. Your child will be taken in return."

Several hours later, I suffered a violent dizzy spell, blacking
out for several seconds. For weeks, I had been breathing the
pestilential air of the cell. The priest instantly reported that I
was ill. I was led off to a medical examination. On the stairway, I was seized with a wild hope that they would take me
to the prison hospital, which is one astral magnitude closer to
life. There, as a political prisoner, I would also be allowed
visits from Gretl and Cella. The physician merely prescribed
that from now on I was to participate in the Aryan walk in the
prison yard. A mouthful of fresh air, and my nerves swung
back into balance. I cursed my behavior toward poor Stich and
I was embarrassed in front of the priest, and also in front of
Hipfinger.

That evening, Jacques Emanuel Weil was brought to our
Burgenland cell. Upon seeing me, he smiled, although without
surprise. He greeted the priest more heartily. Where did he
know him from?

I had always seen Weil only in a formal fur coat, black suit,
stiff derby, and almost never without gloves. I associated him
with something solemn and sheltered: a moving tower with
blind portholes, hermetically sealed off from life. Three gen-

erations of invincible wealth had formed rings of security around him. The entire life's work of imperiled and distrustful forebears had served the sole purpose of making this system of multiple defenses inviolable. And thus the descendant had become a blind tower and a hermetically walled man, who feels disgust. The world enclosing the battlement of his existence was impure and unpredictable, which was why it aroused his nausea. He always wore gloves because he believed he was afraid of germs; however, these germs were not tiny animals, they were the spirits of the unforeseen, insidiously trying to invade his order, which had been made secure by so many ancestral sacrifices. But now, Weil wore no gloves, and his strong neck was bare, for he had been robbed of his collar and tie, and his jacket was spotted and wrinkled. He concealed his small, milky-white aristocratic hands in his pockets so as not to jeopardize them too greatly.

I confess that I was passionately curious about how Weil would behave in prison—Jacques Emanuel, the born aesthete, whose soul was darkened by any disharmonious object. Jacques Emanuel, the tender collector of rare first editions and ancient antiques. Jacques Emanuel, the hypochondriac, who never dined in a restaurant lest his anxiously coddled health suffer from everyday food and everyday silverware. In contrast to myself, the rich man with the most intricate defenses had never gone through the school of trenches, which had thoroughly weaned me from any number of fussy inhibitions dragged along from my childhood. Yet to my amazement, I saw that Jacques Emanuel Weil behaved no differently than we less fortunate and sensitive mortals in the cell. He even ate the gray lentil soup of Liesl, not without meditative appetite, and with the blackish tin spoon, which he held without visible repugnance in his well-protected hands, and he gratefully took the hard sausage that Hipfinger brought him from the canteen. It was only during calls of nature that he did something odd and bashful: he would cover his face with a large handkerchief. It was clear that Weil must have gone through a powerful experience, thus to overcome his nausea so blatantly. At his very first greeting, the priest shook his head.

"For heaven's sake, Baron, explain one thing to me. I saw you in the motorboat that Monday; you were heading toward the Slovakian side. I reproached myself bitterly for not calling you back and asking you to take me along. But I just don't understand *why* you came back."

"It's quite a story, Father," said Jacques Emanuel, "but I'm the head of our firm, and the Gestapo instantly arrested my younger brothers as hostages and gravely threatened them. You see, my brothers have families, and I am a bachelor. That is why I made my decision."

That night, we cellmates did not sleep very much.

Chapter 11

Two Trips; or,
Who Is Nagy?

One day, before our lives changed radically, Herr Franz Stich suffered a dreadful misfortune. It was, to be sure, not the misfortune that he had been expecting for weeks (the stormy winter weather had not cleared up, and the year 1938 was celebrating a white Easter). Maria survived the treacherous invasion of the cold amazingly well; but Clementine Stich, the town councilor's wife, a cheerfully plump woman in her early fifties, had succumbed to an unexpected stroke. This time, the prisoner was not taken to the prison office; instead, in his cell, he was handed a wire from a relative, who reported the death with no cautious circumlocution, coldheartedly indicating the date and hour of the funeral. Stich mutely handed us the wire. We believed that the distraught man, who had told us a lot about his "youthful missus," would now collapse. After all, for some time now, without the least ground for ultimate despair, he had been behaving very strangely, and not just in regard to the harmonica. However, our fears proved unnecessary. He did not collapse. He seemed to find himself. He developed incredible energy. Of course, this energy focused on one single issue. Herr Stich did not fight to see his wife's body one last time or put his home in order during a brief furlough and take the necessary steps to ensure the future of his sick daughter. Not by a long shot. He said absolutely nothing about Maria. He did not wish to go to his house. His whole mind, his wild efforts were set on being granted two hours' leave for the funeral, so that he could follow his wife's coffin to the graveyard. Afterward, they could lock him up for the rest of his life, for all he cared. I had the impression that the bewildered man did not quite grasp what had happened. His dimmed mind clung desperately to externals. The vain urge for ceremonies, that petty-bourgeois secret, had erupted in Stich's soul, breaking through the thin veneer of libertarianism.

When the warden's office turned down his request, he refused to eat, threatening to go on a hunger strike. He was told that only the Party, and no other authority, could decide on the petitions of political prisoners. The little man began scurrying to and fro in the cell, occasionally emitting a dull roar that fitted in with neither his appearance nor his character. Hipfinger's unequal eyes sparkled. "That ain't the way, Herr Town Councilor! Ya gotta find a different way! Watch me!"

Stationing himself at the door, he clenched his fists and performed a short, sharp drum roll on the metal. Stich, who instantly grasped the lesson, threw himself on the door and hammered against the iron not only with his fists, but with his skull, knees, and feet, bellowing, "These are my rights. I know my rights." Pandemonium broke loose. Hipfinger backed him up with his own short, sharp drumming. The neighboring cells awoke. Soon the entire corridor was drumming on the iron doors. Hipfinger beamed. The old steady customer of Liesl had triggered one of those brief noise revolts, which occasionally erupts in every prison without especially frightening the guards, for such an uprising is merely a flash in the pan ignited by desperation. I was ice-cold. I remained fully introspective. I caught Weil and the priest looking at me in amazement. And yet, an unknown madness passed through me. I went over to Stich's side and began to hammer and scream. My innate irascibility helped me to overcome my embarrassment in front of Felix and Weil. Amid my undimmed awareness, a spirit of possession flew out of me. I had swallowed too much during the last few weeks of imprisonment to keep up my composure. (I especially did not wish to look like a jellyfish and bundle of nerves in the priest's eyes, thereby degrading the memory of Aladar Fürst in some manner that was unclear to me.) But now I had had enough. And even though I might easily have managed to control myself, I gave in to the spirit of possession. I had received no further sign from my near and dear since Gretl's terse letter. Her comforting assurance that they would soon obtain my release had proved to be an empty illusion. I was in prison, presumably for life. If they attacked harmless citizens who had done absolutely nothing hostile against the white-stockings, if they drove them across the border with rifle bullets, then why should they usher a secretary of the Iron Soldiers Ring into freedom after a brief, lenient sentence? What nonsense! All my notions of an open file of charges and defenses were the spawn of an incurable sense of lawfulness, unsupported by any reality. My road from prison had only two possible destinations: concentration camp or death. But perhaps these two were one and the same, and the "or" was an "and."

What had happened to Cella and Gretl? During my gruesome sleepless nights in the cell, I did not have the heart to awaken the priest, like Stich, and talk to him about my family. ("For we belonged together, but were not a unit.") While ransacking my office, they must have found all the lists and documents of the Iron Soldiers Ring—a wealth of incriminating material. Something I had feared for many days was now taking on the color of certainty. They had also arrested Gretl and dragged her off into one of the Viennese prisons, inflicting familiar tortures in order to make her confess things about my patriotic activities. And Cella was roaming around, homeless, penniless, for Gretl's family did not dare take in the child of

an outlaw. I could see Cella hurrying through the streets of
Vienna, accosted by drunken brownshirts. Who could help
her? Scherber was no more. Oh, Scherber's bloody head! I
could see him, whom I had not seen under the sackcloth, lying
on the street, the disheveled gray hair, the smashed nose, the
gaping lips, the dentures protruding with the coagulating wave
of blood. Only Scherber, that genius of a teacher, had truly
recognized Cella's gift. What about Nagy? That hope remained. Nagy would protect Cella. But why was the thought
of Nagy so agonizing? I was incessantly haunted by the vaguely
disparaging manner in which Styxi had spoken about Nagy. I
tried to picture Zsoltan's face. It did not work. While all these
things crisscrossed my mind and, with a strangely cool awareness, I simultaneously mused about my chaotic behavior, we—
Stich, Hipfinger, and I—pounded incessantly on the door. I
noticed that my wild shrieks for Cella drowned out Stich's yells
about his rights.

Our guard came with the judicial police.

"You gentlemen are educated people," he cried, "and you
are being treated here like educated people. But if you are going to conduct yourselves like drunkards after a few pints, then,
by God, there are ways to sober you up."

And he pointed to the handcuffs that the two judicial officers
silently exposed.

"Can't you see," the priest said, "Herr Stich has lost his head.
And no wonder."

Hipfinger joined in as if he had been only a terrified spectator
of the thunder concert:

"Yes, can't you see, sergeant? Herr Stich belongs in the investigation section, in the closed division, not here in Liesl.
You know me, Sergeant, I'm a very peaceful man, I've never
caused any trouble in my life. But this is scandalous, it's out-
rageous, even a quiet man can go crazy here, this is no way to
treat innocent people, no investigation, no hearing, nothing,
these men ought to complain, there are laws."

"I don't know," the guard said somberly, "whether you people will be treated any better at the next station. I'm really curious."

But Stich stamped his feet and kept repeating, "It's my human right. After thirty-three years of marriage, always happy . . . I won't be kept away. I insist. I'll go on a hunger strike."

The door slammed shut. Hipfinger snapped his fingers. "Let's go!"

And we threw ourselves at the door again. The bedlam recommenced. But I no longer raged aimlessly; I had a definite purpose in mind. Only the man who surrendered timidly was doomed to rot here. But the man who rebelled had a chance of leaving this cell, if only to be thrown into solitary confinement. The change of scene alone was a desirable goal. And who could tell, perhaps by being refractory, one could be taken in front of a judge—a kind judge of the old school; that was my dream.

I spent my physical energy. The sweat ran from my forehead. I had seldom known such a sense of relief and joy. About half an hour later, one of the top prison officials showed up personally. He was a fat, easygoing man, who amiably patted Stich on the back.

"Don't do anything foolish, Herr Stich, calm down. What good would it do you to force me to take disciplinary action against you? Besides, you're being released tomorrow morning."

Herr Stich's features wore an expression of irrational happiness. "That's different. If I'm released tomorrow morning, I'll be in time. Thank you, warden. I won't go on a hunger strike."

He sat down on his straw mattress and gave each of us in turn a forlorn look. Finally, his eyes dwelled triumphantly on the priest.

"I am a paying member of Flame, a cremation society," Stich declared, "and I won't allow Clementine to be buried. And I won't tolerate any padre either, for the Good Lord is a supreme fascist. It's true, I tell you."

After those words, he stretched out and went to sleep.

g was still trembling with the agitation of our useless revolt. Never had the hours in the cell been as long as on that afternoon. I sat in a corner with closed eyes, prey to the most horrible daydreams. I was haunted by the prison official's words: "Besides, you're being released tomorrow morning." Weil sat down with me. He tried to start a conversation in his strangely remote and blind way, in order to distract me. I did not respond, and I suffered from rejecting his kindness.

That evening, Hipfinger returned to the cell from his KP later than normal. Usually, nothing could get him down, but now he seemed rather worried. He secretly slipped a tiny box, somewhat larger than a watch, into my hand.

"A puzzle, Herr Doctor," he whispered, "keep it as a present from Hipfinger. Look, the red and blue marbles have to get into the right holes; it's not so easy. It's a game for intellectuals. As a souvenir, Herr Doctor."

I held Hipfinger's puzzle irresolutely in my hand. But he leaned over to my ear.

"I don't think Herr Stich'll be going to his old lady's funeral, Herr Doctor. An SS division arrived today. The first transport of political prisoners is being assembled tomorrow."

And he heaved a deep sigh.

"But for a simple looter . . . If ever you need anything from Hipfinger, Herr Doctor, I mean after the whole hullabaloo, under normal conditions, you can always reach me care of Café Bummerl on Taborstrasse."

We were some 150 men, and we had to form a double line in the long corridor outside the prison office. The priest, Weil, and I kept close together so that whatever might happen, fate would not tear apart our comradeship. Stich, on the other hand, did not seem worried. He trusted the prison official's somber words, interpreting them as he wished. The bewildered man's face had shriveled up like last year's apple. His moustache with the thick, wild stubble around it formed a wide gray cuff, swallowing up his chin and mouth. His eyes darted to and fro, nervously and fiercely. He kept shifting from one foot to the other. "If only I can get there in time," he repeated a hundred times, "so that I can make all the arrangements; it's my right, gentlemen, isn't it?"

Hipfinger, who was busy in the corridor, grimaced at us encouragingly. I saw the huge gap in his teeth, which added a pitiable touch to his daring roguishness.

"At the Café Bummerl, please jot it down, gentlemen," he called, and those were his farewell words to us.

We were led in groups of five to the prison office, where the things that had been taken from us at our arrival were returned to us. Beside the official who opened the sacks containing our belongings, a tall man in a black SS uniform stood motionless. He gazed past us as if it were his duty not to soil his eyes through contact with such vermin. Before handing me my pocketknife, the prison official turned inquiringly toward the tall man, who, to judge by his accent and posture, appeared to be a Prussian.

"Go ahead," he said. "Pocketknives, razors, suspenders, belts, string, glass fragments, rusty nails—they're all allowed. We have no objection if Jews and Communists call it quits. The more the merrier. Besides, the right to suicide is one of the philosophical concerns of the Movement."

Now we had to march out double file to the large prison yard. Here, we were awaited by three "Black Marias" and also a large truck. The policemen gazed at us, not without sarcastic pity. For now the SS was receiving us from their mild hands. Several members of this famous model troop marched up, counted us, and subdivided us into groups of seven. The SS men were all handsome, each like the next, tall, narrow, symmetrical, with small blond heads and military haircuts, broad shoulders, and slender hips. I watched them with a cool curiosity, which I found incomprehensible in this situation. If one trusted a first impression, one could truly consider them the astonishingly homogeneous representatives of a new master race. Their faces, however, were—I can describe it no better— virtually faceless. A rock had more face than they, not to mention a tree or a flower.

Everything was present in pretty regularity, eyes, nose, mouth. It all moved and lived, yet the expression was no more personal than an item off the assembly line. I remembered Weil's statement in the Castle Park. (How inconceivably long ago that was!) *"One* single mother could have given birth to this entire generation—an inconceivable mother, to be sure." Weil was right. Mother Nature seemed to have been confused by technology and was now bringing forth only types instead of individuals. What secret goal of hers could this type be serving? In one of our conversations in the cell, Father Felix had called the SS the sons of Lucifer. I now rejected his comment. I picture Lucifer as the Evil One not only in all his evil, but also in the noble sadness of the fallen angel. Evil exists only because there is good. Evil constitutes the other pole of an antithesis, and it is inextricably linked to intellect and criticism. Those men were no more evil than they were good. Whatever diabolism they seemed capable of, they had nothing to do with the devil. The devil is accessible because he has a mind. Even Nature and her tremendous indifference can be overcome now and then if one uses the proper methods. The only thing that proves inaccessible and invincible once it has been set in motion is the machine, the automaton, the golem. The faces of these men showed a grandiose blankness and non-individuality, such as have probably never existed before in history. They appeared to be nothing but transmissions of someone else's will, which, for them, signified life itself. They were as clean, as exact, as mindless, as conscienceless as engines. They waited only to be switched on or off. Their sole morality was to keep their fuel and spark plugs in order. Motor-men. That was why life was so easy for them. That was why their faces had the beauty of mannequins, and none of the thousand torments that they produced every day left the slightest crease in their faces. Those were the men at whose mercy we were—and the word "mercy" could no more be applied to them than "good" or "evil."

Our group was roughly in the middle of the long double file. Aside from us four cellmates, there were three other men. One of them, a forty-year-old worker with a craggy, impenetrable face, carried a worn knapsack. (I myself held my few belongings in a bundle wedged under my arm.) The two others were elderly gentlemen who looked like high-level officials; their faces were deathly pale with white stubble. From the lifelong consciousness of guaranteed privilege, they had plunged into the depths of a disgrace that they were not yet able to feel fully. Their entire crime was the self-evident virtue of colorless bureaucrats; loyalty to the state that gave them a livelihood and honor. In the past, they had served the Kaiser as devotedly as the Austrian republic, whichever party was in power. Now they probably cursed their loyalty, or indolence, which had hindered them from betraying their oath of office, amiably supporting the destructive activities of the white-stockings, and adding their names to the Party register in Munich years ago, like their shrewder colleagues. What devil of decency must have gotten into them that, trusting in their government, they had fought the traitors instead of sucking up to them. Their exhausted eyes gaped with the question of madness: "Is it possible that abiding by one's oath to uphold the law can be a crime?" The handsome motor-men did not concern themselves with the wild eyes of their victims. For them, we were all nothing but an obstruction in the machine, something to be removed. We were only a generation apart. But that gap was enough to free them of the voluntary burden that mankind had been carrying for thousands of years. Their physiques and the blankness of their faces demonstrated that they were "free" in some inconceivable manner.

It started on the left flank. A command snarled: "Right face! Follow me!" The first group was stowed away in the truck.

I saw that Stich was starting to get nervous. "I won't get to the bus in time," he croaked softly. The priest grabbed his arm. "Don't do anything foolish, Stich. For God's sake."

The shrunken face twisted in the gray beard. "But I have to get there in time. I don't want her to be buried."

"You're an old Socialist, Stich," the priest hissed. "Pull yourself together. Think of your fellow Socialists. Do you want them to find out that you behaved like a milksop?"

"Who cares!" the bewildered man clucked. "The warden assured me . . ."

Now I was overwhelmed by anger; I grabbed Stich's other arm and squeezed it. "Stop pretending, Stich," I whispered. "No one believes you're crazy. Do you want to have us all killed? You know very well where they're taking us. Your wife is dead, and mine's alive. But I'll never see her again either in this life."

There were only three groups ahead of us now. A wild energy shot through Stich's small body. His breath rattled. And suddenly he yelled, and his yell went far beyond the bleak prison yard. "I protest . . . A human right . . . I protest."

What happened next came lightning-fast. The motor-men broke into our file. I could hear the priest shouting, "Please, the man's nerves are shot!"

Then I received a punch in the back of my neck, and I saw stars. For a while, I did not know where I was. When I came to, I saw Stich floating off in the arms of some SS men. His shrill "I protest" was swiftly moving away. We were shoved into the Black Maria with kicks and rifle butts. At the time, we did not know what fate lay in store for a "mutineer." My shirt was soaked with ice-cold sweat. A mangy dawn oozed through the barred window. Opposite me, I saw Weil, the blind tower. His face was as rigid and motionless as ever. But huge, round tears, like thick drops of wax, were rolling down his still virtually polished cheeks. Moving his bluish lips, he said, without hearing himself, "This is unpleasant . . . extremely unpleasant. . . ."

I endured it for only one day. As I write this down, I wonder how Jacques Emanuel and Father Felix could suffer through it month after month—they, who were so much unluckier than I, and whom no one helped. Yet, in the very first hour of my brief descent into hell, I felt that secret strength rising in me, the energy that provides a Herculean equanimity for a human being, especially one who is mentally alert. The flow of oblivion increased every second. No sooner had the Black Maria lumbered off than poor Stich vanished utterly from my consciousness, even though I had shared life in a cramped cell with him for so many weeks. The rapids of the tormenting events roared and roared, and I felt as if I were not so much whirling in their midst as standing on the bank, attentive and uninvolved. I was less a victim than a witness of these events. My harrowing of hell occurred in a haze of apathetic dreaminess, which is one of the most ingenious protective devices of life. Of course, I had not been beaten, I had not suffered one of the infamous thrashings, I had not been physically tormented in any way, a kind star shone on me. Otherwise, I do not believe I could have held out.

We were unloaded somewhere or other. I did not recognize the area; there was a very large schoolhouse, and we were again driven through the wide-open entranceway with kicks and rifle butts. We found ourselves in a long gymnasium, where hundreds of men were penned in. I saw the familiar apparatus along the walls—ladders, ropes, rings, horizontal bars, parallel bars, leather horses, leather bucks. The place smelled of fear and sweat and dust and of the equipment. In my youth, I was not a bad gymnast, and we had had a similar gymnasium in our school. But now the equipment seemed like magical works of the archenemy, and I could not comprehend that I had been such a gullible boy, trusting them, making friends with them, whereas they should have been taboo. Half the crowd in the gymnasium consisted of our people, the other half of "Aryans" subject to the law of revenge. The black motor-men were already having a good time fishing real ghetto figures from the timid throng, old men in caftans or other things recalling the cartoons in satirical newspapers. (How well I understood their ugliness! It reminded me of the column of scrubbers to which the leather-jackets had dragged me. Within just a few minutes, the degradation had turned an aristocrat and an elegant old lady into ghostly scarecrows, to the side-splitting amusement of the gapers. In these terms, the ugliness of these cartoon figures here, formed by two millennia of persecution and humiliation, was more endurable.)

The motor-men shoved their finds over to the equipment. There the victims had to climb up and down the ladder with clumsy hands and feet. There, lamentably and helplessly, they clung to the ropes, to the rings and bars, for the men were mostly old. One of the walls sported a gigantic poster. I read the words in scarlet capitals: THE UPRISING OF THE GERMAN PEOPLE IS VICTORIOUS. Where was the people that had risen up? Was this a revolution, playing havoc with the weakest and most defenseless? The dismal, misshapen men climbed and dangled until they collapsed. Then others had to take their places.

However, from a side room—and this was what, strangely enough, produced the horrible, dreamlike impression—came a penetrating voice, a tenor, whose sustained singing, rising up to coloraturas, occasionally broke off with a cry of pain, only to recommence. The motor-men were holding a cantor, forcing him, amid splutters of mirth, to perform his holy prayers in the style of Hebrew liturgy. Sometimes it sounded like a fearful lunatic screeching, but then again it sounded like a full, proud call to the heavens, as if the worshiper knew that he had aroused God's dark attention *de profundis*.

The hours wore on in the stench of this gymnasium. We stood side by side, the priest, Weil, and I, with green faces, hungry, for we had not eaten a bite of food all morning. Names were constantly called out—no, yelled out. Then someone in the crowd would respond with a choked, faltering "Here!" The monkeylike gymnastics on the equipment continued uninterruptedly. The motor-men kicked and punched anyone who wanted to break off his twitching St. Vitus's dance on the rings or bars. The cantor's voice was croaking. Only a hoarse rattle came from the side room every now and then. It was replaced by a bellowed but incomprehensible declamation. They were forcing a victim to read something shameful in a loud voice. Voluptuous bursts of laughter shredded the harried delivery.

One of my joys in prison was that I had been allowed to keep my watch. I would carefully wind it there, twice a day. I always knew the hour and the minute. I looked at my watch countless times, as if to hold fast to the orderly course of waiting. I allied myself with precise time to fight against imprecise time. But last night, after Hipfinger had brought me the anguishing news along with his puzzle, I had forgotten, for the very first time, to wind my watch. Now I had no idea what time it was. Nor did I ask anyone. However, the afternoon seemed well advanced when our names were finally hollered, and we too called out our terrified "Here." We were taken to a room on the second floor. It was the conference room. On the wall, a bright cross in the middle of the green wallpaper indicated the place where the victors over Christ had removed the crucifix. Next to it hung the usual school pictures depicting the *forum romanum* and Emperor Maximilian with his crossbow and spear, straying through the Tyrolian mountains. Aside from a few glass cases filled with zoological and botanical teaching aids, the room was almost completely cleared. It was dominated by a light-yellow desk. The desk stood on a huge carpet which, oddly enough, was half rolled back, exposing the parquet floor. We were virtually standing on the open sea, while the desk and its territory formed an unapproachable continent. Something was ducking behind the desk, promptly reminding me of Peter Schoch's Inbichler, the stationmaster of Pandorf. The priest must have thought the same thing. This person was a short, slightly stunted fanatic with belligerently sparkling glasses. In those days, every troop of handsome, violent men had such a scrawny troll attached to it—in essence, the physically deformed intellect of the attractive muscle power. And this was the case here too. Our motor-men retreated respectfully behind the back of the troll with the glittering glasses. Like most of his sort, this one had risen up, after the eleventh of March, from one of the foul-smelling office vaults of hopeless obsequiousness. For decades, he had probably bared his hateful post-office face to the public, selling it stamps or registering its letters. Showing that public who was boss, letting the impatient wait, slamming the window down prematurely— that was an inadequate pleasure, which could not make up for lifelong starvation wages and the misery of remaining on the bottom forever. But now the clerk-face of all clerk-faces had redeemed him and raised him to a breathtaking heaven of masters. Before us sat the petty bourgeois in an explosive state, reading out our names with an ardent and blissful grinding of his teeth. First he snapped at the priest, "Repeat after me: 'I am a Jew-padre and subhuman.' "

"I am a Jew-padre," said Felix, cheery and straightforward, almost smiling. I myself was utterly calm, as always at such moments. I had, so to speak, "parked" my life and become a mirror of observation, as if I were present with only a trivial part of myself. I concluded that the cowering troll behind the desk was no postal clerk, but a high-school teacher. Subject: geography and history. The presumed teacher now tore into Jacques Emanuel. "Herr Weil! What an honor! Welcome! Did the baron have a good trip? Repeat after me: I am a Jewish pig and a Marxist subhuman!"

The head of the house of S. Weil & Sons gazed blankly at the troll. "A Jewish pig perhaps. But a Marxist? I'm an industrialist."

"That's just it," the troll mocked, "that's a speciality. Exploiting the German nation, extorting from it, poisoning and destroying it. You donated millions to arm the workers. Do you deny that?"

"I do not possess such millions to donate. But anything I

donated was to save Austria and call the hereditary imperial house back into the country."

The history teacher doubled over with mirth. "The Hapsburgs, the Jews' emperors, who screwed up the Ostmark for centuries. They were going to obstruct the führer's plans and block the victorious path of our nation. And all Jewish pigs and Marxist subhumans and moronic counts and lecherous padres and candle women and salon lions and doddery old men and intellectuals—they were all loyal to Hapsburg, to the kings of Judah. And you actually think that your confession can improve your situation? We know everything; we are familiar with every minute of your life, every penny that you gave the Reds to buy weapons with. We know all about you, and about that man next to you, the kike and Marxist, legitimist subhuman, a notorious provocateur."

He glanced at his papers and bellowed at me, "Bodenheim! Repeat after me: I am a Jewish swine and a Marxist, legitimist provocateur."

"More than anything, I'm a war veteran," I said, "and I fought at the front lines in eight of the eleven battles of Isonzo."

There was a hush. The motor-men behind our inquisitor looked at me as I dangled the chain of my medals between two fingers. For the length of five seconds, I had an indisputable success. I had to control myself not to ask the troll, "And at which front lines did you serve, sir?" With great effort, I held my tongue. At the same time, however, I could not stifle a very ludicrous desire: I felt irresistibly drawn to the so conspicuously folded carpet, the continent of the troll. I took a long pace and stood on the forbidden island. The troll turned beetred and leaped up, as if my step had wounded him far more deeply then my reference to the world war. The carpet truly appeared to have symbolic meaning.

"Get back, you!" the party functionary shouted. "Don't you dare. My carpet is not for subhumans."

Then he turned to the ringleader of the motor-men. "It is not my job to discuss things."

The ringleader shook his head.

"I am to determine and dictate."

The ringleader nodded.

"So all three, like the previous ones . . ."

"Up against the wall?" asked the ringleader.

"Up against the wall," said the troll.

We were driven down the steps at a run and shoved into a rather dark room. It was the large toilet of the school; to the right, a row of booths; to the left, a long wall, tarred black to a height of six feet, with water thinly trickling down. The lighting fixture was covered with a black cloth, which explained the darkness. The effect was both grotesque and theatrical. Several men already stood there facing the tarred wall, their toes in the gutter. Two splendid specimens of the SS waited in the door with revolvers ready to shoot. "Don't be afraid," the priest whispered to me when they ordered us to face the wall of the toilet. The ringleader's voice boomed through the hollow room. "If anyone lets out a peep, he'll be taken care of right away. The others after the written order is completed."

The priest did not have to buoy my spirits. I was not afraid. I knew precisely that they were playing a game they had concocted to toy with our nerves. A bogus execution in the children's toilet of a school. People had read about such things. The imagination of the motor-men was excellently animated by detective stories and gangster movies. The electric bulb inside the pall exposed the entire corrupt falseness of their project. And yet, one must undergo such an experience to know what "time" is and "uncertainty," this deepest foundation of human life. I am not speaking of faith, no, our most obvious knowledge hangs on a thread. There are situations in which any certain fact disintegrates. That is why "realism," so renowned, is as taxing on the will as any mystical assumptions. The world can be what it wants to be—but it takes place exclusively in our minds.

I was not afraid. Good! I felt the falsity of the whole busi-

ness. I told myself: Things have gone well so far. I have suffered no harm. It could have been a lot worse. Maybe they'll
send us home after this procedure. And if they take us to a
concentration camp, I can't do anything either. There are no
loose ends in my life. I don't give a damn. How sharply the
children's urine smells, despite the tar. I will now close my
eyes. And I am standing in the toilet of our old high school.
And the boy next to me is Nagy, already elegant back then,
Zsoltan, although his clothes were retailored from his Papa's
cast-off suits. Nagy passionately denied it, but Myslivec could
not be fooled. I am astonished when I think of the richly hung
private gallery of the *père noble,* who was discredited among
decent people (my father, for example), but thrilled me with
the thought of his aristocratic chosenness. Now we stand together, facing the tarred wall, Zsoltan and I, shooting the weak
stream down from our undeveloped bodies. Clumsy Pramer is
probably on the other side of Zsoltan, and Nagy is teasing him
once again. He does so inimitably. Not even I can distinguish
between truth and bluffing in him. What would happen now
if Nagy flashed his cigarette case, the black case, which he says
is made of tula metal and is an old Russian snuffbox. Count
Appony (he says) gave it to Nagy's father. I would do anything
for a cigarette. Nothing matters to me now, except for this
craving, which makes my diaphragm cramp up. Does nothing
really matter to me? Can I really count on this falsity, which I
talk myself into so carelessly? All of us standing against this
tarred wall have long since been crossed out from the registers
of the living. In the French and Russian revolutions, they at
least held trials, so that the semblance of lawfulness would not
vanish from the world. But something completely new is taking
place here: the expulsion of the "subhuman" from the legal
structure of life. Oh, far worse things are happening. We are
not being granted even the rights of dogs and cats, not to mention more valuable domestic animals. An artificial jungle is being set up around us, a technological forest, which is wolfing
us down. One of these motor-men only has to feel like pointing

his mighty revolver at the back of my head and press his finger very lightly on the catch. Shot at this close range, the human skull bursts like a raw egg. If the motor-man gives in to this stirring, he risks nothing. He will most likely even be praised. This is known as a "heroic attitude" and a "perilous life." And it really takes great strength of mind to spatter human blood and brains from a few inches away, even if they belong to a subhuman. I am standing between Weil and the priest. My hands twitch. They no longer wish to be alone. They grope toward the hands of my fellow victims. The priest's right hand is warm and solid. It calmly squeezes mine. Weil's left hand, that milk-white entity, estranged from life, is hot, wet, and slack. We remain hand in hand for awhile. The falsity seems less and less certain to me. But I feel that my doubts will wrestle me down if my mind cannot flee them. My head is already roaring with fear of a dizzy spell, to which I succumbed in the cell just a few weeks ago. I have to evoke proud, resolute, virile memories in me. The war! But I can think of nothing proud or virile. I see only the city of Görz, shelled to bits, a foul-smelling ruin. The line of abandoned trenches, filled with black puddles, heaps of excrement, rusty tin cans, and parts of bodies, meanders through the streets and collapsed houses. Nothing fazes the scores of overly busy rats, as large as cats. But we officers sit and drink amid the ruins in a red-carpeted bar with red lampshades. We are dunned by old frontline whores with bad teeth and desiccated limbs. Someone pointed out the famous Major Grollmüller. If only we had had another week! If only that accursed plebescite had not interfered! We would have raised enough men to occupy the borders. Who knows whether they would have dared to march in. A great struggle for freedom! The world would . . . What would the world have done? I do not know. I know nothing. I do not even know the source of the music I now hear. A piano. Far away, but energetic. The music is not all that remote. I believe the piano is playing inside me. In the pit of my stomach, where a strange warmth is suddenly spreading, as if from an electric heating pad. Just look, Cella has come to me. And it must be Bach, playing tag with a fugue in the pit of my stomach, resounding all the way up to my ears. She does not remove her foot from the pedal. Is Cella thinking of me now? I do not care for this. They say that just before dying, a human being encounters the dearest thing he has on earth. Is that no mere fairy tale? Creaking steps behind us. New motor-men have probably arrived. They are bringing the completed order. Where will they begin? At the right or the left? I am the second from the right. If I cannot turn around now, I will die without being shot. I hear low voices behind my back, which is starting to burn as if it were exposed to the tropical sun. I must, I must turn around and gaze at death. At the other end, a weak cry. Someone collapses. I turn around. We all turn with gaping eyes. A whistle shrills. An order is barked: "In the corridor—fall in! Double time!"

Our train stood far outside Vienna's Western Terminal, on one of the hundred switching tracks, for the liberated nation was not supposed to set eyes on us. There were at least five hundred of us, forming the large transport to the concentration camp of Dachau, near Munich. First they had stuffed us into a shed, where we had waited and waited, for hours on end. We had finally been fed something after that grueling day of fasting. They had actually given us a hot, ample meal, goulash with potatoes and beer and bread galore, and afterward even coffee with milk. The cat had no interest in weakening the mouse ahead of time. We were escorted by fifty motor-men, who were subordinate to Prussian unit commanders. It must have been past nine when they drove us to the train in groups and in double time. Double time was the only pace at which we subhumans were allowed to move. Our train consisted of ancient, sooty, foul-smelling third-class cars, which had been wrested from their sleep of death in some graveyard of worn-out railroad equipment. Each train compartment had eight

seats. Two were reserved for the comfort of the accompanying
motor-man; their limits were indicated by bayonets thrust into
the wood. God help the man who came too close. Every compartment group of prisoners comprised ten men, who had to
make do with six seats. Setting foot into the train corridor was
punishable by death. The commanders solved the space problem without delay: eight men had to squeeze together on six
seats and the remaining two had to sit on the filth-encrusted
floor, one with his back to the open corridor, the other with
his back to the window. This fate was reserved for Weil and
myself, who, according to our warrants, were among the lowest of the low subhumans; after all, in the eyes of the victors,
we combined three inexcusable traits: dishonorable birth, support of Socialism, and loyalty to the Austrian Kaiser. I was
ordered to sit under the window. There, I at least had something to prop myself against, whereas Weil, large and stiff-
jointed, endured the far worse fate of having to sit with his
protruding back toward the open corridor. I could see that
Jacques Emanuel's awkward, perhaps rheumatic body suffered
from the agony of having to sit there. The train was still standing, but the sweat already began to run down his cheeks. It
was strange enough that he kept on his stiff black derby, that
dignified sign of a bourgeois security from which he had been
expelled long ago, a sign belied by his battered clothing.

   Our group had not been torn apart. The worker with the
knapsack, the two high-placed officials, whose faces now
looked blank with bewilderment—they were all in the compartment, along with two younger men, who barely spoke, but
listened intently and sometimes exchanged barely perceptible
glances. We assumed they were informers—rightly or wrongly,
I do not know. Of course, what could they have spied out of
us that the inquisitorial postal clerks, teaching assistants, and
stationmasters did not know? There are only three kinds of
people in any dictatorship: executioners, informers, and those
who are informed on. There was one other man in our group.
He was a handsome, sprightly, dignified old man in an impec-

cable black overcoat, obviously made by a first-class tailor. He had obviously been arrested just a few hours ago in his office or home without being allowed to change clothes. He wore striped trousers and fine, thin, buttoned shoes with patent-leather tips. Everything about him had a deliberately old-fashioned touch. Large, tawny bags hung under his eyes, indicating a gentle, emotional life, diplomatic experience, and a keen sense of all solemn and majestic things. Calculation and decorative charity were neighbors in his face, which was framed by the loveliest white beard imaginable. I, in any case, had never seen such a beard—so frothy, so thick, so well groomed, so vain: the solicitously coddled memorial to a past that now could scarcely be understood. The owner of this challenging adornment of dignity (I instantly felt great anxieties about him) bowed to all sides and gave us his name: Freudreich! Yes, indeed, it was Freudreich, director of the Danube Bank—a supreme star of international banking, whom not even the anti-Semitism that had been making advances for the past five years had managed to drive from office. It is well known that British capital has a considerable share in the Danube Bank, and it is widely known that Freudreich and no other Austrian banker enjoyed the rock-solid trust of London. The Freudreich fortress resembled the Maginot Line: it was safeguarded not only above ground but also below by intricate passages, tricky snares, and a vast system of reciprocity. Until the eleventh of March, none of the insiders who still suspected that international events were a failure of the capitalist system would have nurtured even the slightest doubt that the Freudreich stronghold was invincible. He himself, the old man with the lovely beard and the mild bags under his eyes, seemed unwilling to believe it even here and now, for he flashed encouraging smiles at everyone as if to put our minds at ease. "It must be a mistake, a complete misunderstanding. I have an appointment with the minister of finance tomorrow, because of the developments. My friend, the British ambassador, will take immediate steps. It is a mistake."

The train shoved and moaned as if rolling on the axles of
farm wagons. It stole through the Maytime atmosphere of the
Vienna woods. A full moon shone, and the air smelled of leafy
forests. But we were not permitted to open the window. Now
the motor-man stepped over Weil's body and mine, using our
legs as a path to reach his double seat. He sat down leisurely
between the bayonets, lighting a Virginia cigar, whose fra-
grance I inhaled pleasurably. Then he honored us with an address that he seemed to regard as the acme of upright kindness,
so far as it was allowed by the heroic mentality. "So now listen, you subhumans," he puffed, "and listen good. You're going to a camp for retraining. Dachau, you oughta know, is
several things at once. Everyone there has one foot in a sanatorium and one foot in a mass grave. I say 'sanatorium' because
of the great cold-water treatment, the crash diet, the hardening, and the outdoor physical activities. The fat slobs with
hardening of the arteries can congratulate themselves, for we
guarantee that you'll get healthy, and your lousy lives'll be
extended, even though they're senseless now. Unfortunately,
we can't offer you a private room and bath. But the camp's got
twenty towers, and every tower has two heavy machine guns
and a big spotlight, and every one of those spotlights is aimed
at one of the barracks, where you swine are gonna be sleeping.
And you subhumans oughta know that sleepytime is real special in the camp. For instance, if you talk in your sleep, then
you're a mutineer and you wind up in the mass grave. So just
to make sure you don't talk in your sleep and end up in the
mass grave, the spotlights feel up your straw mattresses like
this, you see. . . ." And his finger slowly and impressively
traced out the path of the lightbeam. "Understand? The spotlight crawls across your face every ten seconds, so that no one
talks in his sleep or has nightmares. You'll have to get used to
that. And just to make sure you get used to that in time, they've
handed down a rule here. You're lucky, the light in this lousy
car is weak.

"So listen carefully: everyone look up there into the light and don't move your eyes, don't turn your heads, understand? I'm going out now, I can't bear your stench, but I see everything. If anyone looks away, turns his head, or falls asleep, I'll give ya a left hook, and you get one point. When you get three points, you'll be killed and thrown off the train, do you understand?"

He stood up and calmly trod on my legs with his full weight, stopping in his tracks, for Freudreich began to speak eagerly. "There must be a mistake, commander. They could not have meant me."

"Don't matter. All the better. Someone else got lucky. We don't care who we get."

"I am Freudreich, director of the Danube Bank."

"What are you? You're a kike!"

"Just a few months ago, Reich Minister Schacht paid me his respects. I have been admitted; without me they cannot . . . It is obviously a mistake."

"So, then we'll retrain you by mistake. You're gonna learn to wipe your ass with your beard. Then you can do your own vaudeville act."

The informers cackled obligingly. The bank director looked around with an astonished and incredulous smile. The motor-man let out a military snarl: "All eyes on the light!"

Then he kicked Weil aside and vanished in the corridor. We sat there, staring at the dirty light bulb with its carbon filaments glowing reddishly. I knew about the famous water torture from cowboy-and-Indian books I had read as a boy: a big drop of ice-cold water falls with dreadful regularity on the shaven head of the immobilized prisoner, whose hands and feet are tied. Within just a few hours he is hopelessly insane. The motor-men too had their romantic side, outdoing themselves with inventions from the sphere of gangland and the Wild West. Peering into light sounds harmless, but it is a torture that increases from minute to minute; the eyes begin to water, the blood shoots into the head, the scalp tightens, the back of the neck stiffens. One would like to die, leap out of one's skin, quite literally.

Weil began to reel; he reached out for the priest, who took his hands; his head sank to the side, he closed his eyes. However, our motor-man was already standing there, and he punched Weil in the back of the neck. The derby rolled into the corridor. Weil's bald head shone with perspiration, as if he had been bathing.

"Number one," the slave driver noted. But Freudreich had gotten to his feet. He was still smiling with mild superiority.

"It is completely out of the question. One cannot just leave home like that. Without soap or a toothbrush. I—"

"Get down, or I'll give you a point," the motor-man threatened.

But Freudreich's mild, dignified face suddenly flashed with unyielding energy. "The matter must be cleared up. I demand my rights. I insist on seeing the commander of the transport."

"You'd better not ask for that, kike," the motor-man guffawed.

But Freudreich straightened up and looked very imposing. "I insist, and immediately. I must point out to you that this mistake will have international ramifications."

The motor-man thrust the half-smoked Virginia cigar behind his ear. "Oh, go on, go on, Herr Director," he smirked.

Freudreich's features instantly grew gentle and solemn again. They seemed to announce: I did not doubt for even an instant that I am a very special case, given my position. Out loud, however, he spoke like a grand seigneur, one of whose virtues is majestic friendliness toward inferiors. "Thank you, commander. That is very kind of you. Everything will be cleared up right away."

Then he gingerly stepped across us in his delicate buttoned shoes. But the motor-man grabbed him by his velvet collar and shoved him along the corridor.

"How can a smart man be so stupid," said one of the informers. He was ignored. After a while, one of the government officials asked, "Where are we now?"

"Maybe half an hour from Sankt Pölten," the other answered.

The first one sighed. "If we go on like this, it'll take us fourteen hours to get to Munich."

"Are you that anxious to get to Dachau?" The other informer laughed. "Here, we're still sort of travelers, tourists."

Weil moaned loudly. "I don't think I can endure sitting like this much longer."

I pushed myself up and offered to change places with him so he could have something to lean on. The guard was gone; we could risk it. It was not easy getting Weil on his feet. When he finally sat under the window, he breathed fast, as if he had been running for a long time. The priest warned us: "Careful. Someone's coming. Everybody look at the light again. I'll tell you a joke I heard recently."

I had never seen the unflappable redhead as pale and earnest as at this moment. He mustered all his strength to serve as our pastor, if only by telling us anecdotes to help us through the torment of this journey.

"In heaven," he began, "the greatest men are talking about the most impressive miracles they have ever encountered. Moses says, 'I saw the burning bush, which burned without being consumed—' "

The priest got no further, for our slave driver stood behind me, yelling, "You changed places. Without my permission. What's your name, kike?"

"My name is Bodenheim."

"Well, you've got something to look forward to, Bodenheim, you mutineer. We're gonna reach Sankt Pölten in ten minutes. Then we're gonna show you."

He turned away, for a bizarre whimpering was approaching, a sobbing singsong that drowned out the noise of the train. Two motor-men dragged Freudreich in and dumped him into our compartment. His overcoat and jacket had been stolen. His white silk shirt was shredded and bloodstained. The blood was running from his beard. But it was no longer the white, frothy, well-groomed beard, the flowing insignia of an almost episcopal rank in the hierarchy of money. It was a thin, disheveled tangle of gray hair and bloody threads. The commander, to ensure enlightenment, had ordered his men to rip out that splendid beard at one swoop. Broad patches of skin had gone along with the white tufts, and the naked flesh was visible. Freudreich's face presented a sight both dreadful and lofty. Within half an hour, it had been transformed from the well-kept mask of the bank magnate to the terrifyingly sincere countenance of the Wandering Jew. It gazed at us with eyes that were a thousand years old: they knew the entire truth. The bloody lips did not yet seem to know this truth, for they kept murmuring as before, "It is a mistake. They did not mean me."

They do not mean you, Freudreich! They do not mean me. Whom do they mean? Israel is not a nation, Israel is an order of the blood, which one enters by birth, involuntarily. There is nothing voluntary in Israel. A prehistoric oath must be honored by the children, generation after generation, whether they wish to or not. This order of the blood is bound not by space, but by time, in an eternal debt without the benefit of any statute of limitation. The people of 1938 are not exempted from the payment day of the people who lived under Nebuchadnezzar, Nero, or Torquemada. Sometimes this destiny lurks for decades, in a leisurely fashion, so that the victim can grow nice and fat from his peculiar debt and stretch out pleasurably in the delusion of ownership and oblivion, a mirage that is permitted other mortals. But then an hour leaps up, and the ancient oath suddenly falls due. For the strange order to which you belong, Freudreich, is thought of as a penitential and mendicant order. You once came to the imperial city of Vienna from some Moravian nest; you were a poor student, and all you had was your father's blessing, two letters of recommendation, and your convoluted acumen. You entered the homes of the wealthy as a tutor in order to help their offspring through school—the already sluggish children of the second and third generation. One of these rich men took you as his son-in-law. Everything you touched turned to gold—money, that self-willed feline, sprang into your lap, purring, so you would cuddle it. And with money came power, and with power came honor, and with honor came splendor, and all these archangels bowed before you, for you grew up in an orderly world and knew nothing about the enigmatic tides, the ebb and flow of our destiny. The Austrian Kaiser himself made you a governor, Freudreich, a pasha of finance and capital, and he shook your hand, and your arm reached around the entire globe, and on the lapel of your tuxedo the grand cordons of all kings blossomed like tropical orchids. And your mansion, which you built in the center of the city, was frequented by princes and barons, ambassadors and envoys, cabinet members and governors, scholars and stage stars, and they all praised you and admired the paintings on your walls and the foods and wines on your table. The beautiful beard that covered your lips and chin turned gray, and you became a patriarch of business life, an epitome, and your life seemed to be concluding in harmony. You had no end of good fortune. Only the end could be its end. From your blood, Freudreich, you expelled memory like a poison, and Israel remained in a separate depth of your soul like black groundwater in a forgotten grave.

Did you not celebrate your seventieth birthday just a few months ago, and did not all newspapers feature lengthy articles about your dazzling life? And then Friday came for you too. And on Saturday, the doormen and stamp lickers of your office no longer greeted you, for they had been told that your greatness owed a debt to their lowness. But you overcame the blow and spun new threads in invincible self-confidence, you golden spider, you even went over to the dragon and his followers. Until this moment! And now you place your disfigured, bloodstained head in my lap, Freudreich. Your true face has broken through as in a child's decal—the face of the Eternal Wanderer, the persecuted, the mistreated, according to the rules of the penitential order. Are you still whispering, half-unconscious with pain, "It is a mistake"?

Yes, it is a mistake, Herr Director, but not the kind you mean, and we are paying for it now—the big mistake.

The train jolted to a halt, shaking all of us thoroughly, those

in the seats and those on the floor. Sankt Pölten! There was a
loud argument out on the tracks. All at once, I heard a shout,
which rang through the car: "Bodenheim, get out! Step on it!"

The priest grabbed my hand. "God will protect you. But
don't do anything foolish!"

Weil also touched me, stammering, "Don't anger them, for
God's sake. Don't anger them."

Had my time come? A mutineer! I wound my way out of the
compartment. I walked as if without legs. Meaningless words
occurred to me, such as: The backs of my knees are chirping.
A kick sent me down the footboard of the railroad car. I went
sprawling. A civilian helped me up, then doffed his hat.

"Herr Doctor Bodenheim?"

I was astonished to hear my own name, as if from far away.

"Delighted to meet you," said the man. "You are expected,
Herr Doctor. The express train from Munich has just arrived.
We have to hurry."

Seeing me stagger, he offered me a cigarette and a light. I
smoked greedily. I followed him. We climbed into the shiny
train. He stopped at a first-class compartment.

"Please go in there," he requested, then said good-bye and
vanished.

I read the words on the door: ONLY FOR OFFICIALS OF THE
PARTY.

I pushed the door open. I entered. The locomotive whistled. A
lone man was gazing out the window; his back was toward me.
The express began moving, soft, supple, fiery. The man wore a
brown jacket with a crease in the back and a hint of a belt at the
waist. A kind of uniform. The lights of the station flashed by.
The man turned around and smiled. I saw Zsoltan Nagy.

I saw Zsoltan Nagy. I saw the gold swastika on his jacket.
I stood motionless in the door. The train charged through the
deep night, barely perceptible. I raised both hands. I had once
hit Nagy in the face. We were children, and he had cheated

me when we were trading stamps. He had taken a plain-looking, but valuable, stamp for the cheap Borneo fiver, a huge, colorful stamp with an exciting tropical landscape on it. I did not hit Nagy in the face a second time. How could I have struck him, today, at eleven P.M., after that day?! I felt bitterly choked by the thought of the priest, Weil, Freudreich. The torture-masters were taking them to Dachau. Perhaps my comrades assumed I was dead. But I was cheating them with freedom, which I owed to that person here. Yes, I was cheating them, and I felt as if I had deserted from drumfire. My arms fell.

"Come, Bodenheim, have a cognac," said Nagy. "You look terrible."

I received the hip flask from his hand and took a long swig. He dropped on his seat by the window and invited me to sit down. Now I sat opposite him, with my tormented limbs; the cushion was soft and warm.

"Bodenheim, be honest! Did you want to slug me?"

I nodded. I could not speak. Zsoltan laughed with his lovely, shiny teeth.

"Imagine, and I was in Munich for a whole week. And do you know why? Only to get you out. I swore to Cella and Gretl that I would do it. But not just for them, I also did it for me, that's something you ought to know, old friend."

"Black and yellow to your bones," I heard my voice, for he had committed himself aloud to the imperial colors.

"Black and yellow to my bones," Nagy repeated, "that's what I am and that's what I'll remain. But it's over for our lifetime. I've known it for years, better than you and everyone else who panicked and called for the Kaiser. No monarchy will come so long as it can be of interest to us. Anyone who believes otherwise is a poor romantic, a deliberate swindler, or a fool. I haven't the knack for any of those professions. And so I am what I now am, and yet at heart I *am* black and yellow."

"You do impress me, Nagy, I have to tell you. Give me some more cognac, so that I can wash it down."

"You really did want to slug me, didn't you, my friend? I've certainly gotten to you. Here, drink, smoke, hold your tongue, and listen to me for a while. I have not yet considered anyone worthy of an apology."

He pushed the flask toward me, along with his cigarette case of tula metal; it was still in his possession. What loyalty in disloyalty! I drank and smoked and held my tongue.

"Listen, Bodenheim," Nagy began, "I'm forty-nine now, seven months older than you. How many years do you and I still have left—figure it out—assuming we don't kick the bucket sooner? Ten or twelve at most, isn't that so? Then we'll be old fogies, and we'll be rightfully thrown on the garbage heap of our generation. You probably know that yourself, Bodenheim, but a man's clock runs according to his potency. When it starts getting weaker, we need a replacement. In my private philosophy, I call that replacement 'potestas,' which means more or less 'mastery.' By fifty, you've got to either have something or be something. In short, you've got to be at the top in some way or other. If not, you belong to the great cannon fodder of humanity, the ludicrous refuse, and your entire life, this unique life, was a bust. Until your fiftieth birthday, luck with women may help you get over that sense of being a loser. But then? Don't glare at me so hatefully, dear friend, I know you've suffered terribly during the past few weeks. But just a little patience, and a look at my life so far. My old man was always impeccable. Pseudogentry through and through! Believe me, he had a much harder time than, say, your old man, and he was quite a master of the art of living, by God. His father's name was Nagel. He Magyarized his name even before I was born, because of the decorative "y" at the end; it fitted his stature. I'm stripping naked in front of you, Bodenheim. My poor mother was a waitress, nobody knew. My father found her in the nightlife of Budapest. She learned quickly and never embarrassed him. Those pillars were the supports of my brilliant youth, during which time I seldom had a real dinner. How often did I envy the other students for their breakfast sandwiches, and the sausages you bought from Subak, the school janitor. *Noblesse oblige* was my old man's favorite phrase, and he would

rather have passed a bad check than appear in public without
patent-leather shoes. He polished those shoes himself before he
went out in the evening; he used a shiny tincture, which smelled
suspiciously of carbolic acid. But while my growling stomach
turned upside down, I would tell you other kids that I was skipping my morning snack for the sake of my slender elegance. You
knew none of this, Bodenheim, when you urged me to join the
Seventh Hussars, which, astonishingly enough, I managed to do,
thanks to various people who interceded on my behalf. But now
you can imagine what an elegant moocher felt like among even
more elegant counts, each of whom had at least ten thousand a
year. But even that was useless after the war and the overthrow.
Did you wish to say something? Voice an objection?"

I shook my head. I lit my third cigarette.

"Just a wee bit more patience, Bodenheim. I'm getting to the
point. I went abroad the same year that Gretl married you,
remember? I'll spare you the description of what kinds of jobs
I had and where—if I started listing them I wouldn't be finished
until we got to Vienna. You know very little or nothing about
all that. I'm not cut out to work for someone, I'm no salesman
and no bootlicker or sycophant. I'm self-indulgent and I don't
much like working regular hours. But I do have one thing: a
raging interest in other people. And they sense it. Maybe that
helped me now and then, along with my linguistic talent in all
nuances. Nevertheless, I remained at the bottom. Or rather,
even worse: I remained in between. You can't imagine what
such a shadowy existence is like, Bodenheim. Something about
me must have a positive effect. People believed that I came
from a higher social sphere. I found friends like Styxi everywhere. Even in old-fashioned England, where the practice of
class distinctions has remained in the nineteenth century. I was
voted into an upper-class club by a normal ballot, I was invited
to country estates on weekends. I was among the accepted who
sit next to the other likable nobodies at the end of the table
that is far from the sun. At forty-four, I was still the attractive
young man from the Central European jungle, who dropped

all sorts of names from home, all of them quite honestly my friends—and whom the hostess used for all kinds of services when the celebrities were visiting. However, to keep myself at this altitude, I had to move every four weeks in order to get away from the hotel managers and tailors, skipping out on them without paying my bills. I suffered from all these things like a hunted deer. For—don't laugh—I'm not a criminal; I long for law and order. I am mentioning only the dazzling eras, so to speak. But then the depression came, and the year nineteen thirty-three came, and at the end of that year, 'they' came to me in London, for they knew about my connections and knack for languages, and they could use such people, the opposites of themselves, outwardly and inwardly."

"Who are 'they'?" I asked him harshly. But Zsoltan placed his hand on my knee.

I saw a large signet ring on his finger. A gem incised with a crown.

"They," he smiled, "the ones who think I'm theirs. I am now putting myself in your hands. You can destroy me. I do not want you to regard me as Myslivec, a subaltern opportunist who could just as easily have become a Bolshevik or goodness knows what if goodness knows who had won. You see, they came to me five years ago, long before their victory was assured. And I did them a few favors. I know a great deal about them. That's the reason they respect me so greatly and even fear me. Now it's my turn finally, just before I reach fifty. And I was able to save Styxi first and now you. Look, Bodenheim . . ."

He produced a few documents from his pocket and pointed to the signatures.

"The second in command in the SS and the third in command—I got them moving for you. This still doesn't seem to change your mood. You're right. So far, I haven't proved to you that I am anything but a banal opportunist."

"You're not even a real German, Nagy, you're—"

"One of the garden-variety mongrels of the Danube monarchy, the usual stuff, one grandfather Hungarian, one grandmother

Croatian, the other a daughter of former military personnel. Fine! What else? That whole nationalism is just a sop for the *misera plebs,* a glue to hold the masses together. The more intelligent ones among them know that we are undergoing a process of disintegration of the old nations and races. You see, you people underestimate them. They have their great side, believe me. Initially, it was just business for me. They had money to burn, I didn't. Later on, I began to understand their wild goal. Listen, they are the first and only people on this earth to strive for world domination without any qualms. All other ruling castes have always shared their power with some sort of gods and moral principles, as a superstitious backup. But they are perhaps the first people in the history of the world without a god or a morality. They are so godless that they don't even have to be atheists like the backward Bolsheviks. But you Jews, understand me, Bodenheim—even as atheists you are so incurably contaminated with religion. You simply cannot grasp the concept of total world domination without ethical fetters—that dancelike lightness of life, familiar only to the man who possesses power with no qualms whatsoever. You know that I'm an old Nietzschean. Remember how often we argued. . . ."

The golden-brown sparks flashed from his eyes more densely than ever. The train switched tracks with a few soft drumbeats. I sat numb. My lips were paralyzed.

"The world domination of the Boches," I said, "the superior strength of the world is as tremendous as its hatred. The world will finally defend itself against you and your germ cultures. And there is still a Church, which has always had the longest arm."

"The world . . ." Nagy shrugged charmingly. "You're mistaken again, Bodenheim, the world is already a ripe fruit in the lap of the Boches. They have discovered a very simple law of nature: namely, that in politics too the water flows from above to below—I mean that lowness is attractive, that the cheap bad instincts devour the expensive good ones, and indeed everywhere. They have brilliantly coupled their two great draws: pessimism and dynamism. Bread and circuses are past

their prime. The masses feed on arrogance, they are starved
for it. And the cat gets its mouse, the eternal enemy for its
murderous game. It doesn't cost much, and the cat toes the
line. You people are the mouse, Bodenheim—I find this dreadful, but is there any better material for blasting the nations?
The terrified mice and their partisans dash about everywhere,
whistling agitatedly—in France, in England, in America. And
the more they whistle, they more they make the local house
cat aware of them. Believe me, the Western nations can no
longer move. They are at death's door. The contagion has
reached a fever pitch, I know them well. The Third Reich will
not have to wage any war, since it has already forced a civil
war upon them. They too will soon get their dynamism. For
the youth of every nation is dynamic. That is, it needs swiftness, because heads and hearts are empty. I have associated
with these young people more than you have. They are all
addicted to swiftness. I tell you, they are alcoholics of every
kind of motion. The powerful internationale of youth has already been won over by the Nazis on the road to world domination. That's how I see it, Bodenheim. Do you finally realize
that your convictions and mine are not as far apart as you
thought in the first flush of terror? And what else? You mean
the Church? How can I believe in the future of an institution
whose dogmatic foundations collapsed long ago? If I could
force a hundred thousand Christians to be totally honest with
themselves, I would not find a single one who truly believes in
the divine nature of that little Jew from Galilee, who truly
believes in the miraculous virtue of the holy sacraments, the
last judgment, and the resurrection of the flesh. What do those
strange words suggest to an auto mechanic, a boxer, a mov-
iegoer? This proves that the Church is standing on quicksand,
that this whole institution has become nothing but a giant
shadow boxing, which a portion of mankind goes along with
out of hostility against the modern world revolution. I saw that
as a Catholic, Bodenheim, for I am well aware of the incom-

prehensible admiration that educated Jews feel for our Church. Religions usually live longer than the foundations of their faith. But eventually they do die. The time is not far off when museums will store our crucifixes as they now preserve the statues of the Greek gods. Perhaps a stadium will then be erected on the ruins of St. Peter's, a kind of Neronian circus, which once stood there. Forgive me, Bodenheim, I believe I have never talked such a blue streak since we were young. I am justifying myself to you. I have been a failure far too long. I cannot, I will not sacrifice my few remaining years to a lost cause. The imperial house— that's history, no loyalty to our convictions will help, I've simply known it longer than you. My conviction is unchanged, of course. But all that's left for me is a smidgen of life."

"And what about me?" I asked. I did not move. I sat there as if under a bell jar of disgust and exhaustion. Strangely enough, my battered limbs enjoyed the smooth gliding underneath me. I gazed into Nagy's face. His wavy, brown hair, his boyish attractiveness—everything as before. To which Party formation might he belong: the Gestapo, the intelligence service? Or was he actually working "on special assignment"? I did not hate him. I had not stopped liking him. I thought of the moment of "communion with the mortal enemy," which I myself had gone through. What could I demand of the others, I had asked myself, who were, after all, merely caught in the middle between me and the mortal enemy? Zsoltan Nagy waited for me to say something, anything after his long confession. I said nothing. The complaisant smile vanished from his lips. He drew a passport from his briefcase and handed it to me. Now his tone was dry and matter-of-fact. "Here is your passport. It's got all the stamps you need for crossing the German border. I promised them that you would take the first train abroad tomorrow. An express is leaving Western Terminal for Switzerland at seven A.M. A second-class ticket is inside your passport. If you fail to use that train and you're caught, then even the Good Lord won't be able to help you, Bodenheim. I have been assured that the Swiss border at Buchs is open to refugees.

In any case, the authorities are alerted. If necessary, you will be taken across illegally. That was really all I could do. However, I think that so far everything has worked out tremendously."

"What about Cella and Gretl?" I heard myself ask.

He leaned far back, half-closing his eyes. "Gretl and Cella will be following you, within three weeks at the latest. Gretl is busy settling your affairs. You know that this is no bagatelle nowadays, especially in your case. We are trying to make everything go smoothly, so she can take along this or that. You'll probably stay in Paris for the time being."

"Naturally Paris," I nodded, barely aware of what I was saying.

"It is the city of cities," Nagy affirmed, "and a man like you, Bodenheim, can slowly build up his life, I'm not the least bit worried."

The first suburban stations were zooming by. After a brief pause, Nagy looked at me from the side. "You know of course that, according to the new laws, Gretl as an Aryan could easily remain here. But your wife loves you, Bodenheim, perhaps more than you realize."

"What about Cella?"

"Cella is your child. . . . Incidentally, for Cella, the whole thing is a stroke of luck. She has to go out into the world. She doesn't need a teacher anymore, I tell you, she is as good as ready. If I were her father, I wouldn't allow her to remain in Austria for anything in the world. The great glaciation is coming here too. That is the payment for the domination of the world. The Romans and British were and are likewise no musicians. By getting out like this, Cella is hitting the jackpot."

"Can't I go to them? Today?" I asked timidly, "I haven't seen them for eight weeks."

Nagy vehemently shook his head. "Are you crazy? It's midnight now. And you have to leave tomorrow morning at seven. The two of them are at home in Eisenstadt. If you show up there, you're doomed. Don't do anything foolish, Bodenheim! Do you want to ruin everything?"

The train entered the railroad terminal. Swastika flags were waving. I reeled through the crowd with Nagy. Outside, a large, beautiful car was waiting for him. The chauffeur doffed his cap. Now Zsoltan, the eternal young man, was a power to be reckoned with, joining in the domination of the world.

"C'mon," he said, "get in! I'm staying at the Bristol. It would be best if you spent the night there."

I could not get into a car with him. It was stupid of me, but I could not get in.

"No. I'll spend the night over there, at the Terminus."

"As you like."

His foot was already on the running board. He reflected for a moment, then said, "It would be better if I brought you over to the Terminus personally. With my recommendation, nothing can happen to you. Gretl made me swear that I would watch out for you." He accompanied me all the way to my room. This time, the wallpaper had red and yellow vetches.

"I'm delighted," said Nagy, "that everything has worked out so dazzlingly. An astonishing sense of organization, don't you think? Your train and my train met in Sankt Pölten right on the dot. Incidentally, the transport commander received the telegram with the order from the number two SS man before the train even left Vienna. Tell me, don't I have the right to be proud?!"

"Yes, you can be proud, Nagy," I replied, adding nothing further.

He placed a couple of banknotes on the table. "You'll need money, Bodenheim. Please don't argue. Gretl will pay me back. . . . Tomorrow morning I'll dash over and report to them that everything is in order and that you're doing fine."

He waited awhile. I sat mutely on the edge of the bed. Then he said good night and left. I instantly asked the switchboard to put me through to Eisenstadt. A few minutes later, I was told that the number had been disconnected on March thirteenth for political reasons. This was the first time in fifty days that I lay down in a real white bed. What luck, the thought shot through my head, in twenty-four hours I'll be saved. I was unable to enjoy my good fortune; my limbs were shaking with cold. The faces of the priest and Weil and Stich and Freudreich and all the others retreated and became distant as if they did not wish to bother me. But the cantor's voice bellowed in my ears, and monkeys were climbing up and down the ladder, jerking on the ropes and rings. I moaned. I tossed to and fro. I heard a church clock strike one. I had already reached the final depth of sleep when suddenly knocks boomed on the door. I jumped up. I did not dare turn on the light. Now they're here, the motor-men. I'm done for. Someone came in; I had not locked the door. Someone switched on the light, while my heart banged against my ribs like a fist. It was Nagy. He sat down on my bed and gazed at me with an utterly lifeless face.

"I frightened you," he said, "forgive me, but I had to come back. . . . You see . . . Well, I gabbed and gabbed today, and it was no apology, it was nothing but intelligent nonsense. One cannot express life in words."

I pulled myself together. My voice was awake and calm. "I can express my life in words, Nagy. Only crimes cannot be explained or glossed over logically."

"Bodenheim, you've gotten to know the beasts. Don't you believe that the same beasts could be unleashed by any other party conviction?"

"No, I don't think so. Like master, like man."

He lapsed into a long silence. Then he stood up.

"This is the last time we'll ever meet. . . . Don't you want to shake my hand?"

I shook his hand.

$$Chapter\ 12$$

The Bridge Between
Nowhere and Somewhere

Most of the passengers left the train in Innsbruck. It was ru-
mored that the Swiss border had been closed to refugees the
previous evening. I took the news without fear or worry. Let
whatever might happen happen. The strange numbness that
had overcome me during my meeting with Nagy was still upon
me through the daylong journey. Outside the window, the Ty-
rolean mountains, to which I had still felt I belonged just a
few weeks earlier, were whizzing by in the radiant evening sun.
Now they had turned into gigantic enemies, armored in racism
all the way up to the region of ice and snow. Indeed, this
region of eternal winter seemed like a severe symbol of that
hatred. Not only the urban buildings had been transformed for
our souls, but also the sky-towering constructions of nature.
The very planet, to which I was bound by gravity, had suddenly become off-limits.

　　There were three of us left in the compartment. Opposite
me, at the window, sat a young, rather corpulent, brown-
haired man, a monocle wedged in the saddened fat of his right

cheek. The other traveler was Lateiner, the music critic. Because of several Prussians who had ridden with us all the way to Innsbruck, we had barely exchanged a word during the entire trip. Now we heaved sighs of relief, for the young man with the monocle looked trustworthy. There could be no doubt about who or what he was.

I was dismayed by Lateiner's appearance, just as he seemed clearly dismayed by the sight of me. The sparse wreath of his tonsure shone snow-white. His features had melted together and were almost cadaverous. If there is a Medusalike mask of offendedness and immeasurable injury, then Lateiner wore that mask. Only now did he ask me about my experiences since that moment when we had stood together on the blood-spattered asphalt of Mondscheingasse, by Scherber's corpse. I tersely outlined my seven weeks in prison and my rescue from the trainload of inmates bound for Dachau. But I said nothing about Nagy.

"I could tell," Lateiner nodded, "that you would fall into a trap. You were ripe, Bodenheim. But even those to whom nothing happened, so to speak, they had no reason for joy, goodness knows. Incidentally, what's the state of your papers?"

I handed him the passport charitably obtained by Nagy's bad conscience. Lateiner put on his large, horn-rimmed glasses and studied the document with increasing surprise.

"Valid for three years," he grumbled. "And no red J on it. You seem to have omnipotent patrons, Herr Bodenheim, since you are not even a marked man."

At these words, the young man with the monocle leaned toward me. "Please excuse me for introducing myself to the gentlemen. My name is Lenz, Siegbert Lenz. My father was General Lenz von Worobiowka. You gentlemen must know the name. I too am going to Switzerland."

"He was in charge of ordnance, wasn't he," said Lateiner, "so presumably your departure will involve no problems, Herr Lenz."

"On the contrary," said Lenz, his eyes scrutinizing us anxiously, "I had very great problems; my house was searched, I was interrogated, and so forth. You see, my father was one of the three non-Aryan generals in the old army, but nevertheless a highly qualified commander, as you gentlemen probably know. Who cared about such things earlier? I didn't even know it myself until I was twenty, I swear, you gentlemen must believe me. There was nothing I could do, they threw me out. I just hope we can get across the border. What do you gentlemen intend to do if we can't get across?"

"In that case, I intend to put an end to my life, like Scherber," Lateiner replied drily, yanking the curtain across the train window, for the setting sun was blinding him. Then he turned to me.

"You ought to know, Dr. Bodenheim, that I am a Dante scholar by avocation. For me, he is the greatest of all poets. But good old Dante Alighieri, the furious refugee from Florence, never dreamed of this, with all his blazing pitch, foul-smelling waters, serpents, and other tortures—I mean the hell of red tape, a genuine and native Austrian hell; the Prussians have awoken it to new life, simply brilliant. You spent seven weeks in a cell, Bodenheim, and I was free; not a proverbial hair on my head was touched; I was able to prepare my emigration during the same seven weeks. Just listen to what it's like.

"It starts on Bräunerstrasse, you know, the old narrow street opposite the castle, that's where you'll find the gates of hell. The line on one side reaches all the way to Josefsplatz and on the other side to the Graben! You naively line up at nine A.M., three times, four times, in snow and rain, no use, the emigration office closes at twelve noon, and you have advanced to within fifty yards of the entrance. By the fifth time, I had seen the light and so I arrived at one A.M. By nine o'clock, I finally got in, and I stood in front of an official of this inferno, who was sweating with hate and laziness. He snaps at me derisively: No information is given here. You are to submit a written request accompanied by a statement that you owe no back taxes. Abysmal words, gentlemen, 'A statement that you owe no back taxes.' And no Dante lives to immortalize them, and all this will go unrecorded by any poet.

"The next two cantos take place at the tax office. I am a poor man, Bodenheim, and I freelanced until I was sixty; no publisher printed my great works. Despite this meager income, the cantos in the tax office last over two weeks and must contain innumerable tercets. Then I line up again on Bräunerstrasse and submit my request with the statement that I owe no back taxes. Now a different bureaucrat is sitting there. His voice crackles with glee, I tell you. New regulations. Smirking, he tells me to note down the certificates that an 'applicant for emigration' has to submit along with the statement that he owes no back taxes. And now listen carefully, gentlemen! Every one of these words is a canto unto itself, taking place in dreadful offices, full of the dust and stench of years and never-emptied cuspidors and dry inkwells and smashed pens and degraded human beings who wait and wait. 'Dog license certificate.' Three years ago, my dog died; he should have been certified. 'Water tax installment,' 'door tax,' 'concession tax,' 'charity tax'—every word an office and a lost day. This is no joke, gentlemen! Even though I own neither a door nor a concession, I nevertheless had to produce a certificate that I owe no back taxes as a nonowner of a door and a concession.

"And after those mildewed government foxholes came the urban caverns, in the old city hall, in the new city hall, and in all possible branches. I had to submit certificates that I did not owe the 'amusement tax,' the 'advertising tax,' or the 'domestic servant tax.' Every word a canto of the bureaucratic hell and a day amid uncomprehending applicants for emigration. The final canto is titled 'Assessment Bureau.' You're a lawyer, Bodenheim, but I bet you didn't know that there's an Assessment Bureau, a baroque agency, which was probably created by Charles VI or, at the very latest, by Maria Theresa."

I shook my head. I really knew nothing about the Assessment

Bureau. My ignorance seemed to fill Lateiner with satanic glee. His long hands molded the air.

"This is a surviving piece of rococo, gentlemen," he exclaimed. "It hasn't been ventilated since 1770, no Dante is alive, nor any Austrian Balzac, to describe it. An antediluvian clerk sits there with a leather protector on his right sleeve and a green visor, an immortal, who was already presumed dead in Metternich's day. His job—pay heed, gentlemen—is limited to the grandiose technical phrase: recovery of uncollected stamp fees. Court judgments, inheritance files, notarial contracts are, as we know, provided with stamps. However, in many cases, the value of these stamps does not correspond to the fees that the state has to levy for these documents. The Assessment Bureau was established by its creators in order—as the so unsurpassably beautiful terminology puts it—to collate the completed documents with the state specifications and charge the insufficiency in fees to the parties involved. Understand? The forgotten clerk walked up and down in this Assessment Bureau from ten A.M. to twelve P.M., together with several assistant ghosts, reading the newspapers, eating breakfast, and impregnating the venerable air with the smoke of a stogey. When noon struck, that was his cock's crow, and he disintegrated entirely. But after the 'recovery' (the very word arouses nausea), the Gestapo put a firecracker up his rear end and he had to delay his pleasant witching hour until six or seven P.M. You see, we emigration applicants were forced to besiege the Assessment Bureau in order to present written proof that we did not owe the state any uncollected stamp-fee differences. Gentlemen, do not look upon it as a senseless, aimless torment of the red-tape hell. Herein lies the vast difference between Austrian and Prussian diabolism. The Austrian harassment is an art for art's sake, it has no other end than itself; the Prussian version, however, is extremely logical and charges ruthlessly toward its ultimate goal. What ultimate goal? Very simple. The Assessment Bureau is a tight sieve. The procedure there takes at least three weeks. Meanwhile, however, the deadline for submitting the emigration application on Bräunerstrasse runs out, and the applicant has to start his journey through the bureaucratic underworld from scratch. And all this will vanish from the minds of men, and no one will record it, for it is too much, by God, much too much. If the gentlemen permit me, I will now open the window."

He shoved the window pane down with a wild thrust and dipped his head into the late golden light and the fresh zooming air. The beauty of the world grazed our powerless hearts. Anyone who did not know would have thought that the three of us were traveling for pleasure, heading into the mountain springtime. Now Siegbert Lenz leaned forward slightly.

"You gentlemen have been through a dreadful time," he said, "but so have I. For instance, do you gentlemen have any idea what the Racial Bureau is like? I made its acquaintance, for three weeks, day in, day out. You see, begging your pardon, I'm a very special case. It was a matter of an excess of three point one twenty-five percent of non-Aryan blood. Otherwise, I would have simply slid through."

Lateiner turned around and guffawed while his face remained deadly earnest. "An excess of three point one twenty-five percent of non-Aryan blood," he ardently repeated twice. The fat youth looked at him, insulted.

"Excuse me, gentlemen, but that is really so; the Racial Bureau computed it precisely. Why, I had to submit all the baptismal certificates and registration certificates of all four grandparents; that was no small matter, I assure you. My paternal grandfather: alas, one hundred percent non-Aryan blood. My paternal grandmother: seventy-five percent. My maternal grandfather: twenty-five percent; my grandmother: twelve and a half percent. Together that adds up to two hundred twelve and a half percent of non-Aryan blood. The Racial Bureau always divides the grandparental sum by four, so that it came up with fifty-three point one twenty-five percent for me. In other words, three percent too much; for with fifty percent, I would have been a pure half-breed, gentlemen, and, as a non-officer and non-government official, I could have remained in my position for the time being."

"Gentlemen, this percentage computation should be preserved for future generations," Lateiner howled, banging his thighs.

But Lenz remained serious, as before. He wedged his monocle more tightly into his eye. "I had a way out. The gentlemen from the Racial Bureau offered me some advice. My dear mama, may she rest in peace, had only eighteen and three quarters percent, which made her almost a full Aryan. They told me to submit proof that I am not my papa's son, that my dear mama, may she rest in peace . . . Needless to say, I refused, as a man of honor. No sir, gentlemen, it was out of the question for me. The officials at the Racial Bureau regretted it, of course."

The compartment door was shoved open. A uniformed motor-man peered at us for a while, then strode on silently. Siegbert Lenz turned pale. No one said another word. I leaned back, closing my eyes for a time. When I opened them again, a greenish twilight had invaded the landscape. The fat young man smiled at me anxiously.

"Do you believe that they will conduct a body search at the border?"

"You can assume the worst," I replied, "and it will be bad."

I could not repress a certain sadism toward this flabby boy with the monocle. Had the nastiness and cruelty that I had suffered made me cruel and nasty? Siegbert Lenz tried to gather the melting features of his face and give them an expression of arrogance and self-confidence.

"I am, still and all, the son of General Lenz von Worobiowka. Papa fought shoulder to shoulder with the Germans in Russia and Italy, I mean in his army headquarters, of course. He was personal friends with Hindenburg and Mackensen. They wrote him warm letters. I have these letters on me. I am convinced that I will be treated accordingly."

"Sir, are you really that naive," Lateiner broke in, "or are you trying to make fools of us? Why did you spend weeks as a star pupil, studying your racial percentage computation! So please calculate. One hundred plus seventy-five divided by two makes eighty-seven and a half—even for a poor mathematician like myself. Thus, for the Third Reich, your venerable father, whom I do not wish to offend, is nothing but a dirty kike mellowed by twelve and a half percent Aryan blood, and that's all. Tear up the letters of the German heroes, for they will not help you, and you will only be compromising Hindenburg and Mackensen."

"Do you really think so?" Lenz was terrified, his mouth twisted upward like a fish. Then he yammered, "If I at least were a real Jew, but I didn't know about it even as a grown man. I give you gentlemen my word."

Night had fallen. The windows were still open. On the mountain slopes, fiery swastikas of burning twigs were still blazing here and there. Not even the night could still be night in the Alps. I thought of Nagy's definitions. This was really a human breed that had never before existed in history. They desecrated mountains and valleys with their shattering will to rule—unprincipled barbarians, but without the innocence and ignorance of barbarians; they practiced the psychology of crafty sideshow barkers, throttling the souls of friend and foe with their gigantic orgies of ballyhoo. Their invincible strength was the perfect shamelessness with which they all denied the better instincts that mankind had acquired during its torments. Nagy was right. They outdid any baseness waiting to be unleashed in the souls of the nations. My throat tightened in ineffable surfeit.

Siegbert Lenz removed the monocle from his eye. His amorphous full-moon face became rigid. He confessed quietly, "Excuse me, gentlemen, but what should I do? You see, I have five thousand on me. Everything that I could liquidate . . ."

"You'll have to figure that out for yourself," I said. "Fifty hundred-mark notes are difficult to conceal."

The young man geared himself up for a daring resistance. "But I can prove my fascistic conviction; I can demonstrate it to anyone. I have various membership cards on me."

"Sir," Lateiner burst in grimly, "what sort of a world do you live in? Don't you know what the penalty is for illegal export of capital? The death penalty! So there! And now please orient yourself accordingly!"

"For God's sake," Lenz breathed.

Landeck was already far behind us. Another hour had worn by. Now we were thundering through the long tunnels of Vorarlberg. We remained silent.

We sat in our places with cramped muscles. We believed we were dashing not toward freedom, but toward an inexorable destiny, worse then anything that had happened before. Surrounded by the crimson army of sparks from the locomotive, a gigantic full moon appeared outside the window. It escorted us, a harshly white border guard, a cosmic customs officer, scrutinizing every move we made.

All at once, Siegbert Lenz got to his feet and gave me a pleading look. "Please, would the gentleman stand at the door and watch if anyone comes."

I went to the door. The corridor was empty. Then I saw Lenz's childishly pudgy hands reach into his breast pocket and pull out a thick wad of banknotes. I too was electrified by all the beautiful money; one after another, the hundred-mark bills were yanked away by the rush of air and whirled off into the moonlit night, to somewhere along the route, to the train tracks, out into the fields. Lateiner rose to his feet and lifted his hand in a salute.

"May this treasure," he said, "reach the right man as in a fairy tale. A decent, honest lineman, for example, a fierce enemy of the regime, whose misery will thus be transformed into a blessing. Amen!"

But Siegbert Lenz, a broken man, collapsed into his seat, moaning, "Now I have nothing left. Now I am nothing. Less than nothing, not even a Jew."

$\mathcal{T}$wo SS men entered.

"Is there a Bodenheim here?"

I almost had to laugh, for I recalled Nagy's futile words: "Hasn't everything worked out dazzlingly?" I handed my passport to the thugs. One of them announced, "There is no legal border-crossing."

When the train stopped, I had to follow them. Lateiner and Lenz wriggled along behind us, dragging their luggage. On the platform of a small, poorly lit station, we were handed over to two country constables, who must have been waiting for us here. They were two artless rustics, speaking an Alemannic dialect, and they treated us kindly, amiably, indeed, with unwonted respect. But perhaps it only seemed like that to my soul, which had been hardened by motor-men, and these representatives of normal justice paid us the same honor as was shown to normal vagabonds and smugglers. We had to climb into a rustic bus, which was parked outside the deserted railroad station. The sign on the bus said: BANNWEIL. Just what was Bannweil (literally "time of exile")? I had never heard of this village. But it had the right name for a jumping-off point for exiles. Where were we heading? The only other passenger was an old peasant woman, who eyed us distrustfully, but then instantly dozed off as the crude bus rattled into motion.

Siegbert Lenz no longer wore his monocle. He looked so waxy with his swollen eyes and nauseated fish-mouth, as if he were about to throw up. He desperately kept mumbling to himself: "No body search . . . What a fool I was. . . ." We had to elbow him energetically to shut him up. The constables had not heard him mumbling. They were whispering together. Finally, the senior officer turned toward us in solemn embarrassment. "We would like to tell the gentlemen that we do not agree with what is happening to them. But orders are orders. There's nothing we can do."

The other glanced at the sleeping crone, winked at us and whispered, "Long live Austria! You gentlemen will come back." Than he offered us a canteen of liquor. We thanked him. We drank. We shook hands with the loyal patriots.

"Yes, we will come back to our homeland," we whispered, and believed it at that moment. I recalled a sentence from Roman law, an echo of my student days: "The day is certain, which day is uncertain." Everything was truly working out dazzlingly. Fortune always smiled at Nagy. These constables had been sent by providence. But my delight was premature. The repertoire of surprises was not yet exhausted.

At the marketplace of Bannweil, in the shade of medieval cottages, a fountain plashed soothingly. However, the constables, our valiant escorts, of whose protection we had already felt so certain, wished us good luck and godspeed. We were paralyzed with fear, unable to talk. Two plainclothesmen with swastika armbands were already standing behind us, as if spirited out of thin air. They carried rifles equipped with bayonets. Our terror was heightened because they were civilians and not uniformed motor-men. The contradiction between the loaded firearm and the tattered clothes of farmhands or jobless men made them look like criminals, gangsters, into whose hands we had fallen. We were beyond the law, they were beyond the law, and even the law was beyond the law.

"Forward march, you kikes!" one of them commanded. "Follow me!"

And our exodus began from the house of bondage to the lands that were not promised us. One thug preceded us, while the other sauntered behind us. The two of them were in no hurry, and so we were allowed to stroll in a leisurely fashion, as if we were not fleeing like outlaws, but ambling through the soft, tender night. The May night is easy on exhausted limbs. Only our fat Lenz—not an inch left of a Siegbert [Victor]—was panting along with his two valises. The moon seemed to grow from minute to minute, almost supernaturally. I had never seen such a huge May moon in my life. One could barely look at it. Death too can blind you. In back of us, the high Alps remained in the bony haze, towering above one another into nothingness. To the right, the hilly region gradually leveled down, surging toward the plain in long roads and swells. Lake Constance must be out there, in the northwest. You stretch from the Lake of Reeds of my childhood to Lake Constance, my Austria, and now you are expelling me. If only your border were already behind me, you alien, you utterly alien homeland! We veered off from the highway. We trudged along uneven paths between hip-high crops and then through pastures and unmowed meadows. Usually the night knows only black and white. But in the reflector beam of that moon, the colors of the meadows blossomed, artificial, rapturous. Especially the excited yellow of the buttercups and huge daisies. I asked my soul: Is this a nocturnal stroll in the outlying meadows of the Castle Park of Eisenstadt? Are you crazy? Do flower colors still speak to you in your situation, as if nothing had happened? Now, between damnation and damnation, are you delightedly inhaling the midnight dew of this planet, which does not care for you? Yes, I saw, I breathed in delight, I cannot deny it. I realized that hatred and mistreatment had not yet ruined me entirely. A wave of warmth billowed up in me. A splendid gratitude! I could say nothing. But to do something consistent with this surge, I heaved Lateiner's valise on my shoulder. He let it happen. He said, "You know, Bodenheim, I was already an old man eight weeks ago, but now. . . ."

We turned into a cart path. It ran upward. Woods surrounded us; chasms opened. A mountain creek gurgled alongside, ran ahead, paused, looked back, leaped away laughing, like a puppy scurrying through the forest with its master. We climbed higher and higher. The water teased us from the depths. The night grew dark. The thugs switched on their flashlights. More than an hour must have passed by the time we reached a huge incision; at the bottom, there was no creek, but a real Alpine river foaming over boulders and tree trunks.

A covered bridge led across this incision, one of those lovely wooden bridges that are native to our mountains. It hung very high over the chasm. Its roof was of age-old shingles. This made it look less like a bridge and more like a long, drawn-out farmhouse hovering in the air.

The thugs switched off their flashlights. They menacingly pointed their rifles. "Bon voyage, you kikes," one of them said. "Get going. The other side is Switzerland. Just follow the path."

I was the first to step out on the house-bridge, its roof shingles fragrant with mildew. The planks swung as if stretched across a tremendous resonator, in whose depth the bottomless murmuring did not die.

The gaps between the planks were often as wide as a hand, and when the moon came out again, we saw the swift curls of foam some thirty yards below. A crucifix hung from one of the coarse roof supports with a tiny oil lamp flickering out at the foot. Did this crucifix belong to the Third Reich or to the other world, or was it the border between them? I thought of Felix and Aladar Fürst.

From the swinging instrument of the bridge we entered the dead forest trail. But we had not advanced more than five paces when three black human figures cropped up from the darkness. A border patrol of the Swiss military. They seemed to have lain in wait specifically for us, for their bicycle lights were dimmed. The junior officer's High German sounded guttural, but not impolite. "Please turn around. This road is prohibited!"

That was all. We ran back to the bridge, which boomed like drums and harp strings under our hurried steps. It was the old song of all borders. Only the rotting wooden cage with the crucifix, the cage in which we hovered over the chasm, added a novel and bizarre touch. The thugs on the other side laughed. They had thrust their flashlights into their belts. We could see them cock their rifles in the circle of light and take aim.

"Anyone who gets within three feet," the spokesman shouted, "will be shot . . . with no challenge and no warning!"

What could we do? Lateiner, who had lost his hat, dashed
to and fro, whinnying, scornfully inspired. Lenz, placing his
valises under the crucifix, sat down upon them, a woeful dis-
ciple of the Lord. Exhausted by the burden, he promptly fell
asleep. His large head swayed. I leaned over the railing. I gazed
down into the confused moon-milky script of the water, which
rushed in an indecipherable tangle. I understood nothing. But
it held me fast like a suspense novel. My heart was profoundly
calm. I playfully estimated how deep the plunge would be. But
my thoughts were shadow boxing. I have never been further
from suicide than at those moments. All at once, I heard Lateiner's voice cracking. He had walked right up to the three-
foot radius of the thugs. His wreath of hair, shining like lunar
silver, bristled in the indulgent wind.

"Why don't you shoot!" he yelled. "C'mon, shoot! Watch it,
gunfire. I'm an intellectual and a subhuman. So why don't you
shoot me, you supermen!"

He spread out his arms and declaimed in a tremendous
baritone, which stirred up the night:

> *You showed me first the steeply sloping path*
> *To Mount Parnassus and its wellsprings sweet,*
> *And you were my first light for nearing God.*
>
> *You are just like a man who bears a lamp*
> *At night. He sees but darkness far and wide.*
> *But those who follow him, they walk in light.*
>
> *And then you spoke! The time will come. I see*
> *A generation rising from the heavens,*
> *Founders of law and order and of justice. . . .*

After bellowing out those verses, he took one step closer to
the stunned thugs and snapped at them, "What's this, you supermen? What? You don't know this? You know nothing about
Dante and his farewell to Virgil, you supermen? I, a subhuman, know it and I can weep over these tercets. My subhuman

heart still beats today at the five-quarter measures in the third act of *Tristan*. I, a subhuman, go crazy with joy because the opening chord of *Falstaff* begins fortissimo in the second, weak part of the measure. Do you understand, you supermen? So, c'mon, shoot, fire, kill the last man who knows these joys."

Our thugs appeared utterly shaken by Lateiner's outburst. They did not laugh. They lowered their rifles. The Swiss had come over. I tore away from the railing and strode over to the junior officer.

"You can see that a misunderstanding has occurred here," I said.

He looked at me, skeptical and embarrassed. He was already planning his words.

"I'm sorry. We have strict orders."

"Which canton town is this?"

"We belong to Appenzell."

"And how far is the next village?"

"Ten minutes by bike."

"Can't you send one of your men over to ring up your superior? Here is my passport."

"Now, in the middle of the night?"

One of the soldiers took our side.

"The man on duty can be woken up. That would be possible."

The Swiss retreated and conferred together. A few minutes later, one of them hopped on his bicycle and glided into the night. I took Lateiner by the hand; he was breathing heavily, coming to very slowly. "These Swiss are nice people, Lateiner," I said. "Maybe we'll be lucky. And now come. We'll sleep for half an hour. Let's sit down side by side. That's right."

We settled on the planks, leaning against the railing. Just a few minutes later, Lateiner's heavy head dropped on my shoulder. Cautiously, to avoid waking him, I reached into my pocket. Damn it, no more cigarettes! However, I was holding Hipfinger's puzzle in my hand. I tried to distinguish between the tiny red and blue marbles. Impossible. During these futile efforts, I had suddenly stepped out on a huge, defective bridge. My knees were trembling, for it was extremely dangerous to walk across this bridge. The gaps between the planks were wider than a human hand. Some planks were missing altogether, and I gazed down, shivering, into yellow, gurgling water, which did not belong to an Alpine rivulet; it was a huge, fat torrent rolling through an unknown metropolis.

And then it happened. The middle of the bridge suddenly snapped over the torrent. A rotten part of the beams had simply plunged into the water. A corrupt town administration! Shuddering, I halted at the edge and gazed hopelessly across at the other fragment of the bridge. The gap was insuperable.

Then I heard soft, quick steps behind me. I knew at once: Cella and Zsoltan Nagy. But there were three people, not two. A shrouded person had accompanied Cella and Nagy. No, it was not Gretl, out of the question, more likely my mother. She paused at my side, unconcerned about me. Zsoltan wore an elegant navy uniform: white ducks, blue jacket with gold buttons, and a navy cap. But where had Cella gotten her yacht clothes? Who had bought them for her? A gift from Nagy, no doubt. He now started running and then soared gracefully to the other fragment of the rotten bridge. What a man, that was a jump of at least thirty-five feet. Then he held his hand out to Cella. I was terrified, but before I could stop this madness, the girl leaped after him, as long and thin as a dragonfly. The two of them waved to me from the other side.

"C'mon, Bulbul," cried Cella, inordinately far away. "Uncle Zsoltan will take you along."

"Jump!" said the shrouded figure at my side; the voice was completely unfamiliar and indifferent. I flew into a rage. It's easy for the two of you. Why? Because you have an easy time of it. You weren't burdened with an invisible sack of coal right at birth. How can I leap that far, a man without a trained self-confidence? My self-confidence was strangled at the very beginning. It could not be cured even by the Kaiser and by having my name in the military roll of honor.

"C'mon, Bulbul," shouted Cella.

Leave me alone, I'm only a part-time hero. I'm a coward.

Then, everything seemed to be forgotten and to start all over again, tormenting, repulsive, shameful, until a new voice came from nearby: "You can enter."

Siegbert Lenz was already standing and excitedly flailing his arms toward Lateiner and myself. It took us a while to stagger to our feet. The Swiss junior officer declared once again in a singsong intonation, "You can enter . . . this time . . ."

He sounded as if he were inviting dubious guests across the threshold of a warm, comfortable house, though not without a strict warning. But where were we? In utter nothingness. The dawn had brought a tremendous fog, which veiled us so thoroughly that we could scarcely discern one another. The nowhere behind us had vanished, and the thugs had vanished with it. The somewhere ahead of us did not reveal itself. The Swiss were growing impatient. Silently, we picked up our belongings and followed the guards into the fog.

Afterword

Here, Werfel's manuscript broke off, and we have only a few notes concerning what he planned. A second volume was to be called *The Bread of Exile (Das Brot der Fremde),* promising that not only Bodenheim but also his wife and daughter eventually escaped to France and then to America. In the course of this flight, though, Bodenheim was to learn that Cella was not really his daughter but rather the child of his old friend Nagy.

We can deduce only the essentials from Werfel's outline of chapters for his second volume:

1. The Adventures of Poverty
2. The Hotel
3. The Dismal Table
4. Zsoltan Nagy Shows Up
5. The Illness—Beginning
6. The Illness—Middle
7. The Resemblance
8. Who is the Victim? (Nagy's Death)
9. The Genius Who Loses His Memory
10. The Great Surprise

At the end, Cella, whose piano debut in Vienna was ruined by the *Anschluss,* makes her triumphant appearance on the stage of Carnegie Hall in New York.

—OTTO FRIEDRICH